THE
SIGN
OF
DEATH

THE SIGN OF DEATH

A VICTORIAN BOOK CLUB MYSTERY

Callie Hutton

CROOKED
LANE

NEW YORK

Published in the United States by Crooked Lane Books, an imprint of The Quick Brown Fox & Company LLC.

Crooked Lane Books and its logo are trademarks of The Quick Brown Fox & Company LLC.

Library of Congress Catalog-in-Publication data available upon request.

ISBN (hardcover): 978-1-64385-582-0
ISBN (ebook): 978-1-64385-583-7

Cover design by Bruce Emmett

Printed in the United States.

www.crookedlanebooks.com

Crooked Lane Books
34 West 27th St., 10th Floor
New York, NY 10001

First Edition: April 2021

10 9 8 7 6 5 4 3 2 1

Dame Agatha Christie,
the Queen of Cozy Mysteries.

CHAPTER 1

Bath, England
January 1891

William, Viscount Wethington, stared in horror at the missive in his hand, the blood draining from his head. He read it a second and then a third time, but the words never changed.

My dearest son,

After much consideration I have decided to retire from our townhouse in London and take up residence with you in Bath. Since the family holding is quite large, there is no reason for me to seek my own dwelling.

I have many things to do to close up the London townhouse, so it will be a week or two before I arrive.

I am so looking forward to spending time with my only son.

Affectionately,

Mother

His mother was coming to live with him.

They had not lived under the same roof for so many years that he'd lost count. He loved his mother dearly, but she consulted her dead husband for advice, found happiness and joy in every second of her life, which could be trying on some days, and had a tendency to get lost if she walked more than a block from her home.

Worst of all, his beloved mother was also determined to see him married with children. He oftentimes thought the sole reason she had given birth to him and his sister, Valerie, now the Countess Denby, was to provide her with grandchildren.

When he reminded her that Valerie and her husband had been reproducing at an alarming rate—seven children so far—she sniffed and said that as much as she loved them, she needed grandchildren she could see regularly. The earl and countess were currently living in France.

He pinched the bridge of his nose and closed his eyes. She was correct, the house was very large, but nothing was large enough to shelter both him and his mother. He folded the letter and dropped it on his desk, relegating it to the list of things to think about after a brandy. Or two.

James Harding, his man of business, was due to arrive any moment. William had an uncomfortable feeling that something wasn't right with his finances, though he had very little to go on.

He'd employed James for three years and had never had reason to mistrust the man. However, some of his own numbers did not add up to the information James had last provided.

William's father, the former Viscount Wethington, had left him a tidy sum when he passed away, but William, wanting to ensure his future—and yes, the future of his one-day children—had used a good portion of the money to invest in various businesses and stocks.

He currently held an interest in two restaurants, one hotel, a small bank, and a printing company. Although James had advised against it, William had also financed a couple of industrial ventures in the United States, which were currently his best-performing investments.

His government bonds were solid as his railroad stock. Yet something wasn't right, and he hoped to discover what it was today and set his worries aside.

He shook his head. Lord knew he had enough to worry about with Mother moving into his house.

"My lord, a note has arrived for you." His butler, Madison, entered the library and held out a folded piece of paper.

William opened the note and frowned. It appeared that Mr. Harding was ill and unable to attend him. He looked up at Madison. "Thank you. No response is required."

He stared at the note on his desk, considering this latest development. When had he started mistrusting James? A little more than three years together, and only recently had he felt a shift in their arrangement. Hopefully the man was legitimately ill and not just avoiding him.

William stood and strolled over to the window, his hands clasped behind his back. The garden was bleak as the day: cloudy, damp, and dismal. This time of the year was his least favorite. The merriment of Yuletide had ended, and nothing would appear on the horizon for a few months.

Shaking off his gloom, he strode from the room and made a last-minute decision to call on Lady Amy. He always smiled when he thought of her. She was a fellow member of the Mystery Book Club of Bath as well as a congregant in his church, St. Swithin's.

Several months before, they'd worked together on solving the mystery of the death of her ex-fiancé, Mr. Ronald

St. Vincent. As unusual as it sounded for there to be a gently reared young lady involving herself in a murder investigation, the subject of homicide was not something completely unfamiliar to Lady Amy. Unbeknownst to the public, she was the very well-known murder mystery author E. D. Burton, a fact he had learned during the course of their investigation.

He still smiled whenever he thought of that.

"I will return in time for dinner," William said to Madison as he shrugged into his coat.

"Very good, my lord. I will advise Cook."

He strode to the small stable at the back of his home to tack his horse, Major. The Cleveland Bay had been carrying him about town for many years.

The familiar, comforting smell of hay and animal greeted him as he approached Major's stall. He ran his palm down the horse's satin nose. "I promise I will take you for a good run sometime soon. I'm afraid right now we're only traveling to Lady Amy's house."

Almost as if the horse understood, he stomped his foot and shook his head. William spoke soothing words to the animal as he finished tacking, then led him from the stable and mounted. With a squeeze of his thighs, he headed away from Wethington Manor toward Amy's house.

★　★　★

Lady Amy Lovell tapped her pen against her desk as she considered the next red herring in the murder mystery she was currently working on. For some reason, she had been having a hard time concentrating the last few days.

It could very well be the dreary weather. She glanced out the window and rested her chin on her hand. Nothing of interest ever happened this time of the year, now that the social events of the holidays were over. It was too early for spring and her annual retreat with Aunt Margaret to Brighton Beach.

Amy stood and stretched, dropping her dog to the floor. She scooped the Pomeranian up. "I'm so very sorry, Persephone. I forgot you were sitting on my lap."

The dog regarded her with disdain. It amazed her how she could ascertain her dog's moods. Of course, no one believed that her dog had moods and that she could determine them. But when Amy did something of which Persephone didn't approve, the dog would raise her nonexistent tail in the air and stroll away as if she were the queen.

What Amy needed was to get out of the house. Go for a walk. Even in the damp, cool weather, a stroll could help clear her brain. Her mind made up, she shuffled her papers and stacked them neatly on the corner of her desk.

"Persephone, let's go for a walk." She reached out and pulled the dog to her chest. "We will take a nice walk and get some fresh air. You are beginning to put on weight and need some exercise." She rubbed her nose in the dog's soft white fur and glanced out the window again. "Well, maybe not *fresh*, but better than indoor air, at least."

Perhaps her close friend, Eloise, would be up for a stroll. They could take a walk to the Pump Room and hope the entire time that the threatening clouds did not dump on them.

She hurried down the stairs, the idea sounding better every minute. She handed Persephone off to her butler, Stevens, while she buttoned up her coat. Just then, the door knocker sounded and Stevens opened the door.

William stood there, bringing a smile to her face. After that ghastly business with her ex-fiancé's murder, she and William had celebrated by getting a wee bit tipsy. Unexpectedly, he had kissed her, and now their relationship had shifted. Nothing about courting had been formally announced, but there was definitely something in the air whenever they were together.

"What brings you here, my lord?" Amy asked, aware of Stevens standing next to her. She felt it important to maintain formality whenever she and William were not alone.

"I thought perhaps you would like some company, but it appears you are on your way out." Was that disappointment she heard in his voice?

"Actually, I was just about to take a walk, possibly to the Pump Room. I felt the need to get out of the house. My brain is having a hard time focusing, for some reason."

"Then I suggest we stroll together." He stopped and considered her for a few seconds. "Unless you were meeting someone else?"

"No." She shook her head. "I thought to stop at Eloise's house to see if she was up for a walk, but now I won't have to drag her out of the house." Amy laughed. "She is not overly fond of walking."

He glanced at the dog snuggled in her arms. "Are you taking Persephone with you?" He tried his best to look unconcerned, but she knew he was not enamored with her beloved dog. He didn't exactly dislike her, but the animal did seem to enjoy snubbing him. Almost from their first encounter, they had seemed to regard each other with uneasiness.

"Yes. I just need to get her leash." Amy retrieved the leash from a hook hanging by the door and snapped it onto Persephone's collar. "There. Now we're ready."

They made their way down the steps, and Amy took William's arm as they began their stroll.

"How is your new book coming along?"

She scrunched her nose. "It was just fine, but I need one more red herring, and I cannot come up with someone."

He patted her hand. "I've no doubt that you will do it. I am still amazed that you write such fearsome stories."

Amy waved her hand. "It's not so terrifying when you're writing it. I mean, I know who is going to get killed and how." She studied Persephone as the little dog moved from one side of the pathway to the other, sniffing and pulling on her leash.

"I will tell you, it is much more fun than when I was the suspect in a murder myself." She shuddered. "I dread to think what would have happened had we not stepped in and figured out who killed Mr. St. Vincent."

"I like to think that our police department would have eventually come to the same conclusion."

Amy looked at him sideways. "You have much more faith in Detectives Carson and Marsh than I do."

They were silent for a few minutes. Then William said, "I received some rather interesting news today."

"What is that?" Amy tugged Persephone's leash. The dog was getting much too close to another dog's leavings for her comfort.

"Lady Wethington is moving from London to Bath."

Amy frowned. "Who?" She tugged again, this time dragging her dog away from a dead bird. Why must Persephone find all the unpleasant things to entertain herself with?

He sighed. "My mother."

Amy almost broke into laughter at the look on his face. William reminded her of a young boy who had just discovered that his tutor was about to pay a visit to his parents.

"Is that a problem?"

"Don't get me wrong. I love my mother. She is everything most mothers of my rank are not. She took daily interest in me and my sister. She nursed us through illnesses and made sure our lessons were done. She read us stories and took us for long walks."

Thinking of her own mother, whom Amy had lost when she was only ten years old, she couldn't imagine anyone finding fault with such a woman. "I believe I hear a *but* in there."

"Yes. You do. The involvement in our daily lives did not stop when we reached adulthood."

"Oh my."

"Indeed. I think if I permitted it, she would read me a story every evening before bed and ask if I had cleaned my teeth and scrubbed behind my ears."

Amy burst out laughing. "I can see your dilemma. Unless, of course, you do not scrub behind your ears." She smirked at him.

William stopped their walk as they approached the end of the pavement. They waited for the traffic to clear, then continued.

"Tell me about your sister," Amy said. "You rarely speak of her."

"Valerie is five years my senior. She married the Earl of Denby about twelve years ago. They have managed to reproduce themselves seven times." He winced.

"Good heavens, they've been busy," Amy said.

"Indeed. I visited her last year before the last one was born, and it was like living in a foundling home. She has plenty of help, but everywhere I turned, there was a small child staring at me. It became quite alarming."

Amy hadn't given a great deal of thought to having children of her own. She'd imagined that if she ever did marry, there would be a child or two. But seven? Now it was her turn to shudder.

"There is also something that you need to be aware of about Lady Wethington, since you and I have become . . . fast friends."

Fast friends. Was that what they were? He'd kissed her a few times since that first occasion, but he always seemed to pull back just when it became interesting.

They came to another stop to allow traffic to proceed. The Roman Baths and the Abbey were a mere block away. She could see the church steeple from where they stood. There were more people about than Amy would have expected for January and the nasty weather. "Of what do I need to be aware?" she asked.

He looked her in the eye, humor clearly written there. "She intends to marry me off. Sooner rather than later."

CHAPTER 2

A light tap on Amy's bedchamber door drew her attention from the bracelet she was struggling to clip onto her wrist. Every time she neared snapping it closed, it slid off.

She blew out a frustrated breath. "Come in."

Aunt Margaret entered and frowned at Amy. "My, you look exasperated. Whatever is the matter?"

Amy held out her arm. "I'm trying to fasten this bracelet. One would have assumed jewelers made these clasps a little easier to affix."

"Why didn't you call for Lacey?" Aunt Margaret moved to Amy, took the bracelet from her hand, and had it closed in two seconds.

"It is Sunday morning, remember? She is off until dinnertime."

The two women shared the Winchester townhouse. Aunt Margaret, the younger half sister of Amy's father, had stepped in to raise young Amy after her mother passed away when she was ten years old.

Aunt Margaret was a wonderful companion; the bane of her brother's existence, since he'd never gotten her married off; and Amy's best friend. Aunt Margaret was the proud owner of a thirty-year-old cockatoo who quoted Shakespeare—unlike

Amy's fluffy Pomeranian, who made her thoughts known with a swish of her missing tail.

Only fifteen years apart in age, aunt and niece were more like sisters. While Amy was of medium height and filled out her clothes quite well—in some cases more than quite well—Aunt Margaret was tall and willowy. And as expected, both women wished they had the other's figure.

"Is William coming to escort us to church?" Aunt Margaret bent to view herself in the mirror over Amy's dressing table. She moved her hat around and stuck a pin in the center. Satisfied, she straightened and picked up her reticule and Bible from the table.

"Yes. He should be here any minute." Amy placed her own hat on her head, made a face, and took it off. She rummaged in her wardrobe for another and pulled out one of her favorites, which unfortunately had been crushed.

"I will meet you downstairs then," Aunt Margaret said as she left the room.

Amy waved her on and pulled out two other hats. Neither of them looked right with her outfit. She sighed and went back to the first one.

She truly had to get herself better organized. While involved in writing a new murder mystery, she let everything else go. The project took over her life to the extent that on occasion she even forgot to go downstairs for dinner. Not one to deny herself food, however, she spent many a late night raiding the kitchen for cold leftovers.

She plopped the original black-and-white straw hat back on her head and anchored it with a pearl hatpin. She picked up her gloves, retrieved her reticule and Bible, and joined Aunt Margaret at the front door.

Aunt Margaret glanced at Amy's feet. "You have on two different shoes again."

"Oh, for heaven's sake." Amy ran back upstairs, frustrated at her lack of attention. She often bought duplicates of the same pair of shoes so she didn't have to worry about wasting time searching for a missing one.

Were she an old lady, they would have called her eccentric. Instead, she was afraid those close to her merely thought of her as harebrained. Except, she assured herself, it took quite a bit of intelligence to write her wonderful murder books.

Back downstairs again, Stevens helped her into her cloak. The door knocker dropped just as Amy finished buttoning up.

"Good morning, ladies." William bowed in their direction, the warm smile he always greeted them with fully in place. He nodded at Amy. "Fix your hat."

She looked in the mirror, readjusted the headpiece, and seriously considered returning to bed and waking up the next day.

"Good morning, my lord." Aunt Margaret smiled back at him.

He stepped out into the cool morning air and allowed them to precede him down the steps.

They were on their way to St. Swithin's Church on the Paragon in the Wolcot area of Bath, where they worshiped every Sunday morning. It was a lovely old church that Amy had attended with her mother and Aunt Margaret since she was a small child.

When her mother was alive, her parents had maintained an amicable relationship but lived their lives separately. Papa and her brother, Michael, had resided in London, and Amy and her mother had lived in Bath with Aunt Margaret.

Mother had hated the noise and smell of London, whereas Papa loved the hustle and bustle of the city. Since there were two children of the marriage, there had to have been a time when they lived together, but for as long as Amy could remember, they'd had separate residences. She'd never questioned the arrangement, because it hadn't seemed odd to her at the time. Not until she became a woman had she wondered about it.

The church was slowly filling up, and greetings and chatter among the congregants almost—but not quite—blocked out Mrs. Edith Newton's organ playing. The poor dear was almost blind and hit the wrong notes on a regular basis.

They settled into their seats, and Amy looked around and smiled. As much as she loved writing about murder and mayhem, she also loved Sunday mornings, when her heart was at peace.

The sunlight streaming through the windows cast an ethereal glow over the congregation. She closed her eyes and took a deep breath.

"Move over."

Amy's eyes snapped open to see Eloise Spencer squeezing into the pew alongside her, pushing with her considerable hips to get Amy to make room.

"Good morning to you too, Eloise." Amy slid over and grinned at her companion, who always looked as if she had just finished a race. Of course, she usually arrived at places having raced there. Between her peculiarity and Amy's unconventionality, they made an excellent pair and had been close friends for ages.

Amy's father considered Eloise a "hoyden." Which was more than enough to recommend her to Amy.

"Have you started the new book yet?" Eloise attempted to rearrange her somewhat disheveled outfit.

Amy reached out and tucked a loose curl behind Eloise's ear. "For the book club? *The Sign of the Four*?"

"Yes. I am finding it quite intriguing."

Eloise, William, and Amy belonged to the Mystery Book Club of Bath, which held meetings every Thursday evening at the Atkinson & Tucker bookstore. They would read a book, then discuss it for a week or two, and then move on to another one.

"Actually, I've been working on my own book and haven't started *The Sign of the Four* yet. I've run into some plotting problems that have me twisted in knots. But I understand *The Sign of the Four* is quite good."

"Yes." Eloise nodded. "I wonder when we will read another one of yours?"

Whenever the club decided to read one of E. D. Burton's books, Amy had a difficult time not blurting out that she was the author. When she received her first contract from her publisher, Papa had insisted she use a pen name so no one would know his delicate, gently reared young daughter felt comfortable writing about bloody body parts and grisly murders.

"Soon, I hope. There are still two more they haven't selected yet."

In the six years she'd been publishing, Amy had written five books, the one sitting on her desk at home being the sixth. She had another month to meet the deadline for that one.

Mr. Palmer, the pastor at St. Swithin's, walked up the center aisle to the front of the church and turned to address the congregation. "Good morning, fellow worshipers. I am happy you have joined us, and I ask that you all stand and greet each other before our service begins."

The man was friendly and had a cheerful demeanor, unlike the last pastor they'd had. The previous reverend had been a sour man, all fire and brimstone. Amy had apologized to God for being happy when Mr. Benson was moved to another church and they got Mr. Palmer in his place.

The pastor stepped down and walked around, shaking hands, listening to sad tales, and pinching the cheeks of chubby babies. Since Amy had greeted everyone as they arrived, she remained in her seat and flipped through her Bible, looking for the verses on which this week's sermon was based.

The church attendees settled down and gave their attention to Pastor Palmer. As usual, the sermon was uplifting, the songs off-key, and the company of friends alongside her comforting.

After leaving the line of congregants wishing the pastor a good day at the end of the service, Amy linked her arm through her friend's and began to walk. "Eloise, please join us for luncheon." She looked up at the Misses O'Neill, who both waved and then walked in their direction.

"I would like that," Eloise said. "Is Wethington joining us as well?"

"Yes, I assume so. I didn't ask him specifically, but he generally does." Amy paused for a moment, regarding Eloise's smug smile, and then said, "Why do you ask?"

"Oh, no particular reason. Just curious."

Before Amy could question her friend further, the two O'Neill sisters stopped in front of them. "Good morning, Lady Amy, Miss Spencer."

William and Aunt Margaret were involved in a conversation with Mr. and Mrs. Hewitt, so all the Misses O'Neill's nosy questions would be directed to Amy and Eloise this morning.

"Good morning, ladies. It's a lovely day, is it not?" Maybe Amy could keep the conversation light and ward off the usual inquisition to which the women were known to subject people.

Miss Gertrude and Miss Penelope O'Neill were sisters who for some bizarre reason pretended to be twins, even though they looked nothing alike and were separated by almost a foot in height. Miss Penelope was short, round, and dark haired, whereas Miss Gertrude was tall and painfully thin, with curly red hair and freckles. Amy found it hard to believe they were even sisters. Their usual flowered dresses matched each other's, as did their navy-blue-and-white-striped straw hats.

The ladies made it their responsibility to be sure everyone was aware of their deep devotion to the church, although their love of gossip canceled out some of the good they did.

"Yes, it is lovely out today," Miss Gertrude said. "Lady Amy, sister and I were considering joining the lovely book club that you are a member of."

Eloise almost choked trying to keep her laughter in.

"Is that right?" Amy said, her eyebrows climbing up her forehead. "You do know we read murder mysteries, do you not?"

Miss Penelope giggled. Actually giggled. "Yes, we know that. We think it might be quite titillating to read about such things." She looked over at Miss Gertrude. "Don't you agree, sister?"

Miss Gertrude nodded so enthusiastically that her hat became loose and slid to the bridge of her nose.

Eloise was now red-faced, and Amy feared the poor girl would choke to death if the conversation did not end soon.

"Well, we would certainly be happy to have you join us," Amy said, as Eloise mumbled something and walked away.

Thank you, Eloise. 'Tis so nice to have the support of friends.

"We meet on Thursday evenings at the Atkinson and Tucker bookstore around eight o'clock. Do you know where that is?"

"Oh, yes. We know where you meet." Miss Penelope linked her arm into her sister's. "I look forward to seeing you

Thursday next." She nodded, and the two of them walked off, their heads together, whispering furiously.

Well, that was certainly surreal.

"Are you ready to leave, Amy?" Aunt Margaret had broken away from the group she and William had been speaking with.

"Yes. I just need to find Eloise. She's wandered off somewhere."

Once they had all gathered, Aunt Margaret, Amy, William, and Eloise climbed into the Wethington carriage, which, fortunately, was a good-sized vehicle.

"Whatever would make Miss Gertrude and Miss Penelope believe they would enjoy reading about murders?" Eloise asked.

"What?" Aunt Margaret asked.

Amy grinned. "It seems the Misses O'Neill have been hiding a penchant for murder mysteries. They said they wanted to join our mystery book club."

Aunt Margaret laughed. "That will be quite an interesting meeting to see. If I didn't abhor reading about grisly, gory, bloody murders, I would go just to see how it all goes."

Amy huffed. "We don't always read about grisly murders. It's a mystery book club, which means we read all sorts of mysteries. The Sherlock Homes stories are not gruesome at all. Well, not usually, anyway."

"But you read Edgar Allan Poe, don't you?"

Amy shifted on her seat. "Yes. On occasion."

Eloise decided to add to Aunt Margaret's condemnation. "And we've read a couple of your books too, Amy. They can be quite terrifying."

"Thank you so much for that, Eloise." Amy glared at her.

Eloise laughed. "Oh, give off. You know I love your books."

The ride from the church to Amy's home didn't take very long. There was continued speculation on why the two ladies from the church wanted to join a mystery book club, but no one seemed to come up with a logical reason.

They all climbed from the carriage and made their way up the steps and into the house. It took a bit of time for them all to remove their outer garments, hand them off to Stevens, and then proceed upstairs to the dining room.

"Oh, I smell lamb," Aunt Margaret set as she sniffed the air. "My favorite."

They each took their regular seats, and Amy shook out her napkin and placed it on her lap. "I have decided to become a vegetarian."

Three pairs of eyes looked in her direction. "What?" Aunt Margaret said, her hand poised over her glass of wine.

"I have decided that it is more ethical for the animals and better for my health to refrain from eating meat."

"No meat?" William asked. "How very odd."

"What will you eat?" Eloise asked as she passed the platter of lamb to Amy, who shook her head and handed it to William.

"Vegetables. Hence the word *vegetarian*." Amy piled potatoes and peas on her plate. She also selected a piece of warm bread and buttered it.

William shook his head. "I don't think that's a good idea, and I'm sure it's not healthy."

"Not so," she said, placing a forkful of lovely buttered potatoes in her mouth. "Did you know we have a Vegetarian Society right here in England? It was established in 1847, and by 1863 it had eight hundred and eighty-nine members."

"A lot of eights," William murmured.

"Have you joined?" Eloise looked at her lamb, shrugged, and popped a piece into her mouth.

"Yes. I have. I haven't yet attended any meetings, however. In fact, I'm not sure they hold meetings, but I sent in my application form and fee two weeks ago."

"Amy, I must say, you never cease to amuse me," Aunt Margaret said, biting into a piece of lamb and making a rapturous sound. She chewed and swallowed and looked over at her niece. "I wonder what you will entertain us with next?"

CHAPTER 3

William tried his best to set aside every Thursday evening for the Mystery Book Club of Bath meetings. It was one of his favorite things to do and he looked forward to it each week.

As he dressed for the meeting, tying his cravat into an acceptable knot, he thought about his life, which was quite pleasant and satisfying. With the book club, seeing friends at his gentleman's club, attending church, enjoying a few dances at the assembly every Saturday, and putting in enough hours each week with his holdings and investments to keep his finances solid, he'd always been a contented man. Until recently.

Despite his mother's pushing him toward the altar, he'd found himself thinking more and more that a wife to come home to each evening and to raise children with might not be a bad idea. A smart, funny, agreeable woman with whom to share his life. He smiled as Amy came to mind.

Whistling an unnamed tune, he grabbed an umbrella from the stand next to the door and hurried down the steps to his waiting carriage. The night was a typical English evening, with mist and a slight drizzle, and the chilly January air supported his decision to wear his heavy coat.

He stepped into the back room at Atkinson & Tucker for the meeting and immediately spotted the one person who had occupied his mind a short time ago. She could easily rearrange his perfect life.

Then perhaps it wasn't so perfect and could use some rearranging.

Amy stood across the room, waving her arms at something she was saying to the group around her.

"Good evening. It looks like you are in a deep discussion. *The Sign of the Four,* I assume?" William joined the small group and took his position next to Amy.

"We were commenting on Holmes disguising himself as a sailor and fooling even Watson," Amy said. "We were considering whether it was really possible for him to disguise himself so thoroughly that even his best friend and roommate wouldn't know him."

"I contend it is impossible for someone so close to the individual not to recognize the man, no matter how well disguised," Lord Temple said.

Amy opened her mouth to speak, then glanced over William's shoulder, and her eyes widened. He turned to see Miss Gertrude and Miss Penelope O'Neill hesitantly enter the room. He looked back at Amy. "They did come after all."

She continued to watch them. "I still don't understand why they want to join a mystery book club."

He frowned. "They do know we read mysteries? And some of them"—he cleared his throat—"especially those by E. D. Burton, are quite, shall we say, intense?"

She elbowed him in his ribs.

"Hello, Lady Amy. Oh, and Lord Wethington." Miss Gertrude hurried to their little group with her sister right behind her.

"Good evening, ladies," William said with a slight bow. "I am pleased you have decided to join us."

"Yes," Miss Penelope gushed, looking around the room. "Sister and I are so excited to join the group." She leaned in close to William and said softly, "Not many people know that we love to read murder stories."

Nothing could have surprised him more. These two older ladies, stalwarts of the church, enjoyed murder mystery books? He shook his head, thinking that one never knew what surprises awaited one when dealing with members of the human race.

Before they could continue their conversation, Mr. Colbert, who acted as moderator for the group, suggested that they begin to take their seats.

While they waited for all the members to settle in, William flipped through the pages of *Keene's Bath Journal*, the local newspaper for Bath. Amy scanned the pages of *The Sign of the Four*.

"Listen to this." William turned to her and glanced back at the newspaper. "An unidentified man's body was found floating in the River Avon early yesterday morning. Attempts are being made to identify the man so his family may be notified."

Amy shuddered. "That's terrible. I wonder who the poor unfortunate man is."

The last few members began to filter in, and William closed his newspaper and tucked it into his satchel. Amy closed her book and gave her attention to Mr. Colbert.

"It is time to begin our meeting." Mr. Colbert stood at the front of the room. He smiled at the members; then his eyes shifted to the doorway, and he frowned. Amy turned, and an unfamiliar man stood there, looking around the room.

"May I help you, sir?" Mr. Colbert asked.

"I'm looking for a Lord Wethington."

William stood and waved the man over. The man held out a folded paper to William. "This is for you, my lord."

William thanked him and returned to his seat.

"What is that?" Amy pointed at the paper.

He shrugged and opened it, his eyes scanning the missive. After a few moments, he inhaled deeply and looked over at her, his face pale. "The police have identified the man found floating in the river."

"And they notified *you*?"

"Yes. He is Mr. James Harding. My man of business."

"How terrible!"

William flicked the paper with his finger. "And strange, too, since we had a meeting set up for Saturday last that he canceled since he claimed he wasn't feeling well."

"Claimed? Did you not believe him?"

"I'm not sure. I had reason to believe recently that there was something very odd going on with my finances." He tucked the note into his pocket. "They want me to come to the morgue and confirm their findings."

Before Amy could comment on that statement, Eloise Spencer came racing through the door, waving her arm. "I'm here!"

Amy rolled her eyes at William. Mr. Davidson glowered at the young woman.

Davidson had been a member of the club since it was formed a few years before. He was not one of William's favorite people, as the man's regard for women was not at all what William thought acceptable. At one meeting when they were discussing *A Study in Scarlet*, he'd suggested that the idea of working with a woman was ludicrous because the only thing women were good for was wiping children's noses and gossiping.

After all the women in the room reacted with shock and sputtering protests, William had taken him to task and was later applauded for his efforts by Amy, a staunch women's rights advocate.

"Must you always rush into the room as if your heels were on fire?" Davidson grumbled.

"How do you know they are not?" Eloise said smugly, as she took the chair on the other side of Amy.

Much to William's delight, Davidson looked at Eloise's feet, bringing a few titters from the group.

Mr. Colbert cleared this throat. "Before we begin our discussion this evening, I would like to introduce to the group two new members, Miss Gertrude O'Neill and her lovely sister, Miss Penelope O'Neill."

The two ladies tittered and giggled as they were greeted with warm welcomes. William still could not understand their desire to join the club. Although he thought most women were too delicate in nature to enjoy murders, Amy had certainly disabused him of the idea that all of them were when she revealed herself to him as a murder mystery author.

Mr. Colbert picked up a copy of *The Sign of the Four*. "I shall begin our discussion by throwing out a question. Do any of you think Mr. Doyle is making a mistake by showing Sherlock Holmes's bad habit of injecting himself with cocaine as he does in the very beginning of *The Sign of the Four*?"

Miss Penelope was the first to raise her hand. "I don't believe so. It merely showed him as a human being, with faults. After all, Mr. Holmes is oftentimes portrayed as imperfect."

"I disagree," Miss Sterling said. "I like my heroes to be perfect. That is why I read fiction."

A discussion on the perfection of heroes ensued.

William tried his best to concentrate, since he had thoroughly enjoyed the book. However, his mind was occupied with Mr. Harding's death.

How very odd that he had been found in the river. Hopefully it had merely been the result of a misjudgment on Harding's part and not purposeful. He shuddered at the thought.

Mr. Colbert nodded as Lord Temple finished his comment. "What is Watson's role in the story? How does he interact with Holmes? Is his presence essential?" He looked around the room for debate.

"I wonder if Watson's presence is ever essential," Miss Gertrude said.

Another discussion followed as William once again allowed his attention to drift to the imminent arrival of his mother. He'd received word earlier in the day that he should expect her to take up residence with him in a few days.

He sighed, garnering a glance from Amy.

"What's wrong?" she whispered.

"Nothing. Just considering my mother's imminent arrival."

"Oh for heaven's sake, William, you are acting like a little boy who is expecting to be chastised by his mother. Nothing will change for you."

He drew back and regarded her with raised eyebrows. "You do not know my mother."

"That is true, and I expect to meet her shortly to form my own opinion."

"Lady Amy, what do you make of the hapless Athelney Jones of Scotland Yard in the book? Do you believe the police are ineffective?" Mr. Colbert asked.

Apparently Mr. Colbert was not happy with William and Amy having their own private conversation, which served to remind William that Mr. Colbert had spent many years as the headmaster of a boys' school prior to beginning his career as a solicitor.

Amy blushed briefly but then recovered. "I can assure you, Mr. Colbert, that the police are not always effective."

No doubt Amy was referring to the two officers they'd dealt with following St. Vincent's murder. Detectives Marsh and Carson had been so focused on Amy that they'd been blind to other suspects.

The discussion turned to Toby the hound, whom Mr. Doyle had sent roaming through London with Watson and Holmes on his heels, bringing comments from Amy about her own dog.

"Not to disagree with a lady, but I doubt a Pomeranian would possess the tracking skills of a hound, Lady Amy." William couldn't help but grin at the picture of the small white fluffy dog sniffing garbage and other noxious things in the more disreputable parts of town in order to uncover clues to a murder.

Within an hour they had discussed and dissected the entire story. It appeared most of the members had enjoyed the book. Including their two new participants.

"Before we finish for the evening, I have an important and exciting announcement to make." Mr. Colbert looked out at the group with a huge grin. "Atkinson and Tucker bookstore is sponsoring a book fair. It will be held in about five or six weeks' time."

Mrs. Morton raised her hand. "That is wonderful news, Mr. Colbert." She turned to Amy. "Perhaps it will become a yearly event."

Mr. Colbert smiled indulgently at Mrs. Morton. "It is my belief that they are going to see how this one goes. I'm sure, if it is successful, they may well wish to repeat it."

Miss Sterling raised her hand. "Will our book club be involved in any way?"

"As you all know, there are several clubs that meet here at the store. From what the store manager, Mr. Dobish, told me, they expect to have all the clubs involved in some way."

"This is very exciting," Lady Abigail gushed.

Mr. Colbert cleared his throat. "I have another announcement about the book festival that I think will please you all." He waited for a moment until all eyes were on him. "Mr. Dobish has been in contact with Chatto and Windus, the well-known publishing house in London."

Sitting next to him, Amy drew in a deep breath and covered her mouth with her hand.

"We are working with them to have the very popular Mr. E. D. Burton appear at our book festival to meet his readers and sign books." Mr. Colbert looked out at his audience with a smug expression on his face.

"Oh no," Amy whispered. She looked over at William. "Oh no. No, no, no."

"Is something wrong, Lady Amy?" Mr. Colbert asked. "You've gone quite pale."

"No. I am fine." She attempted a smile, but it looked more like a grimace.

William was almost as shocked as Amy. She had been writing under that pseudonym since the beginning of her writing career.

"That is delightful news," Miss Penelope gushed. "I love his books, and if I could have him sign my copies, it would make them so much more valuable to me!" She turned to Miss Gertrude. "Don't you agree, sister?"

"Yes. Absolutely, sister."

The group started chattering about the possibility of Mr. Burton being part of the book festival while Amy looked around frantically, as if seeking to escape before the other members could ascertain her secret.

Mr. Colbert stood at the front of the room, glowing at how his announcement had set the room to buzzing.

On the other hand, Amy looked as though she might pass out.

CHAPTER 4

"Will we go to the morgue now, or wait until morning? I'm not sure how late they stay open. But then, I imagine most people don't know that." Amy gathered her things as the members rose to leave the meeting, chatting happily among themselves about the upcoming book fair.

William's head snapped up and he looked at her, his eyebrows practically reaching his hairline. "Excuse me?"

She frowned. "What?"

He withdrew the paper from his pocket where he'd stashed it earlier. "I don't see where they requested the two of us to go to the morgue."

Amy's jaw dropped. "Whatever do you mean? Of course I'm going with you."

He shook his head. "There is no *of course*."

She pointed a finger at him. "Yes. There is. You helped me with my investigation, and now it's my turn to help you with yours."

He drew back in surprise. "My investigation! I have only been asked to confirm James's identity."

"Ha! Do you suppose your man of business accidentally fell into the river? How many people do you know drowned because they fell into a river? Do you know how many I know? None." She crossed her arms under her breasts and glared at him.

The nerve of the man, to think he would leave her behind when something exciting like this happened. Well, actually a man's death was not exciting—she said a quick prayer for his soul—but she would not be left out of it, at any rate.

"No. I don't believe I know anyone who fell into a river and drowned," he said between gritted teeth. "But that does not mean you will accompany me."

"What it means, my lord, is we are in this together." She decided she would need to use her feminine wiles; as much as she hated to do it, she would not be left out. She lowered her voice and attempted to look becoming. "I thought we were partners?"

William burst out laughing. "Don't try that with me, Amy. I know what you think you're doing. I will not be fooled—or felled—by female shenanigans."

She huffed. "Female shenanigans! I will have you know—"

A cough from Mr. Colbert, who now stood in front of them, drew their attention. He had a slight grin on his face as he said, "Excuse me, but the meeting has ended, and everyone has left." He waved his arm around the now-empty room.

Indeed, the room was vacant except for the three of them, and most of the lamps—all but the one next to them and the one by the door—had been extinguished. How could she not have noticed the darkness? Well, arguing with William took all her concentration. That was how.

William stood and held his hand out for her. "I am sorry to hold you up, Mr. Colbert. I am afraid we lost track of time."

"I apologize as well, Mr. Colbert."

Mr. Colbert nodded at the note in William's hand. "Bad news?"

"Yes. You might say that. This is a note from the Bath police. A man's body was discovered floating in the River Avon yesterday. The police want me to identify the body, since it is presumed to be my man of business, Mr. James Harding."

"Oh my. Not good news at all. Nasty business."

Amy left the bookstore, stopped right outside the front door, and waited for William to join her. He and Mr. Colbert exited together. William said something to Mr. Colbert and then joined her. "I shall walk you to your carriage."

"We have not finished discussing your situation."

William placed his hands on his hips. "I have no situation."

Amy poked him in the chest. "Hear this, my lord. I will camp out in front of your house and wait for you to go to the morgue. I will remain there in all weather and at all times of the day and night. Your neighbors will believe you have wronged me. Your reputation will be ruined. You will not be accepted in polite society. Your gentleman's club will probably expel you. Your—"

William threw his hands up in the air. "Very well. Far be it from me to allow you to catch an ague by standing in the rain."

Instead of showing annoyance, as he probably expected, she grinned. "Very well. When shall we go?"

"Tomorrow. I will leave my house at precisely ten o'clock in the morning. I will arrive at your house shortly thereafter." He pointed at her. "Be ready."

She felt like jumping for joy and then realized how very macabre that sounded. She sobered. "I shall be ready."

William took her arm and escorted her to her carriage, which awaited at the edge of the pavement. He helped her in and closed the door, then slapped the side of the vehicle as a signal to the driver to move forward. As she gave him a slight wave from the window, he stood with his hands on his hips, shaking his head as he watched her drive away.

★　★　★

Just to be certain not to give William reason to renege on his offer to allow her to go with him to the morgue, Amy was up and dressed and sitting at the breakfast table well before ten o'clock.

"My, aren't you the early one today," Aunt Margaret said as she drifted into the room. She always moved with such grace that Amy's bumbling through life seemed even more obvious to anyone observing them together. Nevertheless, Amy loved her aunt and honestly did try to emulate her, however meager her attempts.

"Yes. I have an appointment with William this morning."

Aunt Margaret sat in her usual seat and poured tea into her cup. "Indeed? And to where are you two off this early in the day?"

Amy swallowed her bite of egg. "The morgue."

Aunt Margaret's hand stopped, her teacup midway between the saucer and her mouth. "Did you say the *morgue*?"

"Yes."

Her aunt took a sip of tea and carefully placed the cup in the saucer. "I know I probably don't really want to know the answer to this, but curiosity has always gotten the best of me where you are concerned. Why are you going to the morgue?"

Amy leaned forward. "Last night at the book club meeting, William received a note asking him to come to the morgue to confirm the identity of a man who had been pulled from the River Avon."

"Why William?" Aunt Margaret placed her hand on her chest. "Oh goodness, not a family member, I hope?"

Amy waved her hand. "No. They believe the man to be William's man of business."

Aunt Margaret cringed. "First thing in the morning? How awful."

Amy shrugged and continued with her meal. "Best to get it over with."

Her aunt cleared her throat. "Amy, love. I have always admired your—shall we say—spirited personality. I love your ability to create stories that people want to read and the gusto with which you conjure up fake murders and solve the gruesome tales. But even I am a bit taken aback by your enthusiasm about going to a morgue."

Amy put her fork down and looked over at her aunt. "Yes. Perhaps you are right. I must put on more of a somber demeanor when we arrive at the morgue. I don't want to appear too excited by the adventure."

She continued to eat. "Oh, I almost forgot to tell you, what with William receiving the note and all." Amy leaned forward and lowered her voice, lest any of the staff hear what she was about to tell her aunt. "Our book club is having a book festival in a few weeks."

"That's wonderful! I shall love to go to a book festival." Aunt Margaret paused. "What's wrong? You don't look happy."

"No. I am not happy, because apparently the bookstore manager is going to try to persuade my publisher to have Mr. E. D. Burton appear at the festival and sign books."

Aunt Margaret sucked in a deep breath. "Oh no."

"Oh yes."

"What will you do?"

Amy shrugged. "Well, I obviously can't show up as E. D. Burton. I haven't heard from my publisher yet, so hopefully they will be able to come up with something."

Aunt Margaret shook her head and took a very delicate, feminine bite of toast. "It is too bad you can't receive the well-deserved recognition for your work. Even though I don't read your books, I know you have plenty of fans."

"Yes. I know." Amy sighed. "But Papa was adamant that if I were to accept the contracts for my books, it had to be under a pseudonym."

"It will be so nice when women are finally treated as equals and not as children, with men needed to guide them." Aunt Margaret spread jam on her toast. "I wonder if that day will ever arrive."

"One can only hope."

They finished breakfast with innocuous chatter about their day and the coming Assembly dance the next evening.

An hour later, Amy sat by the window in the drawing room that faced the street. It was about four minutes past ten o'clock. William was always on time.

Just as she closed her timepiece, his carriage pulled up. She hopped up and grabbed her gloves and reticule. She had her coat on and fastened before he dropped the door knocker.

Stevens opened the door, and Amy stepped out. "I'm ready."

William moved back. "My goodness. You are anxious."

"Not at all. Well, maybe yes, but more importantly, I didn't want to give you an excuse to leave me behind." She hurried down the steps, afraid he might change his mind.

William followed and helped her into the carriage. "Are you sure you want to do this, Amy? It can be pretty gruesome looking at a dead body. Especially one that has been floating in the river."

"Research, my lord. Research." She settled back and refused to admit to herself that maybe, just maybe, she *was* a bit nervous.

They were both quiet as the carriage made its way through town, stopping for traffic, weaving in and out, making the ride seem interminable.

"You look a bit nervous," William said.

She opened her mouth, about to deny it, then changed her mind. "Yes. I will admit I am a bit unsettled." She held her hand up when he opened his mouth. "But I still want to do this."

The building where the morgue was located loomed before them. She accepted William's hand as she stepped out of the vehicle and took a deep breath.

Inside the building, a young man at the desk right by the front door stood as they entered. "Good morning, sir. How may I help you?"

"Good morning. I am Lord Wethington, and this is Lady Amy Lovell. We are here to confirm the identification of Mr. James Harding."

The man nodded, picked up some papers, looked over at Amy, and gulped. "Are you sure you want to view the body, my lady?"

"Yes. I am sure." *No. I am not sure, but now that I've made a fuss over it, I can't back down and appear a fool.*

"Very well. If you will follow me." He led them down a flight of stairs, around a corner, and then down another flight of stairs. It got darker and damper as they descended. Amy's heart began to pound, and her mouth dried up. She rubbed her palms over her arms, trying to warm herself.

Finally, after a third flight of stairs, they walked the length of a long corridor, the smells noxious enough that she covered her mouth and nose with a handkerchief William handed her.

The man leading them opened a door and stepped aside to let them enter. He pointed to a table in the corner of the room, where a body lay, a cloth of some sort covering it.

Amy glanced at William, who looked quite pale and kept swallowing. She grabbed his hand, and they moved toward the table. The man lifted the top of the sheet to reveal the man's face.

William glanced at the body, then closed his eyes and opened them again. Looking over at their escort, he said, "Yes. I am afraid that is Mr. James Harding."

A loud buzzing sound kept Amy from hearing William's voice very well, which seemed to come from a great distance. The room grew very dim, and she blinked to regain her vision. She noticed that her knees had turned to liquid and her limbs had become quite heavy.

She grabbed William's arm just as she slid to the floor.

★　★　★

When she opened her eyes, she was lying on a sofa in a strange office. William sat alongside her, studying her carefully. "Are you all right, Amy?"

She attempted to sit up, but he touched her shoulder to keep her from rising. "I think you need to give yourself a little time." He handed her a cup of water, which she sipped.

"What happened?" Her head was pounding, and she wasn't exactly sure how she had come to be lying on a sofa in an unknown office.

"You fainted."

She shook her head. Goodness, that wasn't a good idea with her head hurting. "I don't faint."

"Yes. You do."

She looked down. "Who unfastened my dress?"

"I did."

"Why?"

"To let you breathe better. If it wasn't totally improper, I would have cut the strings on your corset too."

"You wouldn't dare!"

"I said I would have, not that I did."

"That was James Harding, wasn't it?" She thought she had heard William identify the man, but since her hearing had taken leave at that moment, she wasn't sure.

"Yes." William put his hand behind her back and helped her up. "It was him. But there was something odd about it."

"You mean there is something odder than being found floating in the river?"

William reached into his pocket and withdrew some papers. "These were found on his body, inside an envelope. They've been drying out, but the ink has been washed away. Tucked in with the papers was my business card, which was why the police contacted me to identify the body."

"What is odd about that?"

"I can't say for certain, since the writing is gone, but I have a feeling these are papers James was to deliver for me a couple of weeks ago regarding a business deal. I'm almost sure these are the contracts I signed, because I remember tucking my card in with the papers and putting them into an envelope that looked very much like this one."

The door to the office opened, and the young man who had escorted them to the morgue stuck his head in. "My lord, how is her ladyship feeling?"

"I am better, thank you," Amy said, fastening the top of her dress.

"Then there are two police detectives here who wish to speak with you."

Taking a glance at her, William said, "Very well, since Lady Amy seems to have recovered from her faint."

"I don't faint."

"I will be right back with them," the young man said, then closed the door.

She smoothed her hair back and adjusted her hat. "We were several flights down to the morgue, yet from the window over there, it appears we are on the ground floor. How did I get up here?"

William raised his brows. "How do you think?"

"Don't tell me you carried me?" For some reason, she felt quite uneasy with the idea of William carrying her up three flights of stairs. First because she really needed to shed close to a stone, and second because it seemed—strange. It appeared he was quite a bit stronger than she'd thought.

Before she could dwell too long on that, the door opened again, and William and Amy looked up. They both groaned as two detectives stepped into the office. Why in heavens name were they to be plagued once more by the men who had harassed them months before during Mr. St. Vincent's murder investigation?

"Well. Look who is here identifying another unexpected dead body." Detective Marsh grinned and slapped Detective Carson on the shoulder. "None other than his lordship, Lord Wethington, and his cohort, Lady Amy Lovell." He strolled into the room and stood before them, his hands firmly planted on his hips. "Who did you kill this time?"

CHAPTER 5

William's annoyance quickly turned to anger. "Detective, must I remind you again that attempts at jokes are inappropriate when discussing someone's demise?"

The prior year when William and Amy had investigated the murder of her ex-fiancé, the detectives had seemed a bit too casual with death for his liking.

"Settle down, your lordship." Marsh took a seat and opened his always-handy notebook. Detective Carson stood behind his partner, his hands clasped behind his back.

"Tell me how it is you are connected to the deceased"—Marsh flipped back a few pages—"Mr. James Harding."

"He was my man of business."

Marsh wrote furiously while Carson addressed William. "What did the man do for you?"

William was certain that Carson continued to stand so he could intimidate him and Amy. Tired of straining his neck to look up at the detective, William stood. "He handled my finances. He negotiated contracts, he collected rents for my various properties, paid bills, and kept track of my various holdings."

Carson nodded. "Why don't you sit down, your lordship?"

"As soon as you do, Detective."

Carson glared at him but took a seat. He looked over at Amy. "I shouldn't be surprised to see you here with Wethington, but it seems to me that viewing a dead body is not something a young lady would want to do. Was this Harding chap your man of business as well?"

"No. I do not employ a man of business. My brother handles all the financial matters for my family."

"Detective, might I ask how Mr. Harding came to be floating in the River Avon?" William inquired.

"All unwitnessed drownings are considered homicides and require an investigation. All we know so far is that Mr. Harding was apparently drunk and took a walk along the river and fell in. It's happened before."

William did a good job of hiding his surprise, since he knew James to be a teetotaler. "And why did you determine he was drunk and fell into the river?"

"He had an empty flask in his pocket that smelled of spirits. Aside from the normal bumps and bruises that a body would suffer floating in a river, there were no other injuries to suggest it was anything but an accident."

"Yet you are investigating it?"

"It is required." Carson looked over at Amy. "Just so we're clear. There is no need for either one of you to do any prying. You were lucky you weren't killed last year, sticking your nose in police business."

"Yet we handed the murderer over to you," Amy snapped.

Marsh looked up from his pad and glowered at her. "Just as we identified the killer ourselves." He waved his finger at her. "If we learn that you are nosing around again, I will notify your father to come and escort you to London."

Amy bristled, and William quelled the urge to plant a facer on the detective. "If you are finished with your questioning, Lady Amy and I would like to leave."

Carson nodded. "Just be sure to remain available for any further questions."

William took Amy's arm and held her elbow as they left the office and exited the building. The weather had turned cooler, and Amy shivered alongside him. He waved for his driver to pull up, and they climbed into the carriage.

"You appeared unconvinced when the detectives said they believed it was an accident." Amy took the blanket he handed her from underneath the seat and wrapped it around herself. He was certain her chill was not just from the cold air but rather from her experience in the morgue.

William leaned forward, his hands resting on his knees. "James Harding was a teetotaler. He never imbibed. He once told me his father was a wastrel who spent a good portion of his income on strong spirits. I have never, in all the time I've known James, seen him take as much as a sip of wine."

"How very interesting," Amy said. She remained silent for a minute or so and then said, "Then it was no accident?"

William shook his head. "Not unless the man did a complete turnaround from the way he had previously lived his entire life."

"Do you have any idea who would want him dead?"

He hesitated. "No."

"Aha! I heard a tiny niggling of doubt in that word." She shifted in her seat and pulled the blanket up farther on her chin.

William stared out the window at the shops and shoppers as the carriage moved slowly through the traffic, carefully considering his words. "As I mentioned briefly before, of late I had a few concerns about James."

"In what sense?"

He looked over at her. "I had reason to believe all was not right with my finances."

"You think he was cheating you?"

"I hate to even say it out loud, since we worked together for a few years, but yes. I was beginning to believe money was disappearing."

"What will you do?"

William leaned back and studied her. "James shared an office with Mr. Ernest Tibbs. He's a barrister, who only recently moved into the space. I think I should go—"

"—*we* should go."

He frowned at her. "*I* should go and tell Tibbs I am going to retrieve my files from Harding's office. While I'm there—"

"—while *we're* there."

He sighed and continued. "I will of course retrieve my files, but I think a bit of browsing through all of Harding's files might not be a bad idea. If he was purposely sent into that river, there must be someone who would benefit from that."

She stared at him for a minute. "Do you honestly think we are about to involve ourselves in another murder investigation?"

William shook his head. "No."

Amy's shoulders slumped. "Oh. I thought maybe that was what you were suggesting."

He cleared this throat. "*We*"—he waved his hand back and forth between them—"are not going to become involved in another murder investigation."

"Now just a minute. If you think Mr. Harding was helped into that river and you believe I will stay out of it, you are mistaken, my lord."

He raised his eyes to heaven. "One could only hope."

The carriage slowed down as it arrived at Amy's house. The driver opened the door and William stepped out. Turning toward Amy, he held his hand out. "I assume I may escort you to the Assembly tomorrow evening?"

"Yes. Of course." She took his hand, and they climbed the steps together.

William placed his knuckle under Amy's chin. "The police detectives were correct. We were lucky we did not get killed when we involved ourselves in St. Vincent's murder."

She shrugged. "I suppose." Her eyes lit up. "Maybe we should get a gun."

"No! No gun. I doubt very much that we will have to shoot our way out of a barrister's office."

With that, he bent forward as if to give her a kiss, but thinking better of it, he gave her a slight salute and hurried back down the steps. When he glanced out the carriage window, she was staring after him.

* * *

The Saturday night Assembly was the event of the week, with those who were in town from London joining the regular Bath citizenry. It was easy to pick out those from Town and those from Bath. The Londoners' clothing was more sophisticated, more expensive, and more daring.

William and Amy joined the circle of friends from the book club who generally attended. Eloise, Mr. Davidson, Lord Temple, Mrs. Morton, and Miss Sterling stood in a circle discussing the upcoming book festival, which William noticed made Amy a bit uncomfortable. That is, if the way she gripped his arm was any indication. He would be black-and-blue in the morning.

"I'm so excited to finally meet Mr. Burton," Miss Sterling gushed. "I just know he will be tall and handsome."

Good lord, she sounded like a swooning young maiden, a status from which Miss Sterling was many years removed.

"Lady Amy, what do you suppose Mr. Burton looks like?" Mrs. Morton asked.

William choked down his laughter. "Yes, Lady Amy. Give us all your opinion. What do you suppose Mr. Burton looks like?" He grinned at her and bit his lip when she kicked his shin hard enough to cause a bruise.

He glanced down at her foot to see if she was wearing men's boots.

"I can assure you, Mrs. Morton, that whatever anyone imagines Mr. Burton looks like, he will be nothing like that," Amy said.

"Who cares what the man looks like?" Mr. Davidson, always the sour one, groused. "Burton writes great books. Nothing else matters." He shook his head in disgust just as the music for the first dance of the evening began.

William held out his hand, and Amy moved into his arms as they began the dance. He wondered how his mother would view his relationship with Amy. No doubt Mother would be quite pleased to meet her. Amy was everything a woman of their class would want for her son. But Mother could also be a bit pushy, which might frighten Amy, who he knew was not as thrilled at the idea of marriage as he might like.

He shuddered to think about the first meeting between the two women.

Once the dance had ended, they headed to the refreshment table to partake of punch and lemonade. They'd each just taken a sip of warm liquid when Mr. Charles Lemmon approached them.

"Good evening, Wethington, Lady Amy." He nodded and picked up a drink from the table behind them. "Bad news about Harding drowning." He shook his head and sighed.

"Did you know him, Lemmon?"

He nodded. "Yes. He was my man of business. I understand he worked for you as well." He seemed to hesitate for a minute, then leaned in close to William. "Did you notice anything odd about Harding the last few months?"

Amy glanced over at William. "I'm not sure what you mean," he said.

Lemmon took William by the elbow and moved him away from the few people near them. Amy walked right along with them.

Of course.

"Something doesn't seem right. Or, I should say, something *didn't* seem right."

"How do you mean?" William decided it was better to see what Lemmon had to say instead of offering his scant information.

"Don't wish to malign the dead, don't you know, but I had a feeling things were . . . not as they should be."

"Can you be more specific? I'm not sure I understand what you're saying."

Lemmon huffed. "He was stealing from me."

Well then. That didn't leave any doubt.

"I see."

"Had you seen the same thing? Or was it only me he was robbing?"

William didn't want to say too much, since he had only just begun to suspect tomfoolery himself, but maybe he could gain more information if he admitted to finding some discrepancies. "Recently, I have had reason to believe that some numbers of mine didn't match Harding's."

Lemmon nodded furiously. "Yes. That's what I have found. A few of the reports he gave me didn't match what my bank was saying." He shrugged. "I'm having my solicitor look into the matter. Now that I have to deal with the estate myself instead of Harding, I'm sure it will take a very long time before I get answers."

"Just so."

They stared morosely at the dancers, both lost in their thoughts. Mr. Marshall approached them and requested a dance from Amy. It annoyed William to no end to watch Marshall take her by the hand and lead her to the dance floor. He could no longer pretend that he was unbothered by the attention paid to Amy by other men. It might be time to seriously consider staking his claim.

No one else approached him with inquiries into Harding's affairs, but two other friends commented on the man's untimely passing. Somehow word had gotten out that he'd been the one to identify the body.

He and Amy danced two spirited cotillions, and with all he had on his mind, he was not unhappy when she asked to leave. He'd spent too much time brooding and thinking about Harding and the mess that was beginning to unravel to really enjoy himself. He also felt a bit of guilt for not dancing with some of the other ladies who were lacking partners, but he had no desire to spend time with any woman besides Amy.

"It appears you were not the only one with questions about Mr. Harding's management of their affairs." Amy pulled the blanket around herself as the carriage rolled away from the Assembly hall. "Did anyone else approach you about Harding beside Mr. Lemmon?"

"No. A couple of others commented on his death and wondered how I had gotten to be the one to identify the body. But no one else mentioned any financial discrepancies."

"I guess it is possible that he wasn't fleecing all his clients. Or no one has learned it yet." She paused. "Or perhaps they have been swindled and don't want to discuss it."

"I need to have access to his files."

She straightened in her seat. "Break in?"

The devil take it, she actually looked pleased. "I do worry about you sometimes, you know."

She waved her hand around. "We've done it before."

"Yes. But it's not necessary in this case. Since the office is not locked up tight with Mr. Tibbs still a tenant, I think I can talk my way into going through Harding's files. That is, provided the police haven't decided Harding's death was no accident and sealed up his office."

"Do you think they might do that?"

"Yes. Once they figure out that his death was orchestrated—if that happens—they will obviously look to his business to see if someone there had reason to remove James from this earth."

"Then we better go there as soon as possible."

William sighed. "There is that word again."

"What word?" She actually looked innocent. But it didn't work.

"*We.*"

"Well, of course, I will go too."

William bowed his head. "In this instance, my dear, you are correct. I want to get in and out as quickly as possible."

"Then when shall we go?"

"Monday. First thing. I want to retrieve my files, but I also want to browse Harding's files to see if we find anything incriminating in his records, like a double set of numbers, that sort of thing. We know of at least one other client he was doing fancy numbers with."

They remained quiet for the rest of the ride. William walked Amy to her front door and waited until Stevens opened it. "I will escort you and your aunt to church tomorrow, I assume?"

"Yes. That would be very nice. And you'll join us for lunch as well?"

He bowed. "It would be my pleasure, and I will see you on the morrow." Again he contemplated kissing her but decided that, until he had time to seriously consider the situation between him and Lady Amy and speak to her about it, it was best to keep his lips to himself.

CHAPTER 6

William appeared on Amy's doorstep at precisely twelve o'clock on Monday, as planned. They'd hoped Mr. Tibbs would be preparing to leave for his noon dinner when they arrived at the offices he shared with Harding, leaving the office empty.

It amused William that Amy was so often late for appointments, church, and other outings but whenever they were doing something that involved snooping, she was always right on time.

He took her arm to escort her down the steps to his waiting carriage. "You look lovely, as always."

Her outfit was very sedate and professional looking. Her dark-brown wool coat and matching hat were certainly not fancy or eye-catching. The perfect ensemble for stealing files. They settled into the carriage and began the ride to Harding's office.

Amy turned to him with a smile. "I just helped Aunt Margaret pack and leave for a week-long visit to her friends, Mr. and Mrs. Devon Woods. Aunt Margaret and Mary Woods have been friends since boarding school." She gripped the strap alongside her head as the carriage hit a bump in the road. "Mrs. Woods married later in life and is now rapidly producing offspring, almost as if she were attempting to catch up."

His brows rose. "Why does that make you smile so devilishly?"

"Because Aunt Margaret will be spending a week with a house full of children, not her favorite humans." She shook her head, her grin growing. "No, not her favorite at all."

After a few minutes of silence, Amy said, "Do you suppose Mr. Tibbs locks the door when he leaves for his lunch?" Once again she grabbed the strap hanging by her head as the carriage hit yet another hole in the road. She rubbed her shoulder, which had struck the side of the carriage. "These roads need to be fixed."

William nodded. "To answer your question, yes, I'm sure he does lock the door. But I remember Harding telling me when Tibbs first took the space with him that he was very particular about his schedule and even had his meals at the exact same time each day. According to Harding, Tibbs leaves for his midday meal at twelve thirty each day."

"Ah, it is so convenient when one's investigation involves a suspect with such punctuality." Her smile turned to a frown. "Is he on our suspect list?"

His brows rose. "I didn't realize we had a list."

"As you so cleverly pointed out, Mr. Harding was not a drinker, so it was highly unlikely he slipped into the river while drunk. That means he was helped into the water. Hence, a murder. Hence, suspects are needed."

"Your mystery-writer persona is showing," William said.

She bowed her head. "Thank you."

The ride didn't take too long, since the building that housed Harding's office was only a few streets from Amy's townhouse. William checked his timepiece. Precisely 12:20.

They entered the building, and William pointed to the staircase. "Next floor up."

They made their way up the stairs and down the corridor to the second-to-last door on the end. The top half of the door was glass. MR. JAMES HARDING, BUSINESS MANAGER was printed in black, with MR. ERNEST TIBBS, BARRISTER directly below it.

William opened the door and ushered Amy inside. There was an outer area with a desk, but no one occupied it. In all the time William had been doing business with Harding, there had never been anyone at that desk.

Mr. Tibbs stepped out of his office, obviously dressed to go outdoors. "Oh, may I help you?"

"Yes." William moved toward him and held out his hand. "I am Lord Wethington. I believe we met once before."

If Tibbs was surprised to see him, it didn't show. "Yes, I remember. How may I help you, my lord?"

"I would like to retrieve my files from Mr. Harding's office. I assume there is no problem with that?"

Tibbs looked a bit confused, then uneasy. "I guess that would be all right. I've been waiting for the police to visit and secure the office."

"Why is that?" Did Tibbs know something that had slipped past William?

Tibbs shrugged. "I just assume they will do an investigation. From what I know of criminal law, an unexpected death is considered suspicious and a routine investigation will take place. I'm sure the first place they would look would be Mr. Harding's office."

"Yes. That is true." Tibbs was a Queen's Counsel, so he clearly knew the law well. He looked at his timepiece. "I guess I can wait while you get your files."

That would not do. They needed time to do a search of other files. But any concern on Tibbs's part could make him deny them access to the office. "If the authorities do visit, please feel free to tell them I took my records. We don't wish to stop you from taking your meal."

Tibbs looked relieved. "Thank you, my lord." He grabbed his hat. "I will leave you to your work, then." He got as far as the door and stopped. "If you will turn this latch when you leave, it will lock the office and I have a key to get in."

Once the door closed, Amy and William headed to Harding's office. Everything was quiet, almost as if the room sensed its occupant was permanently gone. Dust motes danced in the sunlight streaming from the window behind Harding's desk.

"Have you ever visited here?" Amy asked in a soft voice.

"Yes. Most times, Harding came to my home, but on occasion it became necessary for me to visit him here." William moved to stand behind the desk. "I will search his desk, and I suggest you start with the files."

Like most offices, Harding had employed the pigeonhole organization method, using vertical folders to sort and order his various clients.

"What are we looking for?"

"First of all, pull my file, then make a list of his other clients. I'm thinking if someone did want Harding dead for business reasons, it might be one of his clients. That is especially true if he was fleecing others as he was me and Mr. Lemmon. If we have time, we can skim some paperwork to see if there are inconsistencies or anything in the documents that looks odd."

"That will take some time." Amy spoke over her shoulder as she slid out a stack of files. "We only have about an hour. And not even that if Tibbs eats fast. He might not mind us being here to retrieve your files, but it would not take more than ten or fifteen minutes to make sure you have your things."

"We will work as quickly as possible and get out of here before he returns." William opened the center drawer of Harding's desk. Pencils, paper, two pens, and a dried-up inkwell.

The two drawers on the right-hand side of the desk held personal items—the first one a comb, brush, toothbrush, and tooth powder, the second some photographs and an old, bulky sweater. As William shut that drawer, he looked up at Amy, who was frowning and leafing through folders. "What's wrong?"

She continued to thumb through the files. "I've gone through these twice, and there are no files here under your name."

"What? That's impossible. I've been his client for three years." He headed over to where Amy sat in a chair, folders on her lap and stacked on the floor next to her.

"These files are in alphabetical order." She motioned to the piles on her lap and the floor. "Yet there is no file under *William* or *Lord* or *Wethington*."

"How odd." He bent over her shoulder and looked at the stack on her lap. "I can't imagine why, but try my family name. St. John."

Amy reached for a group of folders on the floor. She worked her way through them. "No. Nothing here for a St. John."

This was very, very strange indeed. "I have an idea. Look in the files and see if you find a Mr. Charles Lemmon."

Amy searched both stacks. "No Charles Lemmon." She looked up at him. "Is he not the man we spoke with at the Assembly?"

"Yes. As he said, he had a reason to believe Harding was doing something odd with his businesses."

"Since both files are missing, I would say that is no coincidence." Amy stood and began to place the files back in their pigeonholes. "Now what do we do?"

"It doesn't pay to search the files to see if there were some discrepancies. Since my file and Lemmon's file are both missing, that leads me to believe that the records of those Harding was pilfering were not kept here."

William began to pick up the files from the floor. "Let's put things back the way we found them and leave. We need to discuss this further, but not here." William helped her return the files, not caring too much if they were in order.

They took one last look around the room, fastened the latch as Tibbs had asked them to do, and left the office.

The carriage awaited them at the end of the pavement. A light rain had begun to fall while they were occupied upstairs. Amy shivered as the carriage moved forward. William handed her the blanket, and she wrapped it around her body.

"Since you are always providing me with sustenance, I would like to offer you tea at my house for a change. We will be able to discuss our investigation over the best biscuits in Bath."

Amy nodded. "That sounds lovely, only I believe *my* cook makes the best biscuits."

"We shall see." He grinned.

"Regarding our search of Mr. Harding's office, it appears we now have a few reasons to investigate the man's death."

"True." William began to tick them off on his fingers. "First, Harding, a known teetotaler, falls into the river and drowns while carrying a flask. Second, I had suspicions that things weren't right before that happened. Third, we find out that Mr. Lemmon was also being cheated, and fourth, Lemmon's records as well as my own are missing from Harding's office."

"And perhaps others are missing."

"True, and a very good point, Miss Murder Mystery Author." He looked out at the rain coming down a bit harder, everyone on the street huddled under their umbrellas. February was such a bleak month.

Once they arrived at his home, William escorted Amy to his drawing room and advised his cook that he had a guest for tea. He also left the door to the room open to avoid any suggestion of impropriety.

"What are your thoughts on how to locate the missing files?" Amy settled on the sofa and adjusted her skirts. "I am anxious to proceed with the investigation. There is a murderer out there, and he or she needs to be caught. Who knows when the police might decide Harding's death was not an accident?"

William started a fire in the fireplace, which helped to take some of the dampness out of the room. "Obviously the records have to be somewhere. There is no way Harding conducted all the business he did for me—and now we know for Lemmon as well—without having records of it. The question remains, where are the records?"

"If they are not in his office, the obvious place would be his residence. Do you know where he lives?"

William stopped in front of Amy and rested his hands on his hips. "Yes. He has a flat here in Bath but also a home outside the city on the road to Bristol."

Her eyes widened. "Two homes? It appears the man was doing quite well." She grinned. "At others' expense."

"According to Harding, the home outside the city was an inheritance from a family member."

She studied him, her author's mind obviously going over the facts in her head. "And now you doubt that." It wasn't a question.

William snorted. "I am beginning to doubt everything I knew about the man."

Amy placed her hands in her lap, fingers linked. "There is only one thing to be done."

"And that is?"

"We must break into his flat. And if we find nothing there, we must break into his home outside the city." She gave him a curt nod.

William considered her for a moment. "You have no problem acting the criminal, do you?"

Amy sniffed. "We are not criminals. We are investigators trying to catch a criminal. And in this case, a murderer."

"I agree that with the police still not sure if Harding's death was murder or an accident, finding who killed Harding is our primary goal, but I am also interested to know exactly how much Harding stole from me. I can't reconcile my records without his in hand."

"Therefore, breaking into his flat to retrieve your records is not a crime."

William smiled. "I would love to see the magistrate's face when you offer that explanation for why we were caught rummaging around a dead man's flat."

"There is no reason to be concerned about that, my lord."

"And why is that?"

"I have no intention of getting caught."

William quoted:

The best laid schemes o' Mice an' Men

gang aft agley,

an' lea'e us nought but grief an' pain

for promis'd joy!

"Robert Burns," Amy said.

"Exactly."

One of his maids pushed a tea cart into the drawing room. Mrs. Pringle was right behind her, directing the setup.

"Thank you, everything looks wonderful." Because William's cook seemed to think he would fade away if she didn't ply him with immense amounts of food, she had sent in small sandwiches, tarts, biscuits, cheese, and fruit along with a large pot of tea.

William nodded at Amy. "Will you pour, my lady?" With Mrs. Pringle present, he reverted to formality.

Amy poured the tea for them both, adding sugar and a drop of milk in William's. She handed him a plate. "Choose what you wish. I'm not sure how hungry you are."

He filled his plate with everything offered while she took cheese, fruit, and a small biscuit. He noticed but didn't comment as she eyed the lovely tarts but didn't put one on her plate.

"Have you admitted that breaking into Harding's flat is the best way to move forward?" Amy asked in a low voice.

William wiped his mouth with a napkin and sighed. "I never think breaking the law is the best way to do anything, but in this case, breaking in will not be necessary."

"Oh. Why is that?"

"I am part owner of the building where his flat is located. All I need do is contact the managing agent and tell him I need to enter Harding's flat to retrieve some of my belongings."

Amy sat back. "Well. That was certainly easy enough. Why did you not tell me before that we would not have to break into the building?"

He grinned. "I was far too entertained listening to you planning on operating on the wrong side of the law again."

Amy had opened her mouth—to offer a retort, no doubt—when his attention was drawn by noise at the front door. It sounded as if a whirlwind had entered. "What the devil?" He stood and walked to the drawing room entrance.

"William! I cannot tell you how delighted I am to finally arrive." His mother smiled and tugged on the tips of her gloves. "All my luggage will be here in a day or so. But right now I could use a good cup of tea." She glided up to him and kissed him on his cheek while he stared dumbfounded at her.

She was actually here. She had made good on her promise to move in with him.

Mother leaned back and patted him on the cheek. "My goodness, son, you look as though you've seen a ghost." To his horror, before he could stop her and explain, she moved past him and entered the drawing room. Sucking in a deep breath, she clasped her hands to her throat and said, "Oh my goodness." His conniving, diligent, hungry-for-more-grandchildren, marriage-minded mother turned to him with absolute glee written on her face. "Who have we here?"

William dropped his head to his chest and groaned.

CHAPTER 7

It didn't take much in the way of investigative skills for Amy to determine that the grinning woman standing in the doorway to William's drawing room was his mother. Same hair color, same eye color, and similar stances, although there was nothing masculine about Lady Wethington.

She was graceful, lovely to look at, and well dressed. Amy stood and smiled at her. "Good afternoon. I assume you are Lady Wethington?"

The woman extended both of her arms and walked toward Amy as if she'd just discovered her long-lost daughter. "Yes, my dear. I am William's mother, and so very, very pleased to meet you."

Lady Wethington grasped Amy's hands and squeezed. Amy looked over the woman's shoulder, afraid she might pull her in a for a hug. William's face had gone quite pale.

"Mother, if you will release my guest, I will introduce you to Lady Amy Lovell. She is the daughter of the Marquess of Winchester and sister to the Earl of Davenport."

Lady Wethington let go of Amy, allowing her to take a deep breath, and regarded her with so much happiness that Amy suddenly felt the need to escape. As quickly as possible.

"You are just perfect. Perfect!" Lady Wethington withdrew a laced handkerchief from the cuff of her dress and patted the corners of her eyes.

William cast a look of desperation at Mrs. Pringle, who remained at the window seat but had stood upon Lady Wethington's entrance. The housekeeper hurried forward. "Lady Wethington. How lovely to see you again! We have prepared your room. I am sure you will want to take a short rest after your journey." She took William's mother by her elbow and attempted to move her forward.

Lady Wethington was not allowing that. At all. She pulled her elbow from Mrs. Pringle's grip. "So nice to see you as well, Mrs. Pringle. But I believe I will join my son and his—guest—for tea."

They all took seats, and when Lady Wethington merely stared at the teapot, Amy sighed. Lady Wethington apparently expected her to act as hostess.

"Mrs. Pringle, can you please bring more hot water for her ladyship? I believe this one has chilled." Thank goodness Amy had spent enough time at William's house that the staff didn't seem to resent requests from her.

"Wonderful," Lady Wethington said, and beamed at Amy. She turned to William, who looked as if he had something caught in his throat. "I do hope I am not interrupting anything . . . personal?"

Amy had reached the point where she found the entire situation comical. She'd thought her papa was anxious to see her married off. Absolutely nothing could compare to William's mother. There was no doubt in Amy's mind that Lady Wethington was mentally composing the invitation list for their wedding and would soon join William's cook to work out the wedding breakfast menu.

"No, Mother. You have not interrupted anything personal. Lady Amy and I belong to the same book club. We were merely discussing the current book."

"Book club? How very edifying." She beamed again at Amy. "It must be your influence, my dear."

Amy cleared her throat. "Actually, my lady, his lordship belonged to the book club before I did."

Undaunted by that revelation, Lady Wethington waved her hand. "Women are always good influences on men. Don't you agree?"

Amy had no desire to be an influence on anyone. She had a hard enough time trying to keep herself out of trouble. But she just nodded and offered an innocuous murmur.

A young maid entered the room with the refilled teapot and placed it on the tray in front of the three of them. Lady Wethington smiled warmly in Amy's direction. Apparently it was expected for her to continue to play the hostess, which had thrown her so off guard that it almost had her choking and fumbling.

Lady Wethington appeared to be a lovely woman, but Amy had the feeling that whatever William's mother set her mind to was accomplished posthaste.

William still sat like a stone statue. A terrified stone statue. Amy wanted to hit him over the head with the teapot. She couldn't do this all by herself; she needed rescue.

"How was your journey, my lady?" As far as social intercourse went, that was probably the dullest question she could ask. Right now, however, she was feeling far from brilliant.

Lady Wethington took a sip of the tea that Amy had just poured and fixed for her.

"The trip was not overly unpleasant. I came from London, as I'm sure my son told you, but the roads, in part, have improved. I do believe the city of Bath itself could do with improvement, however."

"Why did you not take the railway?" William asked.

Lady Wethington waved her hand. "I don't trust them. It is risky riding with all those strangers. A carriage is much better. However, as I stated, 'tis past the time the roads were fixed."

Silence fell, since Amy couldn't think of another thing to say. She could see William's chest rising and falling, so she knew he hadn't died from fright; he'd merely been struck dumb.

It would be far too rude for Amy to take her leave so soon, so she would just have to make the best of it. "My lord, how far into the new book have you read?" At this point, Amy was so rattled that she couldn't even remember the book they were currently reading. Hopefully William did.

He took a deep breath, obviously realizing he would have to contribute to the conversation. "I would say about a third of the way through the book." Since he didn't mention the title, she had to assume he didn't remember which book they were reading either.

"What sort of books do you read in this book club?" Lady Wethington took a delicate bite of a biscuit. Amy couldn't help but notice that everything about the woman was delicate, graceful, and elegant. She sighed. Another Aunt Margaret.

"It is the Mystery Book Club of Bath. We meet once a week at the Atkinson and Tucker bookstore." William had actually put two sentences together.

"Oh, I do love mysteries. Do you ever read E. D. Burton's books?"

Amy sucked in a breath just as she was biting down on a biscuit. A full three minutes of coughing, being pounded on the back by William, and hand-wringing by his mother commenced.

Amy patted her eyes with the handkerchief William had handed her—an action, Amy noted, that was not lost on his eagle-eyed mother.

"Yes. We have read one or two of his books," William said.

Lady Wethington leaned forward and lowered her voice. "I have read every one of Mr. Burton's books."

"Mother! I would think they were too—intense for you."

His mother waved her hand. "Nonsense. Men always think women are such weak creatures." She turned to Amy. "I will wager you don't believe that gibberish, do you, Lady Amy?"

"No. I do not believe we are too weak-minded to read Mr. Burton's books." There, she had managed to get that one out without choking. But she really did need to take her leave. She placed her napkin alongside her plate. "I am so sorry to break up our little visit, but I have an appointment later today with my dressmaker." Lie number one. "I would love to stay and chat." Lie number two. "I hope we can have a longer visit another time." Lie number three.

Amy rose, and William stood. "Mother, I escorted Lady Amy here, so I will be seeing her home."

Lady Wethington beamed at the two of them in a most disconcerting way. "That is fine, children. Run along."

William looked as though he would love to throttle the woman, but one did not do such things to one's mother. No matter how strong the urge.

Amy and William hurried to the front door, shrugged into their coats, and practically raced down the path to where his carriage stood. They climbed in and settled themselves.

As the vehicle moved forward, William raised his hand, palm facing her. "Do not say a word. Please."

Amy nodded and grinned. Yes. There really weren't too many words to cover what they'd just experienced.

★ ★ ★

It had taken William two days to get the key he needed from the managing agent to search Harding's flat. Once he received the key, he'd sent a note around to Amy that he would arrive at two o'clock to escort her to the building.

It had been a trying two days with his mother settling in. As much as he loved her, he could see where this new arrangement could be difficult. For him. She had pestered him for hours after he returned from escorting Amy to her home Monday afternoon.

With a pounding headache and his third glass of after-dinner brandy, he'd finally suggested that she retire for the evening because she needed her rest after her journey.

Thank goodness she had agreed, because he'd been about to pull all his hair out. He'd tried very hard to impress upon her that he and Amy were merely friends, that they attended the same church and the same book club.

Nothing more.

Until she learned—he still hadn't figured out how, but his mother was quite clever—that he had escorted Amy to several Assembly dances. Then the questions, innuendos, and hints—the devil take it, they weren't hints but flat-out statements—had begun all over again.

Aside from that, however, his mother had been a help. True to her nature, she'd formed an instant bond with Mrs. Pringle and coerced Cook into making healthier dishes. That was both good and bad. He enjoyed his unhealthy food.

The maids seemed a bit busier, but they all adored his mother. She had a way about her that made people do what she wanted and think it was their own idea. She'd been counting the linens and silverware and sent word to an agency to send over a footman, a lady's maid for herself (since her maid, she explained, had decided to stay in London), and another maid of all work.

If only he could find other ways for her to occupy her time once the house was running to her satisfaction. He knew without a doubt what—and who—her next project would be.

But now he was free of the endless suggestions and on his way to hopefully find his files and any other items that might be of interest. The day was warm for early February, with a bright-blue sky. Not too common, especially in winter.

Amy's maid Lacey opened the door and moved back so he could step in. Amy stood behind the maid, her coat and hat on, ready to go.

"Good afternoon, my lady."

"Good afternoon to you, my lord."

He took her arm, and they made their way down the stairs. Once they were on their way, he said, "I don't think we will have a problem." He patted his jacket pocket. "I got the key from the managing agent's office. And since we have permission to be in the flat, we will not have to hurry through our search. We can take our time and hopefully find the missing files."

"Aside from your business arrangement, how well did you know Mr. Harding?" Amy asked.

"Quite well, I thought. But now it seems I didn't know him at all. I had no idea he was cheating me until recently. We had dinner on occasion to discuss business matters, and he was a member of my club, so we saw each other there sometimes."

Amy looked out the window, her lips pursed in thought. "How did you first come to employ him?"

William leaned back and rested his foot on his knee. "About three years ago, I had been handling all my own businesses and felt the need to have help. Instead of hiring someone to do so full-time, I decided a man of business would suit me better. I asked around, and a few men suggested Harding. I interviewed him, determined we could work well together, and hired him.

"It appeared to be a fine arrangement because I do like to keep my fingers in the pie, so to speak."

Amy turned from the window and studied him. "But not enough to figure out he was stealing from you."

"Yes. I agree. I think what happened was I grew complacent, trusting more than I should. It has only been in the last year or so that I haven't been diligent enough. Since it was my money, I should never have turned it all over to him. You can be sure I will not do so again with my next man."

The carriage rolled up to a very elegant-looking building. "You own an interest in this?" Amy asked, her admiring gaze making him smile.

"Yes. It's one of my investments. I also hold an interest in two restaurants—both in London—a hotel in Bristol, a small bank here in town, and a small printing company. Although Harding advised against it, I also put some of my money into a couple of industrial ventures in the United States."

Amy appeared dutifully impressed. "My goodness. You are quite busy."

"Too busy, apparently. I left too much to Harding." The carriage stopped, and the driver opened the door. They approached the building and found the entrance unlocked.

William rattled the doorknob. "I shall have the managing agency put a lock on this door."

Inside, Amy took in the well-kept entrance hall. The wooden floor was polished to a high gleam. A gas chandelier hung over the space, highlighting a wooden-framed mirror and two plants alongside a small table that appeared to hold mail for the tenants.

"Harding's flat is on the first floor." They made their way upstairs, and William stopped at the first door, which bore the number *1*. "This is it." He withdrew a key from his pocket and slid it into the lock. It turned easily, and they entered the flat.

"I wonder if the police have searched here yet." Amy wandered around, looking at some of Harding's knickknacks, which William felt were far too many for a man to have.

"I'm not sure the police have yet decided that Harding's drowning was not an accident." William moved to the bedroom. Everything was in order. Bed neatly made, clothing all hung up. Shoes lined up against one wall. A brush, comb, and a flowered bowl with a pitcher set inside rested on a dresser across from the bed.

"I will start in here. Amy, why don't you search the kitchen and drawing room?" It would be far better for him, rather than an unmarried woman, to go through Harding's personal belongings.

"That sounds like a good plan. I'll start in the kitchen."

William methodically searched the room. He pulled open drawers, looked under the bed, scoured the wardrobe, and went through a cedar chest at the foot of the man's bed.

No files.

He proceeded to the drawing room, where Amy had moved her search. "Nothing in the kitchen."

William pulled out several books and flipped through them. Amy picked up sofa cushions and looked under chairs and behind drapes.

William put three books back on the shelf and took out two more. An envelope dropped to the floor from inside one of the books. He bent and picked up a letter addressed to Mr. James Harding from a Mr. Martin DuBois and began to read.

"Amy. I think I found something here."

She walked over to him. "What it is?"

"Here." He handed the letter to her.

Her eyes moved back and forth over the paper. When she finished, she folded it up and looked at him. "Your Mr. Harding had a partner."

"So it appears."

"That partner went to prison for embezzlement."

"That's what it says."

"He is out of prison now."

"Yes."

"And he threatened Mr. Harding."

"So it would seem."

Amy tapped the envelope with her fingertip and grinned. "My lord, I believe we have our suspect."

CHAPTER 8

"How much are you willing to tell them?" Amy asked as she stepped out of William's carriage and straightened her skirts.

They had just arrived at the police station in answer to a summons from Detective Carson. The officer had sent around a note to William asking to speak with the two of them and requesting an acceptable time to call. Completely panicked at the idea of the police visiting his house with his mother present, William had offered to fetch Amy and bring her with him to the station.

"I will attempt to answer their questions as honestly as possible," William replied.

Amy smirked. "A very nebulous response, my lord."

William gave her a curt nod and opened the door to the station, stepping back so Amy could enter first. "Just so."

They were quickly escorted to the room in which they had been interviewed during the investigation into St. Vincent's murder.

The room was empty, and William found it difficult to sit, so he paced. The space was oppressive and confining. No windows, sickly-green-painted walls, one long table, four chairs, and nothing else. No doubt these rooms were kept stark as a reminder to those being questioned that this was a police station and the room was strictly for serious business.

The door swung open, and Detectives Carson and Marsh entered.

They were an unmatched duo. Marsh was close to six feet tall, slender, with enough lines around his mouth and the corners of his eyes to indicate that the man had lived more than twoscore years. Carson was round and bald and barely reached Marsh's shoulders.

"Thank you for answering our summons, my lord, my lady." Detective Carson settled into one of the chairs, and William took the one next to Amy. The two detectives sat side by side across from them.

William still wasn't sure why they had requested Amy's presence, but he was certain they were about to find out.

Marsh flipped open his notepad and licked the end of his pencil. Detective Carson took the lead. "We have reason to believe Mr. Harding did not stumble into the river while drunk."

Since that wasn't a question, William and Amy remained quiet.

Carson cleared his throat. "Along those lines, we have opened an investigation."

William nodded.

"Now here is the interesting part of our investigation." Carson leaned forward, his hands folded on the table. "We visited Mr. Harding's office yesterday."

It soon became clear why the two of them had been summoned. He remained quiet. *He who speaks first loses.*

Carson attempted a befuddled look but didn't quite pull it off. "We confiscated the man's files, and do you know what was confusing about that?" The detective tapped his fingers on the table. Very much an annoyance. On purpose or just a habit?

William was not prepared to play games with the detective. They had crossed swords with the men before. "I have no idea why you were confused, Detective, but I have a feeling you will shortly enlighten me."

Marsh grumbled as he continued to write.

Carson leaned forward again, an intimidating move, but William did not flinch. "What was questionable was that there were no files with your name on them."

"Indeed?" William almost smiled; he already knew that, and he also knew his file was not in Harding's flat either. There was no reason, of course, to pass that information along to the detectives. "Is there a question there, Detective? Because if there is, I missed it."

"You know, Wethington, your title and connections will only protect you to a certain degree." Carson slammed his hand down on the table. William, Amy, and Marsh all jumped. "We will not have the two of you interfering again in a police investigation!"

The man's face was bright red, and he looked as though he might soon collapse. William did the man a favor and did not smile.

"You want a question, *my lord*? Well, here it is. Did you or did you not remove your file from Mr. Harding's office?"

"No. I did not." No lie there.

"Then why was there no file with your name on it? The reason you were requested to confirm the identity of Mr. Harding was because he was your man of business." Carson's voice rose. "He had your business card on his person when he was dragged from the river!"

"I will tell you what I know." William glanced over at Amy, who held a completely bland expression on her face. The woman had been through this before.

"Mr. Harding was my man of business for three years. We worked well together. Why my files were not in his office is as much of a puzzle to me as it is to you."

Marsh licked his pencil again and flipped the page. Carson continued. "Yet Mr. Tibbs, who shares the space with Mr. Harding, told us you and her ladyship here visited the office and indicated you were going to fetch your files. Is that true?"

William hesitated, then decided that giving a little information to the police might look like cooperation and get the detectives to leave them alone so he and Amy could solve the puzzle. He had more at stake than just Harding's murder. He needed to find out how far into deception Harding had been. And how much of his money was gone. "Yes, Detective. We did visit the office with the intention of retrieving my files—"

"This is a police investigation! You had no right to interfere and remove possible evidence."

"Ah. It was not a police matter when we visited Harding's office. If memory serves, you indicated when we identified Mr. Harding's body that you deemed it an accidental drowning."

Carson switched his attention to Amy. "My lady, can you vouch for your cohort here that his file was not among those in Mr. Harding's office?"

Amy nodded. "Yes, Detective. There was no file among those in the office of Mr. Harding that had his lordship's name on it."

Carson studied her for a while, no doubt replaying her words in his head to see if he was missing something in the way she had worded her answer.

The detective leaned back. "I have a few more questions."

William nodded.

"Did Harding have any enemies?"

William's brows rose almost to his hairline. "Clearly, since this has turned into a murder investigation, Detective."

Carson flushed and growled, "Any that you can name?"

He thought about DuBois, but further questions from Carson about the man would reveal where they'd gotten his name. William still hadn't decided yet what he would do with that information. Tracking the man down didn't seem to serve his purpose and would only put him and Amy in danger. DuBois might be on their—very short—list of suspects, but William would hold tight to that information for now. Unless the police charged him with the murder, there was no hurry to solve this mystery. He still wanted to find out how his man of business had been cheating him and at least one other client and how much Harding had pilfered from his own funds.

"How well did you know the deceased?" the detective asked Amy.

"Not at all, Detective. I heard his lordship speak of the man on occasion, but I never met him or had anything to do with him."

"He didn't handle your finances?"

"No. I believe I told you at our last encounter that he was not my man of business, that my brother handles all my family's finances. I know nothing about our money."

"Except how to spend it, no doubt," the detective mumbled.

William felt his face flush. "Detective, I see no reason for this line of questioning. If you have some sort of charge you wish to advise us of, I will be more than happy to have my barrister accompany us at another time." He stood and grasped Amy's elbow. "Other than that, I feel we have spent enough time answering your nonquestions."

Both detectives stood. "Now wait just a minute, *your lordship*. I have no further questions—at this time—but I will advise the two of you to remain in Bath, notify us of any plans to leave the city, and most of all *do not involve yourselves in another police matter*."

Rather than arguing that there was little reason for the detective to order them to remain in Bath, William decided a quick exit was in their best interest. If he lingered much longer, he might very well be rightly charged with assaulting an officer of the law.

He nodded. "If that is all you have to say, we will leave now and wish you a good day." With determined strides, he moved to the door, opened it, and escorted Amy—a bit enthusiastically, perhaps—from the building.

★   ★   ★

A mere five hours later Amy sat in her drawing room, awaiting William's arrival once again. He was escorting her to the book club gathering this evening. He had sent around a note to alert her that his mother had decided she wanted to go with them to the meeting.

Amy had laughed out loud when she read it. She could almost hear him saying the curt words, and the sound was not a pleasant one.

She started when the front door opened but was surprised to see Aunt Margaret sail through the drawing room doorway, removing her gloves. "Amy, dear! I am so glad to be home."

"Aunt Margaret. I thought you were to be gone another three days." Amy hurried to her aunt's side and kissed her cheek.

"Yes. I was supposed to be gone longer, but the visit became, shall we say, troublesome?"

"Pray tell," Amy said, taking her seat on the sofa again. Aunt Margaret sat down next to her.

"Devon and Mary Woods are a wonderful couple. How such wonderful, kind, thoughtful, caring, and loving people could produce such horrid children is beyond me."

"Oh dear." Amy smiled.

"*Oh dear* is correct. The little monsters put a snake—nonpoisonous, thank goodness—in my luggage. When I went to reach for my underthings, the creature snapped at me! I thought I would have a heart attack."

"Did you tell Mary?"

"Not the first time."

Amy's brows rose in surprise. "There were others?"

"With the snake? Of course. Then the urchins spread rice on the wooden floor in the bedchamber I was assigned, and in the dark I didn't see it until I slid and fell—quite hard, actually—on my bum."

"Did you tell Mary about that?"

"No. Then the little darlings switched the sugar with salt. I didn't have to tell Mary about that, because she also put salt into her tea."

Amy smiled, not able to help imagining Aunt Margaret, who was not overly fond of little ones, in such a predicament. "That is why you left?"

"Oh no. That was just the beginning. I can't even remember all the tricks they played on me."

"You were only there for a couple of days! How many children does Mary have?"

She waved her hand. "Too many." She sighed. "The last time I counted, I think there were four of them. Although there is a possibility that a couple of them were hiding."

"So you took your leave?"

"Yes." She grinned. "But not before I played my own trick on the devils."

"Oh, good lord, Aunt, what did you do? I don't like the look in your eyes."

"Well, let's see. Each morning they must be fully dressed before they go to the nursery for their breakfast. I helped with that by removing the tie strings from all their shoes. Then I might have put some lard on their doorknob to make it a bit difficult to open the bedroom door. And when the little dears pour honey on their porridge, they will soon learn that the honey jar might be part honey and part castor oil."

"Aunt Margaret, you didn't!"

She sighed. "Not the last one, although I had planned to do that. I really didn't want to hurt them; just a bit of payback. They really are lovely children, but there are far too many of them, and I'd had enough to cut my visit short."

Aunt Margaret leaned back and seemed to notice for the first time that Amy was dressed to go out. "Oh, it's Thursday, isn't it? Book club meeting night."

"Yes. I am waiting for William to arrive." Amy grinned. "By the way, Lady Wethington has taken up residence at William's house."

Aunt Margaret smiled. "Is that good news or bad news?"

"Both, apparently. She is a lovely woman, but her foot is planted firmly on William's back. Pushing him toward the altar has become her goal in life."

"Oh dear. How does William feel about that? I have always seen him as a confirmed bachelor. Although I guess with his title, he will have to marry one day."

"He is feeling quite nervous, actually." Amy laughed.

Her aunt waved her finger at her. "Don't laugh, niece. I'm sure Lady Wethington will soon have her eye on you."

Amy sighed. "I'm afraid she already does. I just happened to be at his home for tea when she arrived Monday afternoon."

Amy did not appreciate how her aunt threw her head back and roared with laughter.

"Now she wants to go to our book club meeting. That's why I'm waiting for William to escort me. I think he's afraid his mother will take one look at all the ladies in the club and begin to drool."

Aunt Margaret turned serious and took her hand. "Actually, Amy, I think William fancies you. If I can see it, I'm sure Lady Wethington does."

Amy hopped up, not ready to have that conversation. "I think William has arrived." She hurried to the entrance hall and shrugged into her coat. The door knocker sounded, and Stevens opened the door.

"I'm ready." She stepped out of the house and moved swiftly down the steps.

"What's your hurry? It's like you're running from something."

"Yes. That is precisely how I feel. Like I'm running from something. An idea, actually." She climbed into the carriage and settled next to Lady Wethington. "Good evening, my lady. It is a pleasure to see you again."

Lady Wethington smiled at her. "So nice to see you as well, Lady Amy. I am so looking forward to tonight's entertainment."

William took his seat across from them and tapped on the ceiling. Lady Wethington chattered all the way to the bookstore while William stared out the window.

Once they arrived, he helped both ladies out of the carriage. Inside the store, his mother gasped and looked around. "Oh my, what a lovely bookstore. I must spend some time here." She looked at William. "Do we have time before your meeting begins?"

William checked his timepiece. "Yes, we have about twenty minutes."

Lady Wethington clapped her hands. "Wonderful. I will join you in a bit. Where is the meeting held?"

William waved to the back of the store. "Just follow this path to the back of the store, and you will come to a door on the right-hand side. We will be in there."

She nodded and walked toward one of the bookcases, her eyes alight with joy.

As William and Amy headed to the meeting room, he pulled her aside and whispered, "I have information that will remove Mr. DuBois from our suspect list."

CHAPTER 9

Before William could tell Amy why Mr. DuBois was no longer a suspect, Miss Gertrude and Miss Penelope jumped from their seats and hurried over to say hello. "Good evening, Lady Amy, Lord Wethington."

As expected, the ladies were dressed in identical dresses. The pretense that they were twins was a mystery Amy would solve one day.

Amy and William returned the sisters' greetings and walked with them to the front of the room, where Mr. Davidson and Mr. Colbert were conversing. "How did you make out with the police last week?" Mr. Colbert asked William.

"I confirmed his identification."

"Oh dear," Miss Gertrude said. "What is that all about?"

William turned to her. "My man of business, Mr. James Harding, was found floating in the River Avon last week. Since he had one of my business cards on him, the police asked me to confirm his identity, as they were unable to find any next of kin."

Miss Gertrude *tsk*ed and shook her head, her eyes quickly darting from William to her sister. The woman did not seem too upset—though if she didn't know the man, there was no reason for her to be wailing and wringing her hands. Then again, Amy had been shocked when the ladies asked about joining the mystery book club. Their enthusiasm had been quite startling. It appeared one never really knew the people one saw on a regular basis.

Mr. Davidson paled but offered his usual scowl, which Amy easily dismissed. Mr. Colbert returned his attention to William. "I received your note that your mother will be joining us tonight. Did she change her mind?"

"No. She is browsing the bookshelves in the store. I will fetch her when the meeting is about to begin."

"Is she visiting you, then?" Miss Penelope asked.

William cleared his throat. "Actually, she intends to take up permanent residence with me."

Mr. Davidson snorted, and the two ladies offered William a warm smile. "How very nice of you to offer your mother a place in your home." Miss Gertrude placed her hand on William's arm and patted it as if he were a small child. Or a pet dog. "Very few children are so considerate."

"Am I in the right place?" Lady Wethington's voice carried to the front of the room, where the group stood.

"Yes, Mother. Come join us," William said, holding out his hand.

Lady Wethington glided up to them and smiled at the group. William made the introductions, and Amy was amused to see a look of stunned admiration on Mr. Colbert's face.

Lady Wethington was an attractive woman. A widow for many years, she could certainly turn heads. Her light-brown hair had a fine thread of gray mixed throughout, while her skin had remained youthful, with mere delicate lines along her mouth and eyes. Eyes that could capture a person's attention—bright, lively, and full of humor. And she possessed a voluptuous figure that would catch any man's notice.

The rest of the group began to arrive, and the chattering went from subdued to loud enough that Mr. Colbert called the meeting to order.

They all took their seats on various sofas and chairs, and just as Mr. Colbert opened his mouth to speak, the door opened, and Eloise raced in. She plopped down next to Amy and placed her hand over her chest as she drew in deep breaths. "I see I'm late again."

"More like always," Miss Sterling offered with a sniff.

Eloise nudged Amy and mouthed, "Who is that?" She nodded toward Lady Wethington.

"I will introduce you later. She is Wethington's mother."

Eloise's eyebrows rose. Then she smiled and covered her mouth with her hand to hold in a laugh. Amy rolled her eyes at her friend as Mr. Colbert addressed the group.

The meeting went as most meetings did. Miss Penelope and Miss Gertrude offered opinions on the club's current book, *The Strange Case of Dr. Jekyll and Mr. Hyde*—opinions that not only surprised Amy but impressed her. Amy was particularly excited and pleased when the sisters mentioned one of her own books.

Lady Wethington remained silent for the most part, but whenever she spoke, Mr. Colbert gave her his undivided attention, a slight smile on his lips.

"I think your mother has an admirer," Amy whispered to William.

"She does not need an admirer," he snapped.

Amy almost swallowed her tongue trying to keep the laughter in. It appeared William was very protective of his mother and had every intention of guarding her virtue.

Later, as the little group from the bookstore who generally stopped at a local restaurant after the meeting convened for a late supper, William appeared no more pleased with Mr.

Colbert when the man finagled his way into a seat next to Lady Wethington's, then focused all his consideration on her the entire time.

Amy had much more fun watching William watch Mr. Colbert. And glower.

Since no one appeared to be paying much attention to her, she turned to William while they were enjoying their meal. She lowered her voice. "Why is Mr. DuBois no longer on our list of suspects?"

William took a sip of his wine and wiped his mouth with his napkin. "I stopped in to see Mr. Nick Smith today after our interview with the police. Do you know the man?"

Amy shook her head. "The name does sound familiar, but I don't think we've ever met."

"He was the former owner of the Lion's Den, a high-class gambling hell in Bath. He sold it several years back after he married his wife, Lady Pamela Manning, the Earl of Mulgrave's sister. He then used the money to invest in hotels and restaurants. Smith comes from a shady background, and although he is now above reproach in all things, he maintains his contacts in the underworld.

"I thought if anyone knew about DuBois, it would be Nick. As it turns out, he did know DuBois and told me the man's been back in prison for the last six weeks."

Amy huffed. "He must have gone back soon after he sent Mr. Harding the note. In any event, it appears we can cross him off our list."

"Yes. Which is probably a good thing, since I had no idea how to unearth the man without us getting killed."

She perked up. "We could always buy a gun."

William drew in a deep breath. "No. No gun, Amy." He shook his head. "I don't like this obsession you have with guns."

"The protagonists in my books always have a gun handy." Amy lowered her voice. "In fact, in my last book, the female character had a gun. She also could shoot quite well."

"Fiction, my dear. You can control the gun in fiction. You cannot do the same in real life."

On William's other side, Miss Sterling asked him a question. Amy took the time to consider how she might buy a gun and where she could practice. Without telling William. Or her papa. Or her brother. She sighed. There were far too many men watching over her.

William turned back to her. "Since the police are now investigating Harding's death, we need to get the files before they do. I am especially interested in getting my file back. The last thing I need is having our favorite detectives pointing their fingers in my direction once they learn that Harding was stealing from me. I am sure that tidbit of information will give them leave to assume *I* pushed the man into the river."

Amy nodded. "They will have legal steps to go through first to do their searches. We should go to Harding's residence on the road to Bristol as soon as possible."

★　★　★

Bright and early the next morning, Amy settled into William's carriage to make the trip to Mr. Harding's home. "Have you decided how we are going to get into the house?"

William tapped on the ceiling, and the carriage moved forward. "Ever since we searched Harding's flat two days ago, I have been asking questions of those who might know. I'm pretty certain there are very few, if any, staff left at Harding's house. Until the estate is settled and the new owner takes possession, there is no reason for the servants to remain. Plus their pay would have stopped as well."

"I don't suppose you have a key to this residence like you did for his flat?"

"No. But with no one around and the home being set back from the street with woods behind it, I think we can go in through the back door."

"You've been there before?"

"Yes. A few times." William looked over at her shivering body and moved across the space to sit alongside her. He put his arm around her and pulled her close to his body.

"Why is it you are always warm?" she asked as she looked up at him.

He smiled down at her. "I don't know, but it's always been that way."

She should have felt a bit uneasy with him being this close, but she was reluctant to give up the toasty warmth coming from him, right through both of their coats.

It wasn't a very long ride, and they spent the time discussing his mother (he had nothing good to say about Mr. Colbert's interest), the current book the club members were reading, and how odd it was for Miss Gertrude and Miss Penelope to be so very enthusiastic about the books.

"Miss Gertrude seemed exceptionally gay last night. Almost, one could say, giddy." Amy smiled again, reminded that the woman had said nice things about her book.

He grinned. "I am still trying to absorb the fact that those two lovely sisters enjoy murder stories."

William had the driver pull the carriage around the back of the house, which hid the vehicle quite nicely from the road.

The house was about half the size of Amy's family estate, which was the largest house Amy had ever seen. Situated in the village of Old Basing, east of Basingstoke in Hampshire, her home had always felt overwhelming to her, and she had been happy to spend most of her life in her cozy townhouse in Bath.

She gazed out the window at Harding's house. "This is quite an elegant home." She turned to William, her brows raised. "I wonder how much of your money is invested in this."

William climbed from the carriage and reached out to take Amy's hand. "As I said, he claims it was an inheritance, but one wonders why he would resort to stealing if he had this kind of money in his family." William continued to hold her hand as they approached the back door of the house.

"Of course, you have since concluded that his story could have been a complete lie." They stopped once they reached the door. "You are sure there are no servants left?"

"As sure as one could be in these circumstances. I checked with Harding's solicitor on the pretense of requesting a final accounting of Harding's work on my finances. During the conversation, I asked about the house, and he said the employees had all left, since it would be some time before a new owner took over."

"That is another thing we should consider," Amy said. "Who will benefit from Harding's death besides those from whom he was stealing? Perhaps a peek at his will would be enlightening."

"Yes. Good point."

They walked down the few steps to the door, the one the servants would have used to bring goods into the house.

William approached the door and studied it, then rattled the doorknob. The door opened. "This was left unlocked. Quite careless."

Before he stepped inside, he looked over at Amy. "I would prefer if you wait in the carriage. There is a possibility that the door is open because someone else is in the house."

Amy shook her head. "No. If we enter quietly, we can determine if anyone else is in the place."

William looked to the heavens and sighed. "Stubborn woman."

"So true," she whispered.

They entered the house and stood very still, listening for any sounds.

Silence.

William went first, still holding Amy's hand as they crept along. They stopped every few steps and listened. There was no noise anywhere in the house. With a bit more confidence, they made their way up to the ground floor.

"Where do you suppose the most likely place would be for the files?" Amy whispered, still uncertain if they were the only ones in the house.

"I'm sure he had an office here, the place being so large. But I think our best bet would be to start with the library. I remember from my visits here that he had a large desk there."

The made their way down a corridor, past a couple of open doors. It felt unnerving to be walking around the home of a man who had been murdered. It left Amy with a feeling of sadness, looking at all his possessions and imagining him being there, relaxing after a long day's work.

A long day of stealing, she reminded herself.

The library was immense. Every shelf was lined with books. There was even a ladder attached to the bookcase so that one could climb up and fetch a tome.

"Your Mr. Harding was quite the reader." Amy stood in the middle of the room and turned in a circle.

"Chances are he inherited the books, either when he was willed the home or when he purchased it. I don't believe

Harding was much of a reader." William moved to the desk and began opening drawers.

"I'll look around the rest of the room," Amy said. There were several chairs and sofas along with tables with drawers. It could very well take them all morning just to search this room.

After only about five minutes, William called over to her. "Amy, I found them."

She hurried across the room. He was holding about four or five files in his hands. "The first one is Lemmon." He waved a folder.

He placed that file on the desktop and flipped through the others. He pulled one out. "Here is mine."

"I think we should make a list of these. One of these could very well be the file of a murderer." Amy shivered.

William dropped the other folders on the desk and opened the center drawer. He withdrew a pencil and pad of paper. "Write down the names."

He lifted the stack and began to read. "Mrs. Carol Whitney. Mr. David Montrose." Amy scribbled the list as he read out the names.

William stopped and took in a deep breath. He looked over at Amy as he held the next folder. "Miss Gertrude O'Neill."

He opened the file and began to look through it. He read the first page, then moved on to the second. "It appears Miss Gertrude started out as one of his clients, but then he must have discovered something about her, because he began to blackmail her."

"Blackmail her?" Before Amy could process that information, the sound of footsteps walking in their direction had them staring at the door to the library in shock.

William was reaching for her, most likely to find them a place to hide, when Detective Carson and Detective Marsh walked into the room.

"Lord Wethington. Lady Amy. What a surprise!" Detective Carson grinned, his hands fisted at his hips.

CHAPTER 10

William could not believe he'd been so stupid as to ignore the fact that there might be others interested in searching James's house. He had been so sure it would not be a problem, since there were no staff left, but he had completely forgotten that the police were right on their heels. Who would have guessed that they would get to this location so quickly?

Amy turned away from the detectives and slipped the paper she'd been writing on into the bodice of her dress. Even if the men noticed, they would not presume to search her. And William would never allow it.

Carson waved to one of the chairs. "Why don't we sit and have a little chat." Before William moved an inch, Marsh walked over and took all the files out of his hands. "We'll take those, thank you."

He nodded at the pile in the detective's hands. "One of them is mine, and I have the right to take it back."

Carson grinned again. "I don't think so, *my lord*. This is now evidence in a murder investigation. But since you brought it up, let's discuss why there is a hidden file with your name on it, here"—he looked around the library—"away from Mr. Harding's office in Bath?"

Amy had taken a seat along with Detective Marsh, who was busy flipping through the pages of his notebook, but William and Carson remained standing.

William crossed his hands over his chest. "I would love an answer to that question myself, Detective. I don't know why my file is here and not in his office."

"All right, then let's move on to my next question. What are the two of you doing here? Are you part owner of this residence?"

"It is quite possible," Amy mumbled.

William had to swallow his laugh. "No. I am not." It would probably pay to give short answers rather than incriminate himself. In fact, he should call a halt to this conversation and demand that his barrister be present.

He decided on an offensive tactic. "Detective, I have a question for you. Are we being charged with something?"

Carson frowned. "Breaking and entering sounds reasonable."

"Except we did not break in. The back door was left unlocked."

William was happy that both Carson and Marsh looked surprised. "We will investigate that."

"Naturally," William said.

Carson continued. "We are working on the theory that someone Harding was cheating and stealing from saw cause to do away with the man. Since the files here—which are no doubt the files that went missing from his office—most likely contain the names of those who had reason to be happy at Harding's demise, your name is now on the top of our list. What other reason would there be for you to be so very anxious to retrieve this?"

Amy bristled at the man's words. "Detective, do you honestly believe that Lord Wethington would shove someone into a river because the man was stealing from him? How about firing the man and turning to legal steps to deal with the situation?" Amy's eyes flashed with anger, and William's heart swelled at how she took up for him.

"Lady Amy, based on experience, we have no reason to believe or disbelieve anyone when involved in a murder investigation. What I can say to you and your cohort here is that, once again, you are nosing around police business."

"I repeat, Detective, I was not nosing around police business but merely attempting to retrieve my file for the sole purpose of comparing the information there"—he nodded at the pile of files—"with my information at home so I could provide it to my new man of business."

Carson shook his head. "As your lady friend said, there are legal ways to obtain that information. Breaking into someone's home is not the proper way to do it."

William's anger was growing. Mostly at himself for being so foolish and getting him and Amy into a position where the police were now looking at him as a suspect. If they didn't quickly make use of that list she'd hidden away, he would find himself sitting in jail.

As had been the case the first time he and Amy dealt with these detectives, the men seemed to have blinders on. Although he was certain that they would check all the people listed in the files they now held, William was the one who had been caught trying to get his file back, which would ensure that they shined the light of their investigation straight in his direction.

Whoever it was who had broken into the house before them could be the real killer or merely someone who too was being blackmailed and hadn't wanted that information to fall into the hands of the police.

But they still had a list of a few of the people whose files had been hidden here instead of at Harding's office. It was a place to start.

"You will not be charged with breaking and entering, since, given your position and title, you will be in and out of jail faster than we can do the booking process. But hear this"— Carson pointed his finger at William—"if you continue to get in our way, you will be charged—both of you—and although it might not amount to much, it will be uncomfortable for a day or so. And I don't imagine it will do much for your business reputation, Wethington, or sit well with your father, Lady Amy."

"Are you threatening us, Detective?" Amy asked, her nose in the air.

William could have placed his hand over her mouth and dragged her out of the room. It was not good to antagonize the police. Certainly not from the position in which they currently found themselves.

"No, *my lady*. That is not a threat but a promise."

Amy stood and shook out her skirts. "In that case, Detectives, we will be on our way."

Carson glared at her but didn't stop William from taking Amy's hand and moving toward the door.

"Once again, I remind you not to leave Bath without permission," Carson said as Marsh closed his notebook. "We will be interviewing everyone in these files, which includes you."

"I shall notify my barrister. Good day, Detective," William said as he hurried Amy down the corridor to the back door. They practically ran to the carriage and climbed in. William tapped on the ceiling, and the carriage pulled forward.

"That was—" Amy took in a deep breath.

"Stupid and our own fault," William added, totally disgusted with himself.

Amy glanced out the window, her expression as annoyed as he felt. "I hate to admit it, but I believe you are correct. We never should have let down our guard that way."

"Speaking of guards, I should have asked my driver, John, to watch out for someone arriving. Not that it was his fault, but he was probably dozing when the detectives arrived."

Amy withdrew the paper from her bodice. "At least we have this."

"Yes." William gave her a curt nod. "I was so caught up with the police arriving I forgot about the list—thank goodness you did not, seeing that we lost the files."

"But we managed to get three names." Amy placed her hand on her forehead. "I have the most incredible headache. I am sure it is from the fright we received. I need a very hot and very large cup of tea."

"I could use a very large brandy," William said.

"Once your driver arrives at my house, I suggest we have lunch. I'm afraid I was quite anxious about this visit and had a scant breakfast."

They rode in silence for a few minutes, collecting their thoughts. "I found it quite interesting that Harding was not only cheating his clients but also blackmailing at least one person."

"Poor Miss Gertrude. Did you see for what reason he was blackmailing her?"

William shook his head. "No. Only the information from when she was a client, with a notation that he had 'uncovered' an interesting fact and would make use of it.

"It might be assumed that the files in the house were blackmail victims as well as those he was cheating. The files of people he was doing normal business with were probably the ones in his office."

"Yet your file was there, and he wasn't blackmailing you." She paused. "Was he?"

"Of course not! There is nothing in my life that would encourage someone to blackmail me. As I said, most likely he kept the files of anyone he was doing shady dealings with—cheating or blackmail—out of his office."

She sighed. "It must be something devastating for poor Miss Gertrude if it became known. Perhaps she is our murderer."

William's brows rose. "Somehow I cannot see Miss Gertrude shoving Harding into a river."

Amy tapped her chin. "She could have hired someone to do it."

"That is a possibility," William said.

"She seemed terribly gay Thursday evening. We even commented upon it. It could very well have been relief at having her blackmailer dead."

"But that didn't mean she killed him or hired someone to do the deed." No matter how he tried, William could not imagine that sweet woman killing someone.

"Maybe so, but she remains on our list. We also have these other names." Amy waved the paper around.

"However, because we didn't have time to go through those files, we don't know if they were also being blackmailed or, like Lemmon and me, being bilked," William said.

"Either case could encourage someone toward murder. Either to remove a threat or as revenge for thievery. Two common reasons for murder." Amy smiled at him. "My research."

"It would have to be more than revenge, I believe. It would certainly not cross my mind to do away with the man because he was stealing from me, and based on what Lemmon said about his solicitor trying to get his papers back, I don't think murder was on his mind either."

Silence reigned for a while. Then William continued. "Blackmail would be a good motive, I think, but since we weren't able to go through the files and sort out those being blackmailed from those being fleeced, we will have to assume everyone on this list is a victim of Harding's perfidy, and thus a potential killer."

"Even Miss Gertrude?" Amy asked.

William nodded. "For now. Yes."

"And there could be one other name that we don't have because based on the opened back door, someone before us could have entered Harding's house and took their file."

"Yes. But we have to start somewhere. I'm afraid, like last time, that our favorite detectives are focusing on just one person. And this time that one person is me. Why they think I am capable of murder is a bit mystifying. And annoying."

"Well, they thought me guilty of St. Vincent's murder. They have no respect for our class."

William laughed. "I get the impression they have no *use* for our class. I'm sure they have run into problems with members of the *ton* before. I know of several people who have used their titles and connections to avoid the law."

They arrived at Amy's house just in time for lunch, which was good, since they were both quite hungry. William hoped some sustenance would help ease Amy's headache.

"Something smells good." Amy sniffed the air, then handed her outerwear to the young lady at the door. "Thank you, Lacey."

"I believe Cook has prepared some sort of fish for lunch. I will tell her Lord Wethington will be joining you." Lacey hurried away, and Amy and William entered the drawing room.

"Lady Margaret, so nice to see you," William said as he followed Amy into the room.

Lady Margaret bowed her head slightly in William's direction. "And you as well, my lord." She eyed them, her lips pursed. "What sort of trouble are you two getting yourselves into now?"

Amy sat on the sofa across from her aunt, William alongside her. "What makes you think we are getting into trouble?"

Her aunt waved her hand in the air. "I don't know. There is something about the two of you together that makes me think there is some sort of discord bothering you."

Amy glanced over at him, and he gave her a brief nod. Her aunt would find out eventually anyway, and perhaps she might have an idea or two that they hadn't yet thought of.

"Remember I told you about William's man of business who was found floating in the River Avon last week?"

Lady Margaret shook her head. "Yes. You did. Such a terrible thing. I remember reading about it in the newspaper, but the man was not identified."

"Well, William and I went to the morgue, as you know. The man's name is James Harding, and I—"

The woman's eyes grew wide, and her hand flew to her mouth. "James?"

William and Amy looked at each other and then back at Lady Margaret. "You knew Mr. Harding?" Amy asked.

Her aunt cleared her throat, and it was obvious that she was attempting to get herself under control. "Yes. For many years."

William was at a loss for words. Not that he knew a great deal about Lady Margaret's life, but it was startling that she and James had been acquaintances. From her reaction to his death, perhaps more than acquaintances.

"May I ask you a question, and if it is too personal, please let me know." William thought for a moment. "How is it you knew James?"

Lady Margaret sighed and looked out the window as she spoke. "We almost married."

CHAPTER 11

The stunned silence was broken a few heartbeats later as Amy shook her head as if to clear her brain. "I've lived with you my entire life; how is it I never knew you were betrothed to Mr. Harding?"

"It was when you were quite young, so you would not have known." Lady Margaret took in a deep breath. "It was before your mother died. I was a mere twenty years at the time. We weren't exactly betrothed, since your father—my brother—disapproved of James."

Lady Margaret glanced at William. "May I ask you to pour me a sherry, please?"

"Of course." William strode across the room and poured a sherry for Lady Margaret and a brandy for himself. "Amy, would you like a sherry also?"

"After the morning we've had, yes, very much."

He placed the glasses on a small tray on the sideboard and carried them to the women. Once they were all settled with their drinks, Lady Margaret continued. "James and I had planned to elope to Gretna Green, but my brother discovered our plans and stopped us. He sent me off to our family estate in Hampshire."

Amy continued to stare at her aunt as if she didn't know her. "Then what happened?"

Lady Margaret shrugged. "I stayed there for a while, then returned to Bath. James had moved on. He was courting another woman, and when we met, he said it was probably for the best, since Miss Daniels suited him better."

"Did they marry?"

"Yes. But she died giving birth to their son, who didn't survive either."

Amy stood and crossed the distance between them and sat next to her aunt, taking her hand in hers. "He hurt you. I can tell."

Lady Margaret patted Amy's hand. "It was a long time ago. James and I met on occasion in town, and we were cordial to each other, but I've always wondered what my life would have been like if Franklin hadn't stopped us." She sipped her sherry, then shook her head. "And now he's dead."

Lacey entered the room and held out an envelope to Amy. "My lady, this just came in the post for you."

"Thank you." Amy took the missive from Lacey and looked up at William. "It's from my publisher." She opened the envelope, and her eyes scanned the note. She groaned and covered her eyes with her hand.

"What is it?"

"They are insisting that I appear at the Atkinson and Tucker book festival as E. D. Burton."

★ ★ ★

"You can't possibly do that!" Aunt Margaret looked aghast as Amy clenched the paper in her hands.

"I know. I shall refuse." Amy folded the wrinkled note back up and returned it to the envelope.

"Just a moment," William said. "There might be a clause in your contract that gives them the right to force you to do this."

Amy and her aunt stared at the man. "Whatever do you mean?"

William shrugged. "I am somewhat knowledgeable about publishing contracts, and it is possible they can do that. Do you have a copy of one of your contracts? If you don't mind, I would like to take a look at it."

"My papa's solicitor gave his approval." Her papa was nothing if not thorough. She studied William, realizing that there was no reason he couldn't have a look at the contract and that to continue to refuse was childish and ridiculous. "Very well, I have the contracts upstairs in my room." She stood and shook out her skirts. "If you will excuse me."

Was it possible that her publisher could force her to appear as E. D. Burton? She had insisted several times on anonymity when she sold her books to them. Mr. Gordon, with whom she'd dealt since the beginning, had assured her that her identity would remain anonymous. It had been one of her requirements when she signed—the only way she could get Papa's permission to sell her manuscript. As an adult, she should have been able to sign her own contracts without getting approval from Papa first.

She yanked opened the drawer of the desk in her small office next to her bedchamber and pulled out the top contract. She made her way back downstairs just in time to hear Lacey announcing lunch.

The three of them made their way to the dining room. Wonderful smells greeted them, reminding Amy again how hungry she was. She handed William the contract as they sat at the table. He took it from her and nodded. "I will look at this once we finish our meal."

A beautiful whitefish with capers in a creamy sauce, roasted potatoes, and carrots had Amy's stomach rumbling and immediately drew her attention. Cook had also provided a jellied salad and fresh rolls.

"I thought vegetarians didn't eat fish," Aunt Margaret said as she eyed Amy's plate.

"Actually, I am the type of vegetarian that eats fish." Amy glowered at William's smirk. She tried her best to follow the vegetarian lifestyle and had no problem eschewing meat, but she had no intention of giving up fish also.

Apparently they were all hungry, because they dove into their food with very few comments as they ate. A few *This is very good*s and *Please pass the salt*s were about all that was said. Good manners held that nothing distressing be discussed while dining. Naught was said about Amy's contract, since, if William found anything that allowed her publisher to force her to appear as E. D. Burton, that would ruin the entire meal.

Once the food had been consumed and they were left with a pot of tea and a tray of cheese, fruit, and biscuits, William sat back, picked up the contract, and began to look it over. He appeared quite engrossed as he read each page, a shake of his head and a frown his only reactions.

Amy and Aunt Margaret attempted some conversation, Amy using the time to tell her aunt about their escapade that morning, but the entire time she kept glancing over to William, who continued to grimace as he read.

"Well?" Amy said as he laid the document down.

He looked over at her and sighed. "I am not a solicitor, but I have read many contracts. From what it says here"—he pointed at the document—"it is possible they can force you to attend."

Amy's jaw dropped. "How? They agreed to keep my identity a secret."

William thumbed a few pages of the contract. "It does say that, but unfortunately, it also says in this clause that the publisher has the right to market the books any way it sees fit."

"But what does that mean?"

He laid the document back down and folded his hands upon it. "Appearing as E. D. Burton at the book festival could be considered a marketing technique. Again, I remind you that I am not a solicitor and I suggest you have one look at this, but my opinion is they can use this clause to enforce it."

Amy let out a huge breath and slumped against the back of the chair. "Father will not be pleased."

A small niggling of joy began in her stomach and slowly spread throughout her body. She had always felt cheated in not receiving public acknowledgment of her work. She had to sit and listen when the book club discussed one of her books and ignore the comments when they praised the writing of E. D. Burton. Frustration was part of the ploy also, because there were times when a member of the book club would swear they knew precisely what E. D. Burton meant when "he" wrote such and such. Oh, how she wanted to correct them.

Now here was her opportunity to have the public know that *she* was E. D. Burton. And *she* could receive all the acclaim without going against her papa's wishes.

But then there was always the possibility he would forbid her to write any more books. Sometimes she hated being a woman.

★　★　★

The next night, William assisted Amy and Lady Margaret from his carriage in front of the Assembly. After their lunch, they had all decided to attend the Assembly, since Lady Margaret had graciously offered to help with their search for Harding's killer.

Actually, she'd announced loud and clear her desire to seek justice for his death, even though she described Harding as an arse.

It was noteworthy that she described him in such a way before William and Amy had even told her the entire story of Harding's duplicity. When they were through with their account, she shook her head and commented that "once a scoundrel, always a scoundrel."

They went over the list of names from the files Harding had hidden in his home. William knew Mr. Montrose from his club, and Lady Margaret mentioned that the man occasionally attended the Assembly. William would watch out for him. Lady Margaret also said there was a chance that Mrs. Whitney would be there as well. If not, she added, looking pointedly at Amy, Mrs. Whitney usually attended the rounds of afternoon social calls.

Amy groaned at that one and stated—quite emphatically—that she did not enjoy sitting around drinking tea with women whose only purpose for being present was to share gossip. But she had reluctantly agreed that if it was the only way to speak with Mrs. Whitney, she would accompany her aunt the next time she made her rounds. Unlike Amy, Lady Margaret was quite the social butterfly.

The Assembly was well under way when they arrived. Since William and Amy were so easily accepted by their circle of friends as a couple, he began to ruminate on their very comfortable relationship. What had been relaxed and happy these past few months now seemed to have reached a point where he needed to consider making it more.

Perhaps much more.

But Amy had mentioned several times that she had no intention of binding herself to a husband who would then dictate her life. Now, with his mother taking up residence at his house, living and breathing her intention to marry him off and be blessed with grandchildren, William wondered if perhaps he should try to change Amy's mind.

Amy was intelligent, high-spirited—sometimes a bit too much—and certainly easy to look at. He felt she would be a wonderful wife if he could convince her that he would not stifle her in any way. Well, he would certainly forbid her from buying a gun.

They approached the small group from the book club who also frequently attended the Assembly. Miss Sterling, Mr. Davidson, and Mr. Colbert all greeted them, as did Miss Gertrude and Miss Penelope, who seemed to have joined the little group as well.

"Where is Lady Wethington?" Mr. Colbert asked, looking behind Amy.

"She had intended to join us, but she had a megrim and stayed home with a cold cloth and a tisane from our cook," William said.

Mr. Colbert's shoulders slumped. "Oh, that is too bad." The man looked as though he'd lost his favorite puppy.

Amy snorted, trying her best to hold in her laugh, but William failed to see what was funny about Mr. Colbert's interest in his mother. She was far too old to be courting. And so was Mr. Colbert.

He took the opportunity to move away from any discussion about his mother. "Miss Gertrude, Miss Penelope, how are you this evening? I don't remember seeing you at these events before."

"No." Miss Penelope grinned. "We never have attended, but now that we are venturing out to the book club each week, sister thought it a good idea to also engage in other social activities."

The music started up, and both Miss Penelope and Miss Gertrude looked in his direction. Bloody hell, did they expect him to push them around the dance floor? Amy's elbow in his side reminded him that dancing with Miss Gertrude might bring information they needed.

He held out his hand and bowed slightly. "Miss Gertrude, would you care to dance?"

She giggled and turned bright red. William did his best not to sigh. Apparently Mr. Colbert thought to follow his lead, as he asked Miss Penelope to dance as well. Mr. Davidson, as usual, just stood and watched the rest of the group. William had never seen the man dance, even though he was at the Assembly just about every Saturday.

He was grateful for his height, since Miss Gertrude was tall for a woman as well as quite slender. She was stiff in his arms, but if he was going to suffer dancing a waltz with her, hopefully he would gain some information.

"How are you enjoying the book club?" That seemed like an innocuous start.

"Very much, my lord. I particularly liked *The Sign of the Four*. Very mysterious, I must say." The woman was also a decent dancer, which helped. If he didn't have to guide her around the dance floor, it would leave his brain clear to ask questions.

"I was surprised to find that you and your lovely sister are interested in mystery stories."

"We never were before, but we suddenly developed an interest in how these things are done."

William stumbled and almost stepped on the woman's foot. Could she be so naïve or unconcerned? He cleared his throat. "What things?"

"Oh, book clubs and such. We always wondered how it worked." Before he could respond to that, she said, "Will we see you at church tomorrow?"

That question seemed to come from nowhere. Unless she was trying to remind him that she was a devoted churchgoer and therefore would never consider killing a man. He had no idea what Miss Gertrude was attempting to do, but he knew she would remain on their suspect list.

He had to find a way to delve into her past to discover what it was that Harding had used for blackmail. "You and your sister have been members of St. Swithin's Church ever since I can remember. Have you always lived in Bath?"

She nodded vigorously. "Oh yes. Always. I dislike London." She wrinkled her nose and shook her head. "Very much." He noticed a flicker of fear in her eyes, which disappeared so quickly that he wasn't sure he'd seen it.

Since he hadn't mentioned London, her answer raised questions. Yes, there were definitely things he needed to learn about this seemingly meek and harmless woman who was interested in mystery books and thoroughly disliked London.

It was time now to bait the lion. "I assume you heard that my man of business, Mr. James Harding, came to an unfortunate end recently. Did you know him?" He watched her carefully for a reaction. He was not disappointed.

Her body stiffened and her eyes flashed. "Whatever happened to that man was well deserved. There are no words vile enough to describe him. He was a rat. A snake. A devil." Once the words were out of her mouth, she smiled at him as if they were discussing something very pleasant, although her face remained flushed.

To say he was taken aback was an understatement. At that moment she looked as though she could kill the man without sorrow or remorse.

The music came to an end, and he returned Miss Gertrude to the group. Amy was just arriving from a dance with Mr. Beckett, an older gentleman who had been eyeing her at the dances recently. That didn't sit well with William. Didn't the man realize he was old enough to be her father? Or at the very least an older—much older—brother?

He would have to keep an eye on Beckett as well as Mr. Colbert, who still looked unhappy about William's mother not being with them. Being the protector of women's virtue was becoming a taxing endeavor.

Amy linked her arm in his. "Why don't we take a stroll, my lord?"

They began their trek around the room. William noticed Lady Margaret conversing with a woman who was unknown to him. "Do you know that woman your aunt is speaking to?"

"No. I wonder if that's Mrs. Whitney."

"If it is, we can count on Lady Margaret to introduce us. But in the meantime, I must tell you about an interesting conversation I just now had with Miss Gertrude."

Amy's brows rose. "Please do."

He repeated the conversation as he and Amy strolled. They nodded at various people they knew as they made their way around the room. Even though Bath's population grew every year and the town was swollen with visitors during the tourist seasons, there was still a group of longtime residents who for the most part—between business, church, various clubs, and the Assembly—knew each other. Or certainly knew someone who was able to introduce them to anyone unknown.

"That is quite interesting," Amy said as he finished his tale. "What I find most telling, besides the fact that she appeared able and willing to shove Mr. Harding into the river, is the fact that she mentioned London when you asked her how long she'd lived here."

"I agree. That left me wondering if whatever occurred in Miss Gertrude's life that Harding found damaging enough for blackmail took place in London."

"My thoughts as well."

They loitered for a bit at the refreshment table, speaking with other friends. After a while they returned to the group, where Miss Gertrude appeared more composed. Shortly thereafter, the sisters announced that they were tired, were looking forward to the book club meeting on Thursday, and intended to take their leave.

"May I escort you to your carriage?" Mr. Colbert asked.

"That would be lovely, Mr. Colbert. Thank you," Miss Penelope said. The three of them departed just as Lady Margaret walked up to them. Accompanying her was the woman she had been speaking with earlier.

"May I introduce you to Mrs. Carol Whitney?" Lady Margaret went around the group, presenting each person. Mrs. Whitney was a pleasant-looking woman and appeared to be in her early thirties. She acknowledged everyone and smiled politely.

Amy, who was standing right next to the newcomer, struck up a conversation with her. Miss Sterling captured William's attention, so he was unable to hear the discourse between Amy and Mrs. Whitney.

Once he was free of Miss Sterling, and as Amy was still in deep conversation with Lady Margaret and Mrs. Whitney, William wandered the room. He didn't see Montrose and hoped to be able to speak with him sometime at their club.

He was about to return to Amy when she and Lady Margaret walked up to him. "I believe I would like to leave now," Amy said.

"Certainly. Lady Margaret, if you wish to stay, I can arrange to have my carriage return for you."

"No. I am ready as well."

They made their way out of the room and down the stairs. After shrugging into their coats, they stepped into the cool, misty air. A footman waved their carriage forward and followed them to open the vehicle's door.

Once they were all settled and the carriage began the ride to Amy's house, Lady Margaret said, "Amy, I think it is time to tell William what Mrs. Whitney had to say. I am sure he will be quite interested."

CHAPTER 12

William listened with growing amazement as Lady Margaret and Amy related their conversation with Mrs. Whitney.

"Much like Miss Gertrude when she was conversing with you, Mrs. Whitney spoke with such vehemence about Mr. Harding that I would have no trouble believing her capable of tossing him in the river," Amy said.

William shook his head at this information. "Mrs. Whitney seems quite attractive. Do you think it's a case of a woman scorned, in addition to being robbed?"

"From experience, I can say it is a possibility," said Lady Margaret. "Although I didn't think about doing away with James when I returned to Bath to find him happily courting Miss Daniels, his blasé attitude about it all did raise an ire in me I had never felt before—and have never felt since."

Amy added, "We did ascertain from Mrs. Whitney that her situation was a matter of stealing, not blackmail. It seems her deceased husband left her with a nice, tidy sum of money that should have lasted her the rest of her life.

"Mr. Harding was named as trustee to the trust established for her benefit under her deceased husband's will. She has reason to believe a portion of it has gone missing."

William gave a soft whistle.

"Additionally, Mrs. Whitney has a stepson, Patrick. With some prodding, we found out that her late husband had been well into his fifth decade when he died and that his son is much closer in age to Mrs. Whitney herself. According to the woman, Patrick was quite angry when he learned about his stepmother's loss."

This revelation left William with quite a bit to think about. Although he'd worked with Harding for three years, it seemed he had never really known the man. There seemed to have been an entire side of himself that he'd kept hidden.

William mused aloud. "At present we have two suspects on our list: Mrs. Whitney and Miss Gertrude. They both have been quite open about their feelings for Harding, none of which were particularly warm. Would they be so open about their animosity if they did actually kill him?"

Amy shrugged. "It's hard to say. I used a female killer in one of my books, but she employed poison, which I felt was more suited to a woman than getting a man drunk and shoving him into the river."

"This is real life, Amy, not fiction," Lady Margaret said. "Those women were mad. Very, very mad. Who knows what they would be capable of in a fit of anger?"

They remained silent for a while, each absorbed in their own deliberations. The cool mist had turned to a slight drizzle, slowing traffic and lengthening the trip, which allowed them time to contemplate what they had learned so far. The clatter of the horses' hooves on the cobblestones gave them a soothing, rhythmic ride.

William presented another thought. "Aside from Miss Gertrude, we don't know if the individuals in the hidden files were being blackmailed or if they were being cheated and stolen from."

"Do you think that would make a difference?" Amy grabbed the strap near her head as the carriage bounced over a hole in the road.

"Probably not. I believe we had decided that the files kept separate were singled out for nefarious purposes. It would be interesting to speak with the men on our list—Lemmon once again, and then Montrose to see if they have the same vehemence toward the man as the two ladies with whom we spoke."

They reached the Winchester townhouse. Once the driver opened the door, William jumped out and held out his hand to help Lady Margaret and Amy out of the carriage. He walked them up the steps, holding his umbrella over them.

"Will Lady Wethington be joining you for church tomorrow?" Amy asked.

"I am certain she will."

"We will see you then," Lady Margaret said, as she entered the house.

"Good night, William." Amy turned to follow her aunt, and William took her hand.

"Good night." He bent and slowly lowered his head and kissed her, enjoying her surprise that turned quickly to acceptance. Aware that they stood on her front steps, he pulled back, offered a slight smile, and hurried to this carriage.

He smiled all the way to his house.

★　★　★

The Church of St. Swithin on the Paragon was a lovely and stately church. The building dated back to the late eighteenth century, but a worship house had stood on its grounds as far back as the tenth century.

Beloved author Miss Jane Austen's father was buried at the site. Amy's parents had been wed in St. Swithin's and she and her brother baptized there. At one time she had thought to be married at St. Swithin's, but as the years passed and she had grown more and more against the idea of matrimony, that thought had slowly died.

Lately, however, the idea of the married state had begun to interest her once again. Provided, of course, it was to the correct man. She wondered if the idea had anything to do with her growing relationship with William and the kiss he had bestowed on her the night before.

You are not a stupid woman, Amy.

As she and Aunt Margaret made their weekly trek to the fine old church, Amy looked forward to the inspiration and peace she always found there on Sunday mornings.

Once free of their carriage, they entered the building, greeting other congregants as they walked along the path. After days of cold, miserable rain, the sun had finally made an appearance, which lifted Amy's spirits considerably. Although they had months to go before spring even began to raise its head, the few good-weather days in the winter reminded her that gloomy, cold weather would not last forever.

Just as they reached the door, William and Lady Wethington walked up to them. "Good morning, Lady Amy. How pleased I am to see you again." Lady Wethington gave Amy a warm hug and another one of those looks that made her a tad nervous. Amy might have been rethinking her position on marriage, but she certainly did not want her ladyship pushing her. Or William.

Amy smiled back. "So nice to see you as well, Lady Wethington. I hope you are feeling well this morning."

"I am. A good night's rest eased my headache tremendously."

"I am so glad to hear that. We missed you last evening at the Assembly." She turned toward Aunt Margaret. "May I present to you my aunt, Lady Margaret Lovell."

The two women nodded at each other. "Do you live together?" Lady Wethington asked.

"Yes," Amy said, "Aunt Margaret practically raised me, since my mother passed away when I was ten years old."

"Oh, how very sad. But I'm sure you received a good deal of love and attention from your aunt."

Amy beamed at her aunt. "Indeed. Aunt Margaret and I are great friends too."

Lady Wethington linked her arm in Amy's as they strolled down the aisle of the church. Normally they sat in the Winchester pew, but this week William led them to his family's pew.

Lady Wethington entered first, with Aunt Margaret right behind her, followed by Amy and William. It did not slip Amy's notice that William's mother purposefully maneuvered them so that Amy and William sat together. It would probably interest her ladyship to know that they usually sat together even without her machinations.

"Ladies, I would love for you both to join us after church for lunch," said Lady Wethington. "William told me you generally entertain him, but I thought it would be nice to return the favor and have you to our home."

"I would like that." Amy touched Aunt Margaret's hand. "Are you free to join us at William's house for lunch?" Amy prayed her aunt did not have other plans, which she sometimes did. Being alone with Lady Wethington and that gleam in her eye made her anxious. The woman seemed to turn most conversation to weddings, something Amy sensed she was growing closer to but didn't want to hear about quite yet.

"Yes, I would be honored to join you. Thank you so much." Lady Margaret got the words out just as Mr. Palmer stepped into the sanctuary and addressed the congregation. Amy settled back and looked forward to her one hour of peace for the week.

As usual, Miss Gertrude and Miss Penelope were in their seats two rows down and across the aisle from Amy's family bench. Amy glanced over at William and smiled when Miss Gertrude's voice could be heard above all the others. Her enthusiasm for life had certainly increased since Mr. Harding's death.

Should they really consider Miss Gertrude a suspect? Yes, she was tall, and though slender, she appeared muscular. But would someone who looked so innocent, with her flowered dresses and straw hats, be a killer? Amy shivered, realizing that, were she writing this story, a suspect such as Miss Gertrude would be a wonderful twist.

The service ended with Mrs. Newton playing the organ with gusto despite her off-key rendition of "Amazing Grace."

As they rode in their carriage toward William's house right outside Bath, Amy said to her aunt, "I'm so glad you agreed to accompany me."

"Why? Lady Wethington seems like a lovely woman. And she seems quite fond of you."

Amy huffed. "You noticed? That's why I'm glad to have you along with me."

"Ah. I think I understand. Do you feel like she's pushing you and William together?"

"I hardly think *pushing* is the word I would use. More like thrusting with a heavy boot."

Aunt Margaret reached over and took Amy's hand. "I know I have been a bad example for you when it comes to marriage. Just because I chose the single life doesn't mean you have to follow in my footsteps."

Amy frowned and dared to ask something she had always wondered. "Why *did* you decide not to marry? You obviously would have had offers over the years. I know my papa has made his frustration known at your not accepting a husband."

Aunt Margaret sighed and stared off into space. "After the disaster with James, I decided to take my anger out on my brother and refused any offers he received for my hand. However, I found as the years went by that I became comfortable with my single life. As you know, life can be difficult for a married woman, although I have hopes that will change soon."

"What about Lord Pembroke? You saw quite a bit of him last year."

"Ah yes, Oliver."

Amy's brows rose. "Christian names?" She grew amused at the flush on Aunt Margaret's face.

Aunt Margaret smoothed her skirts, avoiding Amy's eyes. "Yes, we did see a bit of each other. However, he has various investments out of the country and took a trip a few months ago to visit his properties. I expect him back sometime soon."

"Oh my."

"Never mind." Aunt Margaret waved her finger at Amy. "There is no *oh my* about it. We are merely friends."

"I see. Just like William and I are *merely friends*."

Her aunt stared at her, then nodded. "Yes. The same."

Amy decided to veer from that subject. She would have a difficult enough time trying to avoid Lady Wethington and her suggestive looks without adding Aunt Margaret to the mix.

They arrived at William's house. Amy watched William help his mother from his carriage, which was parked directly in front of theirs. "I think I shall 'gird up my loins,' as Proverbs says, and try to consume my meal without accidentally ending up betrothed." She spoke over her shoulder and then smiled as William opened the door to help her out.

★ ★ ★

The following Tuesday afternoon, Amy pushed her notebook away and tossed her pen onto the desk, ink splattering across the blotter. No matter how many times she thought she had come up with the best situation to get her main character into, it didn't seem right.

"My lady, Lord Wethington has arrived." Lacey poked her head into Amy's small office with her announcement.

Thankful for the break, Amy pushed her chair back and stood. "Tell his lordship I will be right down."

She fussed a bit with her hair, which was generally a lost cause, since the curls never stayed where they were supposed to and the hairpins didn't always help. She plopped a hat on her head, stuck in a pin that scratched her scalp, and grabbed her gloves and reticule before leaving the bedchamber.

They were going to visit the three pubs nearest the site on the River Avon where Mr. Harding's body had been found. William had learned from someone he knew at the police station that the autopsy had revealed that the victim had not been in the water more than twelve or thirteen hours.

William had used the tide, the time of day, and the weather conditions on the day before Harding's body was discovered to determine the general area where the killer had met with Harding to ply him with alcohol—or something to make him lethargic—and then place the flask in his pocket before shoving him into the river. Most likely this had all taken place under cover of darkness, but William had refused to go at night if he was to take Amy with him. He'd insisted it would be too dangerous, and when she'd again suggested that they bring a gun, he hadn't even answered her.

Hopefully the bartenders and tavern wenches they would meet in the afternoon also worked in the evenings.

The first pub, the Owl and the Mouse, was a mere quarter mile from the banks of the river. Amy wore one of her older, less fashionable dresses for the occasion. She borrowed Lacey's coat and didn't look anything like a lady of the *ton* descending upon the underclass.

William had also dressed more like a working-class man, with a cap pulled low over his forehead. "Remember, this is not one of your usual high-class teahouses. It's a low-class pub."

"For goodness' sake, William, I've done research before. I've been in some derelict places," she huffed.

"And I can assure you that will never happen again." He took her by the arm and escorted her into the pub.

Whatever did that mean? Was he already trying to tell her what she could and could not do? Did he think one little kiss—all right, several more than one, and not so little—gave him rights where she was concerned?

Before she could give him the rough side of her tongue, he walked her to a table, one of the few empty ones left in the room. Even though it was the middle of the afternoon, most of the tables were filled with men, all of them with glasses of ale in front of them.

"Why aren't they at work?" she asked.

"They are probably dock workers. The ships that go out of Bristol pick up men here and all along the road. Most of these men are waiting for a captain to arrive and offer them a job."

"And they drink while they wait?"

William shrugged. "It passes the time."

A young woman with a dress sporting a bodice considerably lower than Amy had ever seen approached their table. Amy watched her, amazed that her charms didn't fall out onto the table. "What'll be, laddie?"

"Ale for both of us." William's accent changed a bit, which brought a smile to Amy's lips.

When the lass returned with the ale, William said, "I'm lookin' for someone 'oo I fin' might 'ave been 'ere a couple of weeks ago."

Amy almost choked on the watered-down ale, and the wench snorted. "Good luck wif that, laddie. I ain't got the bloomin' nickle and dime ter keep track of 'oo comes in 'ere. They aw butcher's alike."

"This geeza 'ad a silver flask. It belongs ter me."

She shook her head. "Ain't seen notin' like 'at, laddie." She sauntered off, hips swaying, but not before she gave William a look that Amy found quite annoying.

The next pub they entered, ridiculously named the King's Garden, was a bit more tasteful, but still not something Amy would ever patronize. They took seats at a table. This pub was more than half-empty. The woman who approached their table this time was older, with missing teeth in the front of her mouth. She was bosomy, cheerful, and relatively clean.

William asked his usual questions and got the same results. The woman had seen nothing and knew nothing. He was urging Amy to finish her ale—which she had no intention of doing, since the cleanliness around the rim of the glass was questionable—when a man approached their table.

He was no more than thirty years old, but it was obvious he'd lived a hard life. He dragged over a chair, turned it around, and sat, resting his forearms on the back. "I hear yer lookin' fer a toff what stole your flask."

William regarded the man with casual hesitation. "Yes. Do yer 'ave information about that?"

"What's it worth to ya?"

"It depends on wot yer 'ave ter say."

The man spit on the floor. "I ain't sayin' nothin' till I see a coin."

William removed a coin from his pocket and placed it on the table, about halfway between the man and William. "Talk."

The man edged his fingers toward the coin, but William moved it back. The man finally looked up at William and grinned, the few teeth left in his mouth brown. "There's a toff wot comes in 'ere every couple weeks. I 'eard 'e drahn in the river." He gestured toward the window that faced the water.

"Did 'e 'ave the flask?" William asked.

"Nah, but I thought ye might wanna know 'bout the toff—since 'e's wahn of your kind—that 'e met people 'ere and they give 'im bread and honey. He wrote dahn information in a butcher's book he carried wiv 'im."

Amy took that to mean this "toff" had been receiving money from the people here on a regular basis.

Also, their apparent attempt to dress as though they could fit in and William's attempt at cockney hadn't worked. At least it hadn't fooled this man, who had identified them as members of the upper class with no problem.

William leaned in closer to the man. "Go on."

"The last time 'e was 'ere, there was a big 'rgument."

"And?"

"Wif wahn of them 'igh-flautin' dames." He hitched his thumb at Amy. "Loike 'er"

Amy leaned closer. "What did she look like?"

"Tall, skinny, red Barnet Fair." The man snatched up the coin, bit it, and dropped it in his pocket.

William and Amy looked at each other. "Miss Gertrude."

CHAPTER 13

The carriage rumbled along to the next pub they planned to visit, both of them still in shock from what the man at the last pub had told them. William looked over at Amy when he finally found his voice. "What are you thinking?"

"I'm thinking I don't believe Miss Gertrude killed Mr. Harding. No matter how many times I go over it in my mind, I don't see it."

"If the man was drunk, she would certainly be strong enough to do it."

"William." She sat forward and glared at him. "Think about Miss Gertrude, with the flowered dresses and straw hats. Pretending she's a twin. In church. Every Sunday."

He leaned toward her, coming almost nose to nose with her. "Think about Miss Gertrude suddenly interested in murder mysteries. And think about Miss Gertrude being blackmailed. There has to be something in her background scandalous enough to make her pay Harding for years."

They had decided to continue with the last pub on their list. Just because it appeared that Harding had been meeting some of his victims in the last pub didn't necessarily prove it was where he had met his fate.

Their third stop was an inn as well as a pub. Most likely because of the addition of rooms, this one was fairly decent. The Tiger and the Lion was a two-story building of undetermined years. A groom trotted up to them when they arrived and advised William's driver where he could put the carriage.

The inside was clean, and wonderful smells came from somewhere in the back. "I wonder if it's safe to eat here," Amy whispered as they took seats at a table on the right side of the room.

"I have found in my travels that inns, as opposed to pubs, generally have excellent food. It's what keeps the travelers coming back. When you're on the road, it is not always easy to find a place with clean rooms and decent fare. Once an innkeeper has established himself, word passes among those who need accommodations when they travel."

Amy grinned. "I'm assuming from my simple question and your lengthy diatribe that the answer is yes? I hope so, because I find myself quite hungry."

William smiled back. His Amy was certainly quick with a sharp retort.

His Amy?

Although, considering how much his mother had fawned over her at lunch this past Sunday, no doubt Lady Wethington was now spending her time writing wedding invitations.

And he found himself somewhat pleased at the notion.

A middle-aged woman with an apron wrapped around her considerable belly approached the table, a huge friendly smile on her face. "Good evening, my lady, my lord. I am Mrs. Brodack. My husband and I own the inn. How may we help you?"

"Something smells wonderful. What's for supper?"

With pride in her stance and voice, Mrs. Brodack said, "Aye, I just finished cooking a lamb stew. I have bread ready to come out of the oven and two desserts"—she counted off on her fingers—"my famous lemon tarts and an apple charlotte."

"Good heavens, I believe my mouth is actually drooling," Williams said. He turned to Amy. "What say you, my lady?"

"Yes." She grinned at the woman. "Everything."

The woman hustled away, obviously quite pleased with their response.

"I thought you were a vegetarian. Since you are a vegetarian who eats fish, are you also a vegetarian who eats lamb?" He grinned at her.

Amy raised her chin. "I must be flexible. If that is what the inn is serving, then I must have the lamb stew."

She glared at him as he laughed out loud. Then with a sniff, she said, "I think, since the innkeeper's wife is so friendly, she might be the best person to ask about the flask. Or if Harding was meeting people here as well."

Within minutes Mrs. Brodack returned, carrying a tray loaded with bowls of stew, fresh bread, butter, and both tarts and slices of the apple charlotte. She placed all the items on the table.

"I don't suppose you have tea, do you?" Amy asked.

"I certainly do, my lady." She turned to William. "Ale for you, my lord?"

"Actually, tea will be fine." The ale he'd had in the last two pubs had left him with a sour stomach.

Mrs. Brodack gave a curt nod and left.

Amy stared after the woman as she departed. "How does she know we're lady and lord?"

William laughed. "You might think we can dress in a working-class manner, but our accent and the way we move and walk all deny what we're trying to portray. But," he continued, "dressing this way is still a wise thing to do to avoid drawing too much attention to ourselves."

Conversation ceased as they consumed their meal, until all the bowls and plates were empty.

"Mrs. Brodack, you are a wonderful cook," William said as she took away their dishes.

The woman blushed. "Thank you, my lord."

When she returned with their refilled teapot, William asked, "I am looking for a silver flask that I misplaced. I have reason to believe someone picked it up. It is a family heirloom that I would love to get back. Have you seen anyone in here in the last couple of weeks with such an item?"

Mrs. Brodack placed her hands on her ample hips. "No, I didn't. But funny you ask that, because there were two police officers in here yesterday who had a silver flask with them. They were trying to identify the person who might have used it here."

William glanced over at Amy.

The woman continued. "You might want to check with the police. It sounds like they have your flask."

William nodded. "Thank you. That is a very good idea. I am glad it was found."

* * *

Friday morning, Amy forced herself to sit at her desk and get some writing finished. She'd been too involved in the search for Mr. Harding's killer to devote enough time to her current book. She had a deadline to meet, and it was not going to be met if she didn't spend some time writing. The book was not going to write itself.

She and William had not discussed the murder since their visits to the three pubs on Tuesday afternoon, nor had they talked about where they would go from here. They had others on their suspect list besides Miss Gertrude: Mr. Lemmon, Mr. Montrose, and Mrs. Whitney. However, Amy didn't want to assume one of those individuals was the killer.

William had been busy all day Wednesday and Thursday. He'd told her he would be visiting with his solicitor to have him petition the courts to have Harding's estate reimburse him for the money stolen. The problem with that, he'd said, was that until he received the files from the police department, he had no idea how much was missing, and more importantly, he needed to make sure he was still solvent.

Although he had said those last words with a hint of humor, she could see in his eyes that he was troubled.

The sound of a carriage drawing up to the front of the townhouse had her pushing her chair back and strolling to the window in her office that faced the street.

Her jaw dropped when her papa and brother stepped out of the carriage and made their way to the front door. Papa had not written that he was going to be visiting.

Then her stomach clenched. Had he heard about her publisher wanting to have her appear at the book fair? She wasn't quite ready to face him with that matter yet. She was still toying with the idea of agreeing to the publisher's request.

And therefore bringing Papa's wrath down onto her head.

She took a quick look in her mirror to make sure she wasn't disheveled enough to warrant comments about her untidiness, then left the room.

"Papa!" She walked into his outstretched arms and received a warm hug. For as much as she hadn't seen much of her papa over the years, what with her living mostly in Bath and him staying in London, they still had a warm relationship.

Except when he wanted her to do something she did not want to do. Then they butted heads, and he used those occasions to remind her that she was too much like him. And then when she rejected marriage offers, he complained that she was too much like his sister, Margaret. Amy liked to think she was too much like herself. And she wanted to stay that way, thank you very much.

"I didn't know you were coming for a visit. Why didn't you write?" She turned to her brother, Michael, the image of her papa. They looked alike, walked the same way, used the same facial expressions, and had a similar stance. If it hadn't been for the lines on Papa's face and a few extra pounds he had gained over the years, they could have passed for twins. Papa had even retained his full head of hair, although it was streaked with silver.

"Michael, you too! I can't believe you are both here." She drew back from hugging her brother and turned to her papa. "Is something wrong?"

"Nothing wrong, my dear. We're here for Lady Wethington's dinner."

"Tonight?"

Papa draped his arm around her shoulders and led them to the library. "Is there more than one dinner?"

Amy shook her head, confused. "Not that I'm aware of, but I didn't know Lady Wethington had invited the two of you."

Aunt Margaret glided into the room. "Me as well."

Amy swung around. "You too?"

A sinking feeling hit her stomach. Why in heaven's name would Lady Wethington invite her entire family? She broke into a sweat when she came up with the most obvious reason. Surely William would not do something so foolish as to propose marriage in front of everyone? Lord, she felt like running to her room and hiding under the bed.

"Yes. The invitation came earlier in the week. I'm surprised that *you* are surprised." Aunt Margaret looked closely at her. "Are you well, Amy? You look rather pale."

"No. I am fine." She tried a smile and doubted that she carried it off. She had to speak with William before this dinner tonight. Didn't they have enough on their hands with this murder investigation without something as foolish as a marriage proposal in the middle of it all?

She turned her mind off and hurried back upstairs. Papa would never allow her to take the carriage to William's house by herself. Yet she didn't want to take Lacey or Aunt Margaret with her.

She grabbed Persephone, found her leash, and hurried downstairs. "I'm taking Persephone for a walk," she called out to whoever was still in the library. She shrugged into her coat and opened the door.

And was met with a virtual downpour.

She stomped her foot like a toddler and didn't even care if someone saw her. From the voices coming from the library, it appeared that her brother, papa, and aunt were in a lively discussion and had forgotten about her.

Sucking in a deep breath, she looked at the carriage still parked at the end of the pavement. The driver, Malcolm, was just starting to move the horses forward toward the mews at the back of the house. With a quick look over her shoulder, she raced down the stairs, dragging Persephone, who howled the entire way.

"Lord Wethington's house, Malcolm." She jumped in and kept staring at the front door, waiting for Papa to come barreling out to stop her.

Once they were on their way, she took a deep breath and let it out. Her mind was a jumble of thoughts, all of them scrambled. She wasn't even sure William was at home, and if he wasn't, whatever would she say to Lady Wethington about her visit without sounding like a half-wit?

She tapped on the carriage ceiling. Malcolm slid open the small door in the roof and looked down at her. "When we arrive at Lord Wethington's home, please drive around to the back first to make sure his carriage is there."

The good servant that he was, Malcolm merely nodded and continued on his way, the rain dripping off the brim of his hat. It occurred to her now that Malcolm might have been parked at the front of her house waiting for Papa or Michael to go somewhere. No, she assured herself. The man had definitely been moving the horses toward the mews. She gave her full attention to the prospect of speaking with William.

The traffic had been light, so they arrived at the Wethington townhouse sooner than she would have thought. Once she was free of the carriage, with Persephone wailing in distress, she hurried up the steps. A man Amy had not seen before opened the door and gave her a slight bow.

"I am Lady Amy Lovell, here to see Lord Wethington." Her words came out breathless from her jaunt up the steps. She stepped into the house as he moved back. "Is he at home?"

"I shall check, my lady." He waved toward the drawing room. "If you will be so kind as to wait here, I will see."

As he started to move away, she said, "Wait!"

Startled, the man turned back. "Yes, my lady?"

She moved closed to the man and lowered her voice. "Is Lady Wethington at home?"

"I shall check on that also."

"No!"

His eyebrows rose. Good gracious, the man must think her a lunatic. Like all good servants, however, he merely stopped and stared at her with no indication that he thought there was anything odd about her behavior. She could picture him laughing wildly when he returned to the servants' quarters and told all and sundry about the daft woman who had just called on his master.

"I, um . . . I do not wish to, um, disturb her." She patted her upper lip with her gloved finger. Why did she always get herself into these messes?

"Very good, my lady." He bowed again and left the room.

She paced as she waited for William to arrive. She glanced out the window, the rain still coming down in torrents, as if she should be preparing for another great flood.

At the sound of footsteps, she turned, then breathed a sigh of relief when William stepped into the room.

"Amy! Whatever are you doing here?" He walked over to her and took her hand in his. "Is something wrong?"

She pulled her hand away and placed her hands on her hips. "Why are we having dinner tonight?"

He stepped back, his brows rising to his hairline. "Because we will most likely be hungry?"

She waved her finger at him. "Don't try to dodge that question. Your mother invited my entire family to dinner tonight."

"Yes. I just found out myself."

Her hands dropped to her sides. "You didn't plan this?"

"Plan what?"

"I don't know. Did you?"

"Did I what? Amy, you are not making sense. I feel like I'm in some sort of a crazy dream."

The man who had answered the door entered the drawing room. "My lord, you have guests."

"Already?" He turned to Amy. "I thought dinner was at eight o'clock tonight."

Amy shook her head and shrugged as Detective Carson and Detective Marsh sauntered into the room.

"Well, look who we find together again. Sherlock Holmes and Dr. Watson." Detective Carson grinned.

CHAPTER 14

Before William could even begin to make sense of what Amy was talking about and attempt to answer her nebulous questions, he was faced with the two men who were as irritating as a swarm of mosquitoes.

William ran his hand down his face. "To what do I owe the pleasure of this visit, Detectives?" He attempted a smile, trying to at least be well-mannered, although his first instinct was to toss the men out the door. Headfirst.

"We have a few questions for you." Detective Carson walked farther into the room. William, Amy, and Detective Marsh followed him to a grouping of chairs near the fireplace. As if the man was the host, he waved at the chairs. "Shall we sit?"

William and Amy took the chairs next to each other. Carson and Marsh sat across from them.

Detective Carson removed a flask from his inner jacket pocket. He waved it in William's direction. "I hear you've been looking for this."

Deciding that silence was his best response, especially since Detective Carson had not raised a direct question, William said nothing, his brows rising slightly.

Visibly annoyed at William's lack of response, the man continued. "In the course of our investigation—and by that

I mean *police work*—we visited a few pubs near where the late Mr. Harding's body was found floating in the River Avon."

Again, no question, so William remained silent.

"Imagine how confused we were to discover that a man and a woman had visited one of these places asking about a 'stolen' flask."

Still no question. Still silence on William's part.

"Do you know what is peculiar about that?" Carson asked.

Finally, a question. William looked the man straight in the eye. "No. But I assume you are about to tell me."

"You are bloody right about that, lad." He glanced in Amy's direction. "I apologize for the language, my lady."

Amy waved him off, and Carson continued. "We warned you two before about staying out of police business. There can be only one reason why you would be nosing around those establishments asking questions."

Again, William rewarded the man with silence.

"Remember, *my lord*, you are a suspect in a murder investigation."

"What!" Lady Wethington had quietly entered the room, unnoticed by any of them. Her face was pale as she stared at the two detectives.

William groaned. This could turn into a catastrophe. "Mother, all is well. The detectives are asking questions about my man of business, who drowned recently."

"And they suspect you? Of murder? A peer? A member of the *ton*? An upstanding, moral, loyal, and honorable man?" Her voice rose as she spoke, and her face now turned bright red.

Carson looked over at Marsh. "His mother. No surprise there."

William walked over to Lady Wethington, taking her hand in his. "Mother, this won't take long. I suggest you retire to your bedchamber, and I will attend you once the men have left."

"Not at all!" She straightened her shoulders and glared in the detectives' direction. "I demand to know what this silliness is all about."

Detective Carson stood—something he should have done when Lady Wethington entered the room—and arranged his features into an almost-pleasant mien. "Lady Wethington, I suggest you do as your son said and remove yourself from the room."

"Remove myself? This is my home, sir." She raised her indignant chin. "I will not be ordered about by the likes of you." With those words, she let out a soft sigh, her knees crumpled, and she slid to the floor in a faint.

"Shite," Detective Marsh mumbled, and slapped his notebook closed.

William and Amy both rushed to his mother's side. Amy got down on her knees and turned to Carson. "I suggest you leave now, Detectives. Apparently the stress of your assumption has thrown her ladyship into a faint. She needs our attention."

Carson gritted his teeth, then pointed his finger at William. "I am warning you"—he swung his attention to Amy, still on the floor—"and you as well, Lady Amy. Stay out of our business." And with that, the two detectives left the room.

Once the sound of the front door closing had reached them, Lady Wethington opened one eye. "Are they gone?"

William and Amy burst out laughing.

★   ★   ★

Later that evening, Amy joined her papa, brother, and Aunt Margaret in the front hall as they prepared to leave for William's house. After she and William had helped his mother up from the floor that morning and he had assured her he was not a murder suspect, Amy had taken her leave, never having learned what this two-family dinner was all about.

Since William had seemed confounded by her questions and had told her he'd had no idea her family had been invited until that very morning, she felt a bit more confident that she would not have to endure an embarrassing moment.

Once they all settled in the carriage, Amy looked to her papa. "Papa, I find it hard to believe you and Michael traveled all the way from London for dinner."

"We were invited, daughter, and you know I am quite fond of your young man. It would be nice to meet his mother. Additionally, we are considering another business venture here in Bath, and 'twas a good time to investigate that potential acquisition."

Amy bristled. "He is not my young man, and why would you be interested in meeting Lady Wethington?" She still felt a bit uneasy. Not that she was as much against marriage as she'd been at one time, but she certainly wasn't interested in being pushed to the altar anytime soon, which seemed to be Papa's favorite pastime.

Papa shifted in his seat so that he was able to look her in the face. "Amy, Lord Wethington appears to be a nice lad. I've been asking around, and he is well thought of in both London and Bath. Furthermore, it seems every time I visit Bath, he is hanging about the place."

Amy groaned. Papa had been "asking around" about William? She gritted her teeth. "And?"

"And perhaps Lady Wethington also feels as though you and he would suit."

"Aha!" she almost shouted. "I knew you had ulterior motives in this."

Papa frowned. "Settle yourself, daughter. We have no ulterior motives. I merely plan on having a nice dinner with a well-bred family of the nobility and then spending some time perusing the business in which we are interested."

They were all silent for the rest of the trip.

Amy had to smile when they were led to the drawing room and William walked toward her. He looked fine and dandy in his charcoal trousers, striped waistcoat, fashionably tied cravat, and deep-blue jacket.

"Good evening, my lady." William turned to Aunt Margaret, bowed to her, and addressed Papa. "My lord, may I present you to my mother, Lady Wethington?"

Lady Wethington glided across the room, moving much like Aunt Margaret. Amy feared she would never acquire that grace. She would forever fumble her way through life, always looking for the handle.

William's mother extended her slim hand, and Papa accepted it with all the dignity and arrogance of his station. He bowed. "Good evening, Lady Wethington."

William continued. "Mother, this is Lord Winchester, his son, Lord Davenport, and of course you are already acquainted with Lady Amy's aunt, Lady Margaret."

"How very delightful for you all to join us this evening." Lady Wethington turned to Amy with a warm smile. "I have simply fallen in love with your daughter, my lord. Lady Amy is charming, witty, and a pleasure to visit with."

If only the floor would open, allowing her to drop through, Amy would donate her yearly allowance to the church.

Sensing her embarrassment, William stepped in. "Why don't we all relax with a drink before dinner is ready?"

Beverage preferences were noted, and William and Michael poured for everyone while Amy, her papa, and Aunt

Margaret joined Lady Wethington in a cozy corner of the room between the long windows and the fireplace, which gave off toasty warmth to those within its reach.

Michael and William delivered the drinks to Papa and the women. Instead of sitting, they both chose to stand as they swirled their drinks. Amy knew she was not imagining the looks her brother cast at William. Good grief, they looked like two warriors from times past, eyeing each other up for a duel.

Amy glanced at William, who winked. Perhaps he was as uneasy about this cozy family gathering as she was.

Despite Amy's misgivings, the dinner was fine, the food wonderful—no one commented when she ate the roast beef—the conversation light and harmless. Lady Wethington and Papa got on quite well, and it disturbed her the way the two of them glowed with happiness whenever William spoke to her. If William noticed or felt uncomfortable with the attention, it didn't show.

After dinner, they retired back to the drawing room for tea. It had grown close to the time for their departure when Lady Wethington said, directing her comments to Papa, "I was quite pleased when I visited the book club the children belong to."

The children? Amy almost lost her dinner. She threw William a side glance. He looked as stunned as she felt.

"It's a lovely place, but the most exciting thing I heard was that the bookstore is having a book festival."

Papa smiled. "Indeed? That sounds wonderful. I am a great believer in reading, myself."

"And"—Lady Wethington stopped to make sure she had everyone's attention—"the owner of the bookstore has promised to have the very well-known author E. D. Burton at the festival to meet his readers and autograph books!" She grinned at the great news.

Aunt Margaret choked on her tea.

William closed his eyes and groaned.

Michael laughed and downed his brandy.

Papa glared in Amy's direction.

Amy offered him a sick smile and again prayed for the floor to open and swallow her. Two years' allowance to the church.

★   ★   ★

The following Monday, Amy's ears still blistered from the tongue-lashing Papa had given her on the ride home from William's house. To say he was displeased was a gross understatement.

It had been quite surprising—and painful—when Lady Wethington made her announcement. If she noticed the strange reactions from everyone else in the room, she did not show it.

Shortly after that, Amy and her family had taken their leave.

Presently, she was waiting for Aunt Margaret to join her in the drawing room. They were making afternoon calls, something Amy viewed as akin to suffering from ague.

Her main motivation was Aunt Margaret's assurance that Mrs. Whitney would be at one of the three places they planned to visit. Amy prayed she was at the first one so she could return home with her brain still intact. Gossiping women turned her mind to mush.

"I'm ready." Aunt Margaret sailed into the room, pulling on her gloves. As always, she looked wonderfully put together.

Her deep-green wool suit with black piping accentuated her warm brown eyes. Although her aunt bemoaned her straight brown hair, she always managed to keep every hair slicked back and in place.

Amy, on the other hand, dealt with her messy curls by fixing them into a sort of chignon from which obstinate strands escaped before she had even put on her hat. Whereas Aunt Margaret was always impeccably dressed and graceful as a swan, Amy was not at all graceful or stylish, and considered herself well dressed if her shoes matched.

Giving her niece a quick once-over, Aunt Margaret rolled her eyes and turned toward the door. "Time to leave."

Amy looked down at herself. Did she truly look that bad?

Their first stop was the home of Lady Ambrose, a woman Amy had difficulty tolerating. Lady Ambrose loved gossip and scandal more than most. She had relished telling Amy all sorts of newsy gossip last year when Amy was forced to abide the woman's company to gain information on Mr. St. Vincent's murder.

Lady Ambrose also hosted a sewing circle each week in which the ladies made baby clothes for the unfortunate. Amy liked to think that this at least revealed some goodness in the woman.

When they arrived, one of the first women they spotted was Mrs. Whitney—*thank you, lord*—enjoying tea, along with Miss Everhart and Mrs. Welling.

With a little help from Aunt Margaret, Amy managed to finagle her way into the seat right next to Mrs. Whitney's.

The ladies were listening to Mrs. Welling tell the story of her daughter and how ungrateful the young lady was because she refused to allow Mrs. Welling to move into her house with her husband and five children.

Amy couldn't help but think that Mrs. Welling must be a difficult person to live with, since her daughter had passed on the opportunity to have her mother's help with all those children.

Once Aunt Margaret began what Amy knew was going to be a very lengthy story about her recent visit with the Woods family, Amy used the time to strike up a side conversation with Mrs. Whitney.

"It's so nice to see you again, Mrs. Whitney. Did you enjoy the Assembly dance last week?"

The woman smiled brightly, the fine lines at the edges of her eyes more visible. "Yes. I did. It was a pleasure meeting you."

Mrs. Whitney bent closer to Amy and spoke softly. "I heard that you and Lord Wethington are trying to uncover who killed Mr. Harding."

Well then. It seemed gossip and news did spread fast in the community.

"We are asking a few questions, but only because Lord Wethington employed Mr. Harding and he is now concerned about some of his holdings."

Mrs. Whitney snorted. "I certainly didn't trust him. I wasn't happy when my husband's will was read and I learned that Mr. Harding was the trustee of my trust. I just hope that when the court appoints a new trustee, he can learn how much Mr. Harding stole from me."

Mrs. Whitney paused as she took a sip of tea. "I will tell you what my main concern is." She leaned even closer and lowered her voice again. "My stepson Patrick."

"Oh, why is that?"

She twisted the handkerchief she held in her hands. "He was also concerned that Mr. Harding was stealing from me and made some vague threats. Patrick disappeared right around the same time Mr. Harding was killed. I haven't seen him since."

CHAPTER 15

Amy sat patiently in the drawing room, waiting for William to arrive. She'd told William at church two days before that they needed to discuss Mr. Harding's murder and their next steps. After Mrs. Whitney's revelation at Lady Ambrose's tea yesterday about Patrick going missing, she felt they had a genuine lead to follow. It was too much of a coincidence that the stepson had disappeared the same night Harding was killed. Especially if he had learned that Harding was stealing from his stepmother's trust.

It had stuck her as quite odd, however, that a stepson would be so concerned about his stepmother's finances. Unless he was expected to support her once the money was gone.

Papa entered the drawing room, breaking into her musings. "Good afternoon, daughter. It looks like you're planning on stepping out today. With Lord Wethington?"

Amy gritted her teeth. "Yes."

Papa and Michael had taken up residence while they explored the possibility of purchasing the new business they were considering. Ever since the dinner at Lady Wethington's, whenever Papa hadn't been scowling at Amy about the book fair, he had been watching her with a gleam in his eyes.

For that reason, she was reluctant to have William visit, but they needed to get together to continue their investigation.

She glanced out the window, happy to see William climbing the steps to the front door. "He is here."

"Excellent!"

She gathered her things and moved around Papa. "I'm leaving."

"No. Wait a minute," Papa followed her to the front door. "Good afternoon, Wethington. I see you and my daughter are off for a jaunt this afternoon."

William attempted to remain friendly, but Amy saw the unease in his stance. "Yes, my lord. We are off to the Pump Room, then to a shop for tea."

Papa slapped William on the back. "Good, good. Have a wonderful time. No need to hurry back. I know my daughter is in good hands."

Amy pushed William toward the door. "Good-bye, Papa."

Once they settled in the carriage, she let out a deep breath. "I apologize for my papa, William. He's been acting quite strange since dinner at your house the other night."

William chuckled. "You want to see strange, stop by and visit with my mother." His eyes grew wide. "No. Forget I said that. Do not stop in to see my mother. She will send for the modiste to take measurements for your wedding gown."

Shocked at his words, they stared at each other. William swallowed. Amy cleared her throat. They both looked out opposite windows.

Silence reigned as the carriage made its way through town to the Pump Room next to the Roman Baths. Even though the weather was cold—normal for February—the unexpected sunshine had encouraged strollers to leave their homes. The mall, surrounded by shops, the Abbey, and the Roman Baths, was crowded with visitors.

Amy and William wandered the Pump Room, paused for the obligatory drink from the famous waters, and stopped to chat with friends and acquaintances.

"We need privacy to discuss our information. I believe it's time for tea," William said as he steered her out of the Pump Room.

They walked onto the cobblestone pathway, which had dozens of shops on either side, and found a teashop that looked large enough to give them some anonymity. Once they settled into their seats and ordered tea, Amy glanced around the room and lowered her voice. The shop was busy, but no one seemed to be paying them any attention.

"I had time to visit with Mrs. Whitney Saturday afternoon when Aunt Margaret and I made afternoon calls," Amy said. "Well, actually only one call, because Mrs. Whitney was blessedly at the first place we stopped."

The waiter returned with the tea and a tray full of small sandwiches, tarts, and biscuits. Amy eyed them, then shook her head and poured their tea. She handed William a plate, which he immediately filled up.

"Aren't you having anything besides tea?"

Amy sighed. "I'm afraid not. I think I need to cut back on treats."

"Why?" He looked genuinely surprised, which warmed her heart.

"Because I need to lose a bit of weight."

He shook his head. "No you don't." He popped a piece of lemon tart into his mouth. "This is very good."

Attempting to distract herself, she said, "Mrs. Whitney is beside herself with concern over her stepson, Patrick. Mr. Harding was the trustee for the trust Mrs. Whitney's deceased husband set up for her in his will. She is afraid Patrick learned that Mr. Harding was stealing from her and went after the man."

"Does she think Patrick may have had something to do with Harding's murder?"

"She didn't say that exactly, but she *did* say that her stepson went missing around the same time Mr. Harding was discovered in the river."

"I'm beginning to believe James was truly a wicked man." William picked up a tart and placed it on her plate.

She eyed the treat but attempted to ignore it. With one finger, he pushed the plate closer to her. When she looked at him, he winked. She picked up the tart. "Just one bite." She closed her eyes and groaned. "This is delicious."

William laughed. "Continue."

Amy wiped her mouth. "She didn't say, but I got the impression from her demeanor that she is worried his disappearance might have something to do with Mr. Harding's death."

"Based on that, we will place him firmly on our list."

"Exactly."

William slid his empty plate aside. "Another thing that I've been considering lately. The man we met at the King's Garden who told us about Harding meeting people there on a regular basis mentioned he marked information down in a book."

Amy's face lit up as she straightened in her chair. "Yes. You are right. We have to get our hands on that book." Amy scowled. "Unless the police already have it."

William shook his head. "No. They were thrilled to get the files. I don't have a lot of faith in our police, so it's quite possible they would not consider a general ledger for recording names and payments to be important."

"My lord, I believe I will turn you into a private detective yet."

He bowed toward her. "Clearly."

Once William paid their bill, they strolled back to where they had left the carriage. "Will you be at the book club meeting this Thursday?" Amy asked.

"Yes. I am mostly caught up on my work. Without my file from the police, however, there are some facts I am missing. I visited the bank, and their numbers do not correlate with mine, but I'm sure Harding's file of my affairs from his end will give me an idea where the discrepancy lies."

"I am going to attempt to have a private conversation with Miss Gertrude Thursday. She and her sister generally arrive early and spend some time browsing the bookshelves in the store before the meeting."

William helped her into the carriage, and they both settled in. The beautiful sunny day had turned cloudy and cool. Amy shivered, and William handed her the blanket from under his seat.

"Are you up for another visit to Harding's house to look for the ledger?" William asked.

"Yes." Her answer was out before he finished his sentence. She was always up for a chance to do some snooping and investigating. "Just tell me when."

"I will come up with a plan, and we'll go over it when we meet Thursday at the club. Shall I stop by to pick you up?"

Considering her papa's enthusiasm for William and his visits, it would probably be better to travel there herself. "No, I will take my own carriage. But thank you."

"Why?"

Amy fidgeted on the seat. "No particular reason."

He grinned. "Are you sure?"

Amy raised her chin. "Of course I'm sure. I traveled by myself to the book club meetings for two years before you began calling for me."

William burst out laughing.

She narrowed her eyes at him. "What, pray tell, is so funny about that?"

He leaned back in his seat and rested his foot on his bent knee. "What is funny, my lady, is you trying to convince me, or perhaps yourself, that your father—with his eager greeting every time I arrive at your house—has nothing to do with your decision."

She huffed and looked out the window. They had just arrived at her house. Once the driver opened the door, William stepped out, turned, and took her hand. She stepped out, and they made their way to the front door. "Good night, Amy. If you change your mind about having me call for you Thursday, just send around a note."

She nodded. "And don't forget to make your plan for our next trip to recover the ledger."

Stevens opened the door, and Amy stepped inside. Once the door was closed, he said, "This came for you this evening." He handed her an envelope from her publisher. With a certain amount of dread, she opened the missive and scanned the page, groaning as she read.

My dear Lady Amy,

This letter is to advise you that, in accordance with your contract with Chatto & Windus, Publishers, we require you to appear at the book festival to be held at Atkinson & Tucker Booksellers. The date shall follow.

Yours truly,

Mr. Edmond Gordon, Editor

★ ★ ★

On Thursday evening, William arrived at the Atkinson & Tucker bookstore with his mother once more in tow. Hopefully she would not spend all her time chatting away with Amy, trying to push her toward the altar.

He had to admit that he'd gone from *marriage is not for me* to *maybe it wouldn't be so terrible with the right woman* to *Lady Amy is most likely the right woman to give up my bachelorhood for.*

Although he'd eschewed marriage for a long time, he'd always known in the back of his mind that, being the only son, he had an obligation to produce the next Viscount Wethington. If he should die without issue, the title would pass to an obscure relative currently residing in the American states with some Indian tribe.

But when he decided to make that huge change in his life, it would be his decision to make, and his proposal to make, and her acceptance to give. Trying to keep his mother and her father out of it had become trying.

He was pleased to see Amy and Miss Gertrude conversing in the bookstore while they pretended to browse the shelves. He hurried his mother into the meeting room, not wanting her to see Amy and break up their conversation.

Several people had already arrived and were gathered in a circle. When he reached the gathering, Mr. Davidson introduced a friend, Mr. Christopher Rawlings, who was new to the club. With the O'Neill sisters, William's mother, and now Davidson's friend added to their numbers, the group was growing into quite a sizable crowd.

Eventually the two Misses O'Neill and Amy arrived from the bookstore. Mr. Colbert seemed to have to drag himself away from fawning all over Mother, who was blushing like a debutante. William shook his head in disgust.

The man eventually called the meeting to order. Once he had everyone's attention, he began the discussion of their current read.

With all that William had been dealing with in trying to get his finances in order, he hadn't spent much time reading his copy of "A Case of Identity," another Sherlock Holmes story.

"Do you think it was wise of Holmes not to tell his client what he had discovered about her missing lover?" Mr. Colbert tossed out the first question.

Amy quickly related the plot of the book to William as the group began to share their opinions.

William spent his time studying the members of the club. Had any of them also been clients of Harding? How had Harding learned whatever it was he knew about Miss Gertrude that had made her willing to pay him to keep it quiet?

He needed to speak with Amy about the conversation she'd been having with the woman when he first arrived. Miss Gertrude did not look upset, leaving him to wonder if Amy had addressed the question of her being blackmailed at all. Assuredly there must be something lurid in the woman's background for Harding to have been able to get money from her on a regular basis.

Once the story had been torn apart by the club members and put back together again, Mr. Colbert made one final announcement.

"Friends, it gives me a great deal of pleasure to announce that the date for the book fair here at Atkinson and Tucker will be Wednesday, the twenty-fifth of March, so please make your plans. Also, I have heard from Mr. Dobish, the manager of the store, that it has been confirmed that Mr. E. D. Burton will make an appearance at the book fair." He glowed with happiness as he made this declaration.

William looked over at Amy, who looked back at him and shook her head furiously.

Right after that, the meeting broke up, and the members began to filter out of the room. "Since we have separate carriages, we won't be able to exchange information." Amy looked annoyed as she mumbled to him on their way out of the bookstore.

" 'Twas your idea," William said. "Although in all fairness, since my mother has decided to continue attending the book club meetings, we would not have been able to converse anyway."

Amy and William stood apart from a small group, including his mother, who waited in front of the store for their carriages to be brought around, chatting away with Mr. Colbert.

William glared in their direction as he spoke to Amy. "I have come up with a plan to visit Harding's home again. All I can tell you is be ready tomorrow night around midnight."

"Midnight!"

"Shh." William glanced over her shoulder, but her comment hadn't garnered any interest. "Yes. It is not too far, but a large house, so it may take all night, but that's our best chance of searching without running into the police again."

"Very well. I probably won't have trouble getting out. I can go down the back staircase and leave through the servants' door. Papa has usually retired to his room by that time. But depending on how long it takes, it might be tricky for me to get back in when we return."

"We'll work something out. Just be ready."

CHAPTER 16

Just as Amy stepped out of her room to head to the back staircase and meet William, Persephone began to bark. Amy sucked in a deep breath, closed the door, and turned back to the dog. Going down on one knee, she ran her hand over the animal's soft fur. "Quiet, Persephone. You will wake everyone."

Persephone licked her hand and settled into a slumber position, a slight sigh coming from her tiny mouth. Amy stood and walked to the door. The minute she opened it, Persephone rose up on all fours and began to bark again. Amy rushed back to her dog. "Persephone, stop. I have to leave, and you must stay quiet." She petted the Pomeranian some more until the dog's eyes closed and then was comforted by the sound of soft snoring.

Already late for meeting William, she hurried to the door. *Bark, bark.*

Amy leaned her forehead against the door. She turned to see the bloody dog running in circles, barking her fool head off. With no other choice, Amy scooped Persephone into her arms and left the room. Clamping the animal's mouth shut with her hand, she raced down the back stairs and out the door.

William stood right outside, and she ran into him, knocking him off his feet. They both tumbled to the ground, Amy flat on top of William. As they untangled themselves, Persephone licked William's face.

"What the devil were you thinking to bring that dog with you?"

Amy rolled off William, her skirts a tangled mess. He stood to offer his hand to help her up and then brushed off his pants. "Are you crazy?"

"She wouldn't stop barking every time I moved toward the door. She would have awakened the entire household if she kept it up. Then it would have been investigated, and you can imagine the rest." Amy swept her hand over the back of her dress and, carrying a happy Persephone in her arms, followed William down the path to the gate that led to the street, where his carriage stood.

His driver jumped from his seat and opened the door.

"Have you thought about what would happen if she continues to bark when we leave her in the carriage?" William helped her into the vehicle and climbed in after her.

"We will simply have to deal with that issue if or when it arises. We might have to bring her with us into the house if she does start up again. I don't understand what is going on with her. She has been acting very strange lately."

William smirked. "How can you tell?" Then he shook his head and glared at the dog, who glared right back. Amy rolled her eyes at the two of them.

"Since we found the hidden files at the house, I'm assuming Harding would have hidden the book he was keeping there also rather than at his office or flat," William said once they were well under way. "Also, it's quite possible his things have been cleared out of his flat, since I know the manager would not leave a place empty for long."

"I wonder if Mr. Harding had relatives who would claim his things."

"If he does, they aren't local, or they would have shown up to claim the body. From what I heard through my contacts, Harding's body was left unclaimed, and the authorities were forced to arrange his burial."

"How very sad," Amy said. The man might have been a scoundrel, but he still deserved family or friends to see him off to his final resting place. "Sometimes it pays to attend the funeral of a murder victim. The theory is the killer will show up."

"Yes. I have heard that. Is that what you do in your books?" She shrugged. "Sometimes."

"I have been in touch with a few people in an effort to locate Mrs. Whitney's stepson, Patrick. He is not known in the clubs I belong to in Bath, so we might need to get more information from her about his employment and activities. Where was it you spoke with her again?"

"It was at Lady Ambrose's house." She shuddered. "I dislike that woman, with all the snide remarks she made to me last year when the police were focused on me for Mr. St. Vincent's death. I sometimes think she was actually sorry when it was proven I was not the killer."

"Women can be more destructive with their tongues than men with weapons," William said.

"I heartily agree. I don't think it will be too difficult to obtain Mrs. Whitney's direction. Since she is friends with Aunt Margaret, I'm sure my aunt knows it. I can send around a note to set a time when we can visit with her. She seemed quite distraught when I saw her at tea. I think she would like to know that someone is interested enough to unravel the puzzle. And that all is well with her stepson."

"Then we shall put a visit with her on our list of things to do. I'd like to find out more about her relationship with her stepson."

Amy's brows rose. "I wasn't aware of a list of things to do."

"You might consider yourself a great detective, but my expertise lies more in organization." William offered a smug smile. "I've already made up a list of what we need to do and when it should be done."

Amy smiled. "Well done, my lord."

After a few minutes, William said, "I meant to ask you how your conversation with Miss Gertrude went last night at the book club."

Amy ran her hand over Persephone's fur. "She confirmed that Mr. Harding was blackmailing her. However, she stubbornly refused to say why. She said now that he was dead, the secret had died with him and she had no interest in bringing it up again.

"She seemed so very cheerful about the man's death that it disturbed me a bit. It is almost impossible for me to seriously consider her a suspect, but given the fact that she confirmed he was blackmailing her and her joy at his demise, I believe we should keep her on the list. For now, anyway."

After a moment she added, "Oh, I can't believe I forgot the most important part. She also confirmed there is a book where he recorded her payments. She said it was about the size of a journal and he had it with him every time she visited him. If it helps, she said it had a black cover. And she said the meetings took place in the pub we went to, where the man told us Mr. Harding met with people on a regular basis."

"Well, that's good to know. At least we are not on a fool's errand, looking for a nonexistent ledger." William shifted in his seat. "Keep in mind that if Miss Gertrude knows about the book, so does everyone he was blackmailing. Let's hope no one else knows Harding's direction and has been there before us."

"Or the police," Amy added.

"Except we know he recorded his payments in a book, while the police might believe they have everything they need by taking his files. I'm sure the files might say why they were being blackmailed, but it will take some time for them to go through the paperwork and accumulated information on each person."

They remained mostly silent for the rest of the trip until they arrived at Harding's house on the road to Bath. Again William's driver pulled around the house to the back, where the carriage could not be seen from the street.

After a quick reminder to the driver to watch for anyone else arriving, they climbed out, and Persephone opened her eyes, enjoyed a huge stretch, and when she saw them climbing out of the carriage, began to bark.

And bark.

And bark.

William ran his hand down his face. "Is there any way to shut that animal up?"

"If there were a way to shut Persephone up, she would right now be sleeping soundly in my bedchamber," Amy growled at him, when she should have been growling at the animal. "We will have to bring her with us."

"I don't think that is a good idea, but since there seems no alternative, go fetch her."

Amy returned to the carriage and scooped Persephone into her arms. "You are being a very bad dog tonight, Persephone. Whatever is wrong with you?"

The dog ignored Amy's words and licked her hand.

They made their way to the back door of the house. It appeared the police must have arranged to have the house locked after their previous visit. However, with one swift punch, William broke the corner of the glass, reached in, and unlatched the door, and they were inside.

They stopped for a minute and listened to make sure they were the only ones in the house. At William's nod, Amy followed him up the stairs and down the corridor to the library.

Once inside, she put Persephone on a small sofa and joined William at the desk. "Since we already went through the desk the last time we were here, I suggest we search the bookshelves. That would be the best place for a ledger or other record-keeping book to be kept."

He nodded at the desk. "Take that lamp, and I will get the one from that table over there." He waved at a small table next to where Persephone snored. "We will go slowly and thoroughly through the books. Based on what Miss Gertrude told you, we can skip any book that isn't black. If it's anywhere in this house, this seems to be the best place."

Amy nodded and lit the lamp and then moved to the bookcase on the south wall. Persephone raised her head and watched. When Amy didn't attempt to leave the room, she settled back down and closed her eyes.

Amy had no idea what was going on with Persephone. She had never been this clingy before. Hopefully her beloved pet wasn't getting sick.

They began the tedious job of pulling out a book, flipping through it, and returning it to the shelf. The area she had chosen to search for the ledger contained shelves of biology books. She found herself stopping to look at pictures, thinking there might be something in these books she could use in her novels.

A good hour and a half passed before William pulled out what seemed like the five hundredth book and flipped it open. "Yes!"

Amy dropped the book she was holding and hurried over to him. "Did you find it?"

He walked to the desk, laid the book down next to the lamp, and flipped back to the beginning. He ran his finger down the list of entries and looked up at Amy. "It's in code."

"What?" She pulled the book toward her, looked at the writing and groaned. She chewed on her lip and studied the crazy entries. There were regular letters and some numbers, just jumbled up. Looking up at him, she grinned. "We'll have to crack the code. I could use it in one of my books."

William tugged the book back and slammed it shut. Persephone let out a bark combined with a screech. She jumped from the sofa and raced out the library door.

Amy and William stared at each other. They turned and sprinted from the room. "Persephone," she called.

★ ★ ★

"I can't believe this," William mumbled as they dashed up the stairs after the dratted animal. "I swear that dog spends its time thinking of ways to bring chaos into my life."

They reached the top of the stairs and looked right and left. The doors to the rooms on the floor had been left open, and moonlight through the windows gave them enough light to know that Persephone was nowhere in their range of vision. "This is a nightmare. Do you see how large this house is? How many rooms are here? It might take us hours to find her."

Amy leaned on the banister and panted, sweat breaking out on her forehead as she tried to gain her breath. "It won't take long."

"We need light. We'll have to go back down to the library and take those two oil lamps with us to do a proper search."

"Wait," Amy said. "Persephone, where are you?" She called softly, in a singsong voice, apparently trying to keep the beast quiet.

She held her hand up to keep William from speaking and got down on her knees. "Persephoneeeeeeee."

Silence.

"I'm going for the lamp." Just as William spoke, the blasted dog came strolling past one of the doorways, her missing tail in the air. She walked up to Amy, climbed right into her arms, and nudged her hand until Amy began to run her palm over the dog's fur.

Amy climbed to her feet. "See. It wasn't so hard."

William growled and headed toward the stairs. They made their way back down, William holding Amy's hand to keep them from stumbling in the dark. As they entered the library, their attention was caught by someone in the room. The stranger looked up at them, grabbed the ledger off the desk, and raced to the window. Within seconds the culprit had climbed out the window and disappeared.

William and Amy both ran toward the window, but no one was visible by the time they looked out into the darkness.

William clambered out and ran in the only direction the escapee could have gone. In the pale moonlight, William saw the shadow of someone as he rounded the corner of the house.

The offender turned to look back at William and stumbled, dropping the ledger. Leaving the book there, the thief raced away, disappearing into the woods behind the house. Aside from William's heavy breathing, the only sound in the night was the echo of small branches cracking as feet pounded across the ground.

As it was too dark to attempt to follow whoever had absconded, William stopped in front of the ledger and bent over, resting his hands on his knees as he tried to catch his breath. After a minute or so, he picked up the book the mysterious person had dropped and turned to join Amy.

By the time he reached the house, she was outside, clutching the infernal animal in her arms, moving her head back and forth, peering in the dark, trying to see him. "Did you catch whoever that was?"

"No. But the thief stumbled and dropped the ledger." William waved the book in the air. He moved toward her, grabbed her arm, and tugged her forward. "Let's get out of here."

Just as they made it to the carriage, a shot rang out. Then a second one. William pushed Amy into the carriage and climbed in after her. "Move!" he shouted at the driver.

William slammed the door as the carriage took off to the sounds of another shot being fired.

"Someone is shooting at us!" Amy yelled.

William shoved her to the ground and jumped on top of her. "Stay low until we're back on the road."

The carriage swayed as the driver urged the horses faster. William closed his eyes and took a deep breath. He looked down at Amy before moving onto the seat, pulling her up next to him. "Are you all right?"

She dusted off her coat and had the nerve to glare at him. "I told you we should bring a gun."

CHAPTER 17

"No guns. We would only have ended up in a gun battle, and someone would have been hurt. Or killed." William moved his hand to his upper arm and winced. "I believe I've been shot."

"Shot!" Amy shifted on the seat and fumbled to light the oil lamp anchored to the wall of the carriage next to the window. "Let me see."

He shrugged out of his greatcoat and jacket and turned his arm toward her. She leaned in very close, then looked up at him with wide eyes. "You've been shot!"

After she composed herself, she said, "Take off your shirt so I can see how bad it is."

William complied by removing his cravat and his waistcoat. "You need to help me pull the shirt off."

Amy tugged the shirt out of his trousers and gingerly removed it over his head. She got up, holding onto the sides of the carriage, and moved to his other side.

Kneeling close to him, she said, "It looks like the bullet grazed you. But there is a lot of blood. Do you have a handkerchief?"

"Yes. In my right-hand trouser pocket."

Amy reached in and withdrew the handkerchief. She pressed it against the injury.

"Ouch." He sucked in a deep breath.

"My apologies, but we need to stop the bleeding."

"What the bloody hell—excuse my language—am I going to do about this? I can't show up at my house with a bullet wound. Mother would pass out and then demand to know how I got shot."

Amy shook her head. "We can't go to my house either, since it's close to dawn, and no one even knows I'm gone. If Papa wakes up, well . . ."

They remained silent for a few minutes, and then Amy said, "I know. We shall go to Eloise's house. I can throw stones at her bedchamber window to wake her. She can let us in and get you fixed up. We did that for years when we were younger."

"Why am I not surprised? I think your father made a miscalculation in allowing Lady Margaret to raise you."

"I beg your pardon? Aunt Margaret is a wonderful aunt and companion."

"Yes. She certainly is, but I don't think she was as diligent as she should have been at keeping you in hand." William leaned his head against the squab and closed his eyes. The pain was not unbearable, but damn, the thing hurt.

"You had better tell your driver where to take us." Amy watched him carefully, no doubt afraid he might pass out on her.

He had no plans of swooning like an overwrought debutante. He reached the opening in the roof of the carriage and slid the door open. "John, do not take us to Lady Amy's house or my house. We will go to Miss Spencer's home. Do you know where that is?"

"Yes, my lord," came the answer.

Amy narrowed her eyes at him. "I will not ask you why your driver knows where Eloise lives." She raised her chin. "It is not my business."

Despite the pain, William grinned at her obvious suspicion. "Do not fear, my dear; you may recall that we have both traveled to her home on the way back from our book club meetings once or twice."

Amy smoothed out her skirt. "I knew that."

"I think I could use the blanket underneath the seat across from us. Can you get it for me?" He had begun to feel chilly and knew it was probably from the shock as well as being bare chested. Soon he would be shivering.

Amy helped him back into his shirt and then wrapped him in the warm blanket and sat close to him, most likely to share her warmth. What a mess! He would have to keep his mother from knowing he'd been shot, and there was still the issue of getting Amy back into her house before her entire household awoke.

Despite all the hysteria surrounding them, the blasted dog had been sound asleep since Amy dumped her on the seat once they threw themselves into the carriage.

He must have dozed off, as it was near four o'clock when they arrived at Miss Spencer's house. "Stay here, and I will wake up Eloise." Amy left the carriage and went around to the back of the house. William closed his eyes and willed the pain in his arm away.

About five minutes later, Amy returned. "Eloise is coming down to the front door. We will bring you up to her bedchamber, where we can take a closer look at your injury and get you patched up."

Amy helped him into his greatcoat, leaving off the jacket, cravat, and waistcoat. The pain in his arm was becoming a steady throb. As he started to climb from the carriage, he said, "I think John should take you home once Miss Spencer has let me in. It is already past four o'clock."

Amy shook her head. "No. It won't take long to clean you up and put some ointment and a bandage on your arm. I will stay."

William couldn't help but think that Amy did not want him in Miss Spencer's bedchamber alone. Had it not been for the pain in his arm, he would have laughed. "Very well. But if it gets too late, I will insist you return home. The last thing we need is your father seeing you waltzing back into your house at dawn."

"Nonsense. Eloise's house is only a short distance from mine."

Naturally, once they made to leave the carriage, the dog woke up, stretched, and began to bark.

"Amy, do something with that dog. She is going to wake up the entire neighborhood, and I have no sensible explanation as to what the devil is going on here that won't result in police summons, outraged fathers, and promises of duels at dawn."

Amy took the annoying animal in her arms. As he left the carriage, William stopped to speak to the driver. "John, this should not take long."

The man tugged on the brim of his hat. "Very good, my lord." It always amazed William how John showed absolutely no concern, criticism, or disapproval regarding the various things William requested him to do. He imagined how entertaining the driver must be to the other members of the staff when they visited over glasses of ale and he shared stories of their employer's shenanigans.

By the time they reached the front door, Eloise was already there, holding an oil lamp up in the air and waiting for them.

She had thrown on some sort of a dress and had the look of someone who had just been roused from a deep sleep. "Whatever happened? Why are you both here in the middle of the night? Together?"

"Just get us upstairs to your bedchamber, and I will explain everything."

The three of them hurried up the stairs and down the corridor to Miss Spencer's bedchamber. If they were caught, it would be a disaster. Here William was, in the middle of the night, in an unmarried woman's bedchamber with another unmarried woman. If caught, he would be forced to remove himself to Australia or the American states for the rest of his life. Maybe there was something to be said for an Indian reservation.

Except Lord Winchester and Eloise's father would beat him to a pulp first, which would most likely render travel impossible. For many years.

"Eloise, we need bandages, some sort of ointment, and a pan of hot water and a cloth." Amy barked out her orders like a drill sergeant.

Miss Spencer smirked. "My goodness. Had I known I was to become a medical clinic in the middle of the night, I would have had all those things at hand."

"Never mind the humor; just please get the things we need." Amy turned to William. "Sit in that chair by the fireplace, and I will help you remove your coat and shirt."

Eloise left the room, mumbling something about a pending calamity and forced marriages.

Amy dropped Persephone onto the floor. The little dog wandered the room, then settled in for a nap near the fireplace. Amy eased his coat, waistcoat, and shirt off. "Does your arm hurt?"

William winced each time he moved. "A bit. I've had worse."

Her eyes grew wide. "You've been shot before?"

"No. I meant I've had worse pain before." He closed his eyes and leaned his head back on the chair.

"Where is the ledger?" Amy asked.

"It's in the carriage. But I must warn you that during the chase through the woods, the ledger was dropped on the ground. Since the woods were quite damp, it's possible some of it has been damaged."

"So now we have a book that is in code and possibly illegible," Amy said, shaking her head.

William shrugged. "We won't know until we can examine it in the light. I'm just glad we retrieved it."

The door to the bedchamber opened, and Eloise stepped through. "I had to wake my maid, Jenny. I couldn't figure out where to get all the stuff I needed."

A young girl walked in behind Eloise, carrying some supplies, wearing a dressing gown, and also looking as if she had just climbed from bed. Wonderful. Now he found himself in a bedchamber, with the door closed, with *three* young, attractive, unmarried women surrounding him.

With his coat, waistcoat, and shirt off.

In the middle of the night.

His reputation would never recover. On the other hand, in certain circles he would be revered and receive many slaps on the back.

Luckily, all three women were quick and competent, and it seemed that within minutes he was cleaned up, bandaged, fully dressed, and on his way out the door. Since the bullet had only grazed his arm and taken out just a small chunk of flesh, there had been no need for stiches.

William, Amy, and the dog returned to the carriage after Amy gave Miss Spencer and the maid a hearty hug, and he offered a huge thanks.

Miss Spencer's final words to Amy were, "I want the entire story."

They had traveled only about the length of a full street when they arrived at Amy's house. Once William got her and the blasted dog inside, he would return home, order his valet to burn the shirt, jacket, and coat, and then pour himself a very large brandy.

Perhaps two.

★ ★ ★

Amy tiptoed up the back stairs, avoiding the boards that she knew from years of sneaking out of the house made noise. Perhaps William did have a point about Aunt Margaret's supervision.

She kept Persephone's mouth clamped shut with her hand wrapped around the dog's nose. They were too close to safety to have the dog start barking again. Holding her breath, she stepped onto the second-floor landing. Everything was quiet.

She moved quickly past Michael's room, Papa's room, and Aunt Margaret's. She breathed a sigh of relief and opened her door.

Aunt Margaret sat in a chair by the now-dying fire, sound asleep with a book in her lap. Keeping her eye on her aunt, Amy quickly divested herself of her clothing, pushed it all under her bed, and slipped on a nightgown. Easing the counterpane up, she climbed into the bed with a sigh of relief.

"Where were you?"

Amy almost jumped from the bed at the sound of Aunt Margaret's voice. She placed her hand over her heart. "Good heavens, Aunt, you scared me to death."

Aunt Margaret stood and walked toward her. "Is there something I should be concerned about? Do I need to begin wedding preparations?"

"Goodness, no! Why in heaven's name is everyone suddenly talking about weddings? It's making me itchy."

Her aunt sat on the bed. "Perhaps because you were out of the house all night, and I have a strong suspicion that you were not alone."

"Maybe."

"Is this the murder investigation again?"

Amy nodded. "Yes. William and I returned to Mr. Harding's house to look for a ledger or some sort of book. We learned that Mr. Harding carried such a thing with him in which he wrote information—probably payments—when he accepted money from his victims."

"Did you find it?"

"Yes. We did find it, but unfortunately we were not the only people there looking for the book."

Aunt Margaret groaned.

Amy shifted so that her head rested against the headboard. "There was another person in the library when William and I returned after finding Persephone, who had run off."

"Were you seen?"

"Yes. The thief grabbed the ledger and then climbed out the window. William gave chase, but the burglar stumbled and dropped the book."

"Did William manage to get the book back?"

"Yes." There was no point in further distressing her aunt by telling her that William had been shot and that they had no intention of stopping their investigation. William was on the police detectives' list of suspects, and it was up to him and Amy to clear his name.

Aunt Margaret sat and, taking several deep breaths, appeared to calm herself. "Now I will tell you why I spent the night in that chair." She pointed across the room. "When I got home last evening from the Mallorys' musicale, you father was in the library. He waved a letter at me and was quite upset by its contents."

Amy did not have a good feeling about this.

"Since he thought you were already abed"—her aunt stopped and glared at her—"he said it could wait until this morning. I thought perhaps I would give you a warning about what the letter said."

"Did he tell you what it was?"

"Yes." She sighed and took Amy's hand. "Mr. Gordon from your publisher, Chatto and Windus, wrote to your father and told him if you did not appear at the book fair as E. D. Burton, you would be in violation of your contract and they could sue you."

Amy groaned and dropped her head in her hands. Good grief. Could this night get any worse? Then she said a quick prayer, not wanting to urge the good Lord into showing her how that could happen.

CHAPTER 18

William winced as he reached for the door handle of the building where Nick Smith had his offices. It had been three days since he'd been shot and the pain had lessened, but when he forgot about it and used his arm in a certain way, he was all too quickly reminded.

Thankfully, the wound had not become infected, and he'd managed to suffer through the Assembly on Saturday and church on Sunday, not wanting Mother to know he was not up to snuff. At least he'd had the pleasure of dancing with Amy, and they had managed to sneak in a few conversations about their investigation. He had also surreptitiously handed off the ledger to her when they left the Assembly.

Amy had sent a note around earlier this morning and told him she was working hard on trying to decipher the code Harding had used in his ledger. She'd confirmed what he'd thought when the unknown thief dropped the book: the name at the head of one section was smeared.

Soon they would have a list of Harding's victims. In the meantime, William hoped Nick could help him locate Patrick Whitney.

His thoughts turned to the night they had gone to Harding's house. Neither William nor Amy had gotten a good look at the individual they had chased and who had mostly likely shot at them. It was dark and the culprit had moved fast, never turning his head toward them.

From what William remembered, he'd seen a person a bit above medium height, of medium build, and wearing a hat so that no hair color was visible. One of the thousands of citizens of Bath. Or one of the unfortunate people being blackmailed and anxious to get the book before anyone else saw it.

Now William climbed the stairs to the second level, where Nick's office was. The man was expecting him, and William hoped he could lead him to Whitney, since he'd helped him before in locating DuBois, who had turned out to be safely behind bars when Harding was killed. Smith was a remarkable source, and William was grateful the man was willing to help him.

William was immediately ushered into Nick's office by his secretary, a young man who looked as polished as one would expect in this office.

"Good morning, my lord." Nick stuck out his hand, and they shook.

"Good morning to you as well." William settled into one of the two comfortable blue-and-white-pinstriped chairs in front of Smith's desk. "I would prefer it if you called me William. Sometimes my title seems a bit stuffy. Especially in the circumstances in which I find myself, assisting in a murder investigation when I am on the suspect list."

Nick grinned. "Yes. I imagine that can disrupt a man's days." He leaned back in his chair and rested his hands on the desk. "What can I do for you?" His fingers were slim, nails clean and buffed. He wore two rings, one on each hand. Everything about Nick Smith exhibited grace and polish. It was hard to reconcile this man with his early background.

"I am trying to locate a Mr. Patrick Whitney."

Smith's expression did not change. If he knew the man, he was very good at keeping his cards close to his chest. Nothing in his expression or movements revealed his thinking.

"He is one of the people on the list Lady Amy and I have gathered as suspects in the murder of my man of business that I spoke with you about before. It seems he had some ill feelings toward Harding and disappeared around the time his body was found in the River Avon."

"And you have reason to believe Whitney is implicated in this?"

"Whitney's stepmother had a trust left to her by her late husband. Harding was the trustee, and Whitney believed Harding was stealing money from the trust."

Nick blew out a low whistle. "Not well done."

"Not at all."

Nick tapped his desk with his fingertip. "I don't know Whitney personally, but if he has gone into hiding anywhere in Bath, I can roust him out. I will send a message to you when I find him."

William stood, not wanting to take up any more of the man's time. "Thank you. I appreciate it."

Nick stood also and walked him to the door. He stuck out his hand. "If I can do anything else, just let me know."

With that behind him, William needed to see Amy and discuss whether the two of them could figure out the code in the ledger. What baffled him was why Harding had kept the names in code. Perhaps he was afraid someone would come across the book and attempt to take over his thriving black-mail business?

Whatever the reason, they needed to get more names to investigate. Mrs. Whitney didn't seem a plausible murderer.

Since her money was tied up in a trust, there would have been no gain for her in getting rid of Harding; the trust would just pass into another trustee's hands. Of course, hopefully that trustee wouldn't steal from her.

Miss Gertrude, based on her demeanor and what he had known of her for years, didn't seem likely to have gotten Harding drunk and tossed him into the river, but she obviously had something dark in her background if she had been paying blackmail money, so she would remain near the top of the list.

Although William did not consider himself an expert in solving murder mysteries, he had read quite a few stories, and Patrick Whitney had possessed motive—revenge for his stepmother—to kill Harding. Granted, not a very strong motive, since doing away with Harding wouldn't give her the money directly anyway. But his anger at Harding and then his own disappearance around the time Harding had been found moved Patrick Whitney's name a few positions up the list.

On the other hand, everything inside William screamed to forget the whole thing. Either he or Amy, or both of them, could have been killed the other night. Whoever had shot at them was serious.

Someone now knew what they were up to, unless the culprit hadn't recognized them and had come only for the book and then shot at them in an effort to stop them from running off with the ledger. It was plausible that the shooter was one of Harding's victims.

His head had begun to pound with all these thoughts, ideas, and theories running through his mind. He'd also found that his energy had dropped since he'd been shot. Even though he'd suffered only a flesh wound, his body had still suffered a shock, and he had lost some blood.

He decided that luncheon at his club and some socializing would be a good balm. Later he would visit with Amy and see how she was proceeding with unraveling the code.

William handed off his coat and hat to the footman and entered the main room of the club. The place was about half-full. He had started toward the dining room when Mr. Colbert from the book club waved him over. Colbert was seated with Mr. Davidson and the friend Davidson had recently introduced to the club members, Mr. Christopher Rawlings.

William had always liked Colbert and enjoyed the way he kept control of the book club meetings. However, since the man had begun to show interest in William's mother, he now viewed him differently.

One did not like the idea of a man eyeing one's mother with such eagerness. It was not done. When William had broached the subject with his mother, she had merely laughed and walked away.

That had concerned him.

"We were about to retire to the dining room for luncheon. Would you care to join us?" Colbert offered a genuine smile, which made William mad, because he truly wanted to dislike the man.

Well, he wanted socializing, so there was no reason to turn down the invitation to join the men. "Yes. That sounds like a wonderful idea."

The four of them made their way into the dining room, where they were seated at a table close to a window overlooking Queen's Square. It was a pleasant day. Unfortunately, there was no sun, but the air was cool and crisp, so there were strollers out and about.

Once they ordered their food, Colbert looked away from the server and regarded William. "Have you heard any more about your man's death?"

William groaned to himself. He had hoped to forget about Harding for the afternoon.

★ ★ ★

Frustrated, Amy balled up the paper she was working on and tossed it toward the fireplace to join several others already there. She was a murder mystery author. Why couldn't she figure out this code Mr. Harding had used?

A slight tap on her door drew her attention, for which she was grateful. She needed to clear her mind, and hopefully this would do it. "Yes?"

Lacey entered. "My lady, Lord Wethington requests your presence. He is in the drawing room."

"Wonderful!" Amy jumped up and grabbed the ledger and headed downstairs. Right before she reached the staircase, she came to an abrupt halt and turned toward Lacey, the poor girl almost crashing into her. "Is my papa at home?"

"No. He left earlier this morning with your brother for a meeting."

Amy sighed with relief. At least she needn't deal with Papa eyeing William as if he were to be served up at the next meal. She'd also been avoiding Papa because of the E. D. Burton predicament. He had been livid at the letter sent from her publisher.

After haranguing her about the problem of her possible exposure as the murder mystery author, he did a complete turnabout and very calmly told her she should put it from her mind and he would deal with it. She hadn't heard any more about it since then.

Downstairs, William was standing in front of the window that faced the street, his hands behind his back. "Good afternoon," she said as she joined him.

He turned and offered her a smile. Something in his eyes warmed her insides.

"I came to see how you are doing with the ledger coding."

"Join me." Amy walked over to a small sofa on the north wall and sat. William settled alongside her.

"No luck so far. It looks to me like it should be quite simple, but it eludes me. I've been working on this one entry: 'Rg42UY 74OHEEB9.' That name appears quite a bit. One thing I did learn from the ledger, however, is that if these are the names of those he was blackmailing, he had three victims. The only one we know for sure is Miss Gertrude."

"Does having her name help at all in figuring out the code?"

"One would surmise, but that's not the case."

He studied her. "The names on the files the police took from us at Harding's house were probably clients he was stealing from. And that fits, because along with my file, we pulled Lemmon, Montrose, and Mrs. Whitney from those folders, who we know were clients. I can't imagine he would need a file on someone he was blackmailing. Thus the use of the ledger."

William took the paper she'd been working on from her hand and scrutinized it. "We know about Miss Gertrude, that it appeared from her file that she started out as a client of Harding's and then he began to blackmail her. Therefore, with three names in the ledger, that means there are two others who would had a good reason to kill Harding."

"And until you can find him and speak with him, Patrick Whitney is also on our list."

William took the ledger from her and flipped through the pages. He let out a low whistle. "This has been going on for some time."

Amy nodded. "So it seems." She leaned over his shoulder and looked at the book. "It appears, the way the book is set up, that each person has their own section where Mr. Harding recorded their payments." She pointed at the ledger. "If you study the entire book, there are a few names in sections where no payments were recorded for some time. I'm thinking they either died or found a way to get out from under Mr. Harding's clutches."

William flipped through the book and ran his finger over some of the headings, which appeared on each page as a strange combination of letters and numbers. He shook his head. "Between the two of us, we should be able to figure this out."

"I've tried." Amy hopped up and walked to the desk in the middle of the room. She opened the center drawer and withdrew several sheets of paper and two pencils, then handed a pencil and a piece of paper to William. "Let's try again."

They sat for about fifteen minutes, playing with various letter combinations. Soon her eyes grew wide, and she looked back and forth from the garbled name to what she'd written. She sucked in a deep breath and looked up at him, her eyes sparkling. "I think I have it."

William looked up from his paper. "Pray tell."

She opened her mouth to speak just as Stevens entered the room. "My lady, there are two detectives here to see you."

"What?" She quickly shoved the journal under the settee cushion and turned to William. "Why would they come to my house?"

He shrugged just as Detectives Carson and Marsh entered the room. Carson looked directly at William. "Ah yes, my guess was correct. When your man at the door at your residence said you were not at home, we assumed we would find you here, my lord."

William's jaw tightened. "What is it you want this time, Detectives?"

"My goodness, aren't we on the querulous side today." Carson waved to the sofa. "Why don't we all sit."

The four settled into their seats. Amy placed her hands in her lap, her back stiff as if waiting for a blow. She did not like the look on the detectives' faces. She glanced over at William, who appeared more annoyed than concerned.

Carson looked at William. "My lord, we have reason to believe you are solely responsible for the purposeful drowning of Mr. James Harding."

CHAPTER 19

William was more shocked by the detective's words than he'd been when he found himself shot in the arm the other night. However, years of handling difficult business matters and maneuvering through the treacherous maze of polite society had served him well. He took a deep breath and looked the detective in the eye. "Am I being charged with something, Detective?"

"Maybe." Detective Carson remained silent after that one word. The only sound in the room was the ticking of the long clock in the corner. It was as if all the occupants in the room were holding their collective breath.

William had always dealt with business matters by remaining silent. He remained silent. He felt he was doing a good job of hiding the shock he'd just received, which was twisting his stomach and making his heart pound. Although he'd known in the back of his mind that the detectives would love to involve him in the murder for various reasons, he had never thought it would get this close.

Detective Carson placed a folder on the small table in front of them. William immediately recognized it as the file they'd seen in Harding's library before the police arrived and confiscated it.

William, Viscount Wethington (St. John).

The man opened the folder and looked at the top page and then over to William. "You and Harding were involved in some pretty shady deals, my lord."

The shocks continued. "What?" William stood, his hands fisted at his side. "I have never involved myself in anything shady in my life."

Carson continued to stare at him. Then he tapped on the open file. "Not according to this." He flipped the cover of the folder back. "It says right here, 'William, Viscount Wethington (St. John).' Is that you?"

William's eyes flashed. "I will not play games, Detective. You know very well that is me. However, regardless of what it says in that file"—he nodded toward the folder sitting on the table—"I have no idea what you are talking about with regard to shady deals."

The detective picked up a shaft of papers and flipped through them. "Fraud, embezzlement, stock manipulation . . ."

This visit had turned into a nightmare. William had only just begun to suspect that Harding was playing fast and loose with his business matters, but this! The man must have been dealing in dirty business almost from the time he'd employed him.

William reached out. "I want to see those papers, Detective."

For reasons unknown, the man handed him the file. William looked through the documents, his rage growing and his stomach sinking as he read. Harding had forged William's signature on a number of contracts that he knew nothing about.

"I don't care what those papers say, I am completely unaware of any of these dealings. My signature on the documents is a forgery."

"I take it that is your official story?" Carson leaned back in the chair and studied William as if he were a bug under a glass.

"It is no story, Detective. It is the truth. I have never done anything illegal in my life." The sweat began to form on his body, and he hoped it would not reach his face, which would only give the detective reason to believe he was lying.

William turned to Amy sitting next to him, needing to cling to a lifeline. "You believe me, don't you, Amy? You know I would never do anything illegal?"

The panic grew as she hesitated and just looked at him. Surely *she* would know the truth about him.

★ ★ ★

Amy studied William and saw the man she'd known for years, whom she'd grown close to over the past year. He was smart, polite, caring, and the most upstanding man she knew, aside from her own papa and brother. In those few seconds while William waited for her answer, she realized she believed him with her whole heart. She trusted him, and aside from a few illegal break-ins—necessary to their investigations, of course—he would never do anything criminal.

She reached out and took his hand, despite the idiot detectives grinning at each other. "Of course I believe you, William. I trust you and would trust you with my life. I know you well. You would never do those things."

Carson looked at them with disgust. "That's all very nice and cozy, but we still believe these papers are solid evidence that you and Harding were involved in nefarious activities. Together. Then the man turns up floating in the river. Leads me to believe you didn't want to continue to share your gains anymore."

William fisted his hands at his side. "No gains, Detective, because I was not aware of this."

"So you say."

William tried assiduously to control his temper. Lashing out at the detectives would not serve his cause. "I will ask once more, sir, am I being charged with something? If that is the case, then I demand a barrister be present to represent me if the questions continue. If not, I then ask you to leave. Lady Amy has nothing to do with this, and I strenuously object to you coming to her house and involving her."

"My, my. Aren't we protective?" Carson stood, apparently tired of William hovering above him. "I disagree, my lord. Lady Amy was found at your side when you identified Mr. Harding's dead body and when you—illegally I might add—broke into the man's home in search of your file. Like it or not, she is involved, or rather, she has involved herself."

The detective bent over the table and gathered the papers and shoved them into the folder. "There are further questions. Many of them. At this point I suggest you retain a barrister and report to the police station at ten o'clock tomorrow morning."

Marsh flipped his notebook closed and stood. The two men lumbered from the room. Amy wrapped her arms around her middle, sick to her stomach. "What are you going to do, William?"

He ran his fingers through his hair and sat alongside her, his hands dangling between his spread knees. "I am going to do exactly as Detective Carson said. I shall spend the rest of this day retaining a barrister." He shook his head. "I cannot believe this."

"Do you know what else this means?" Amy asked.

"What? Don't tell me things could get worse."

"Probably, but now that the detectives have you at the very top of their list, they're going to do to you what they did with me last year when St. Vincent was killed. They're going to spend all their time and resources attempting to find you guilty rather than looking at other suspects. It is up to us to find the killer first."

William gave a slight laugh. "I'm not sure I can concentrate on finding a killer now that I have this mess on my hands." He slumped back against the sofa. "Do you realize how much time I will need to go over my financial records? And how many fires I will have to put out with the damage Harding has done to my name? I have always enjoyed a stellar reputation, and now it appears there are some people who view me as a scoundrel."

"There is no reason why I can't continue with the investigation while you are busy."

"No!"

Amy jumped back, her hand at her throat. "Goodness, William. You frightened me."

William blew out a breath. "I apologize. But under no circumstances are you to pursue this matter on your own. We've already been shot at. I agree that we must continue to search for the killer. With the detectives telling me to meet them tomorrow and to have a barrister with me, there is no doubt that they are considering me a suspect."

They were both silent for a few moments, staring off into space. Their reverie was interrupted by the sound of the front door opening and Papa coming through the door. From the sounds of their voices, he and Michael were in the middle of a disagreement. Between William's troubles and Papa's irritation with her publisher, it was probably not the best time for Papa to arrive.

"Good afternoon, Amy." Papa's eyes lit up at the sight of William sitting alongside her. "And Lord Wethington, good to see you, lad."

Amy groaned to herself. She really wished Papa would stop referring to William as a lad. He and Michael were the same age, and with all the business Papa and Michael did together, she doubted her papa considered her brother a lad.

William stood and shook Lord Winchester's hand, then turned to Amy's brother. "Good afternoon." He stopped, looked down at Amy, and turned back to Papa. "My lord, may I have a few minutes of your time?"

Papa's face broke into a huge smile, but Amy was sure William was not requesting an audience with her father for the reason the poor man thought. Being a smart man, William was going to turn to Papa for help.

The two men left the drawing room, most likely headed to the library. Michael grinned at her. "Should we be planning a wedding?"

"No." She wasn't quite sure if she should tell Michael what was going on, but she didn't want him harboring the idea that William was drawing up marriage contracts.

"William has a problem, and I believe he wishes Papa's counsel on it, since his own father is deceased."

"That sounds serious."

Amy sighed. "I'm afraid it is." Knowing her brother to be very discreet, she told him the tale of Harding's death, relating that William's business card had been found on him so that he was requested to identify the body. She left out the part where she was there as well.

She skipped over other parts too, especially breaking into Harding's flat and house—twice—and their compilation of a list of suspects. The men in her family were so squeamish about her doing anything except attending balls, gossiping at afternoon teas, and selecting gowns for social events. If Michael knew of their escapades, especially the part where they had been shot at, she would find herself hustled back to London and confined to her bedchamber until she was old and wrinkled.

When she finished the story of the detectives' visit and what they had accused William of, Michael let out a low whistle. "Sounds like your young man is in trouble."

Amy sighed, irritation springing up again at his words. Then she reconsidered and sighed again. "Yes, my young man is in trouble."

★ ★ ★

Once they entered the library, William took the seat across from Lord Winchester and, based on the man's demeanor, immediately realized Amy's father was expecting him to make an offer for his daughter. William had been so rattled by the police visit that the first thing he'd thought of when his lordship walked into the room was that he could use some serious advice. Now he was about to not only disappoint the man but lay out some grim allegations regarding his reputation.

He remembered when Amy had been under suspicion last year and her father had retained a barrister for her. William cleared his throat. "My lord, I find myself in a bit of trouble, and I need the advice of someone with a few more years of experience than I have. Were my father alive, I would seek his counsel, but since he is not . . ."

Lord Winchester frowned. "What is the problem?"

With fits and starts, William laid out the entire situation before Amy's father. He conveniently left out the part about him and Amy investigating the murder. There was no reason to cause her father any further alarm.

When William was finished, Lord Winchester leaned back and rested his elbow on the arm of the chair, cupping his chin with his index finger and thumb. After a few minutes of silence, he said, "I agree, Wethington, you have a serious problem on your hands."

"I blame myself for being neglectful of my duties to my own financial well-being. But I had no reason until very recently to imagine anything was wrong. Harding has worked for me for three years, and never has there been even a hint of misdeeds."

Winchester shrugged. "Perhaps something changed in his life that encouraged him to begin this duplicitous life."

"That could very well be, but my most pressing need now is to hire someone to represent me. I suppose I could contact my solicitor and get a recommendation for a barrister from him, but I remember the man you secured for Lady Amy last year seemed quite competent, and I don't have a great deal of time."

"I agree." Winchester nodded. "I shall send a note around to my man immediately. I suggest you gather your financial records, so you have some proof of what you thought was going on as opposed to what they found in Harding's files."

William breathed a sigh of relief. Lord Winchester was a competent businessman and had reason to hope that one day William would be his son-in-law. Although William did not wish to play to that expectation too much, at least at this time, he could use the man's advice and help.

"I will do that. And I appreciate your help in this matter." William stood, as did Lord Winchester. Just as William reached the door, his lordship added, "If you ever want to discuss anything else, please feel free to request a meeting."

Knowing exactly what Winchester had in mind, William nodded and returned to the drawing room.

He found Amy alone there.

"How did it go?" She eyed him with concern.

"Your father was quite helpful. He made the good suggestion that I gather my own financial records, and he will contact the barrister he hired for you last year. I believe his name was Mr. Nelson-Graves?"

"Yes. I remember him as being quite somber and excellent at thwarting the detectives when they tried to trick me into answers by confusing the questions they asked."

"I will take my leave now. I want to go over all my papers and get ready for the meeting tomorrow."

"I understand." Amy stood and walked him to the door. "Oh, with all the excitement, I forgot to tell you I figured out the code."

"That's right. I remember you saying so just as the detectives arrived." They stopped in front of the door. "Are you going to tell me or make me figure it out myself?" He was sure his grin was a bit forced, but he had a great deal on his mind.

"I will tell you this much. The name we were trying to figure out is *Ethel Burrows*."

"Interesting." William accepted his coat and hat from Stevens and turned to her. "Continue on with the other name, and perhaps tomorrow afternoon we can get together. I still want to pursue this investigation. Especially now that I am front and center with the police. I don't much care for that position."

Stevens opened the door for William, who nodded, then turned back and wrapped his arm around Amy before leaning in to give her a kiss. "For luck."

He hurried down the steps to his carriage, thinking he needed much more than luck. Right now, what he needed was a miracle.

CHAPTER 20

Amy was tired of pacing in her room, waiting for William to arrive. He was with his solicitor and the barrister Papa had arranged for him, and at the present time they were all at the police station.

She walked to the window and pushed aside the drapes to gaze out at the traffic below. So many people out and about, having a perfectly normal day, when William's world was crashing down.

Instead of wasting her time here, she should be out and about herself, trying to find the true killer and save William. She checked her timepiece and decided it was not too early for a social call.

Miss Gertrude and Miss Penelope would be only too happy to visit with her. Since Miss Gertrude had acknowledged to Amy that she had, in fact, been blackmailed by Mr. Harding, perhaps she could give Amy some more information without revealing the reason for the blackmail. Although a tad curious, Amy would not broach that subject unless Miss Gertrude brought it up.

She pinned her hat to her head, fighting with her unruly auburn curls, tugged on gloves, and grabbed her reticule. As she approached the front door, she saw Aunt Margaret standing there, being assisted by Stevens into her coat.

"Are you doing morning calls?" Though they were called morning calls, they usually took place well after noontime.

"Yes." Aunt Margaret raised her brows. "Don't tell me you are interested in making visits?"

"Actually, yes. But only to a particular person." Amy turned and allowed Stevens to help with her coat. "I am off to see Miss Gertrude O'Neill."

"Ah," Aunt Margaret said. "She is on your list of suspects, is she not?"

"Yes. But this visit isn't about tripping her up, since I really don't believe she could do something so hideous, but in gaining information that only someone who has been blackmailed by Mr. Harding would know."

"All right. You have gotten my interest up. If you have no objection, I would like to accompany you."

"That would be lovely. As you know, I am awkward at these things. I always seem to say the wrong thing, or drop my tea in my lap, or trip over a chair leg."

Aunt Margaret grinned. "Yes. That about covers your visits." She looked down at Amy's feet.

Amy sighed. "Yes. My shoes match."

Stevens opened the door, and she and Aunt Margaret descended the steps and climbed into the carriage.

Fluffy clouds floated like giant pillows across the sky, blocking the sun, then retreating, allowing the warmth and light to bathe the earth again.

Once they were settled and on their way, Aunt Margaret asked, "William is with the police this morning, is he not?"

"Yes. I am quite anxious. You know how these detectives seem to work, since we've dealt with them before. They focus on one suspect and then devote all their time to proving that person was the killer instead of casting their net wider."

"You were there when the police arrived. What sort of evidence do they have?"

"Apparently one of the ways Mr. Harding was cheating William was by forging his name on contracts that turned out to be questionable at best and criminal at worst. William, of course, knew nothing about them, but it didn't look good for him. The detectives took the stance that with all the shenanigans going on, Harding and William had formed a partnership and William decided to do away with Harding and claimed the other half of the ill-gotten goods."

"How horrible for William. I know him to be an upstanding man, and to think they believe he would do illegal and perhaps criminal things with his business dealings is disheartening."

"Yes. But more than disheartening to William, since he now has to spend time and effort restoring his good name with all those people and businesses that Harding swindled."

"How does all of this tie in with wanting to visit Miss Gertrude, since you believe she couldn't have shoved Harding into the river?"

"From what William and I have uncovered, Harding met his victims at the same pub on a regular basis to collect the money. I am hoping Miss Gertrude might have seen other victims in her comings and goings."

"This leads me to believe you intend to keep on with this investigation."

"We have to. If we don't, they're going to charge William, and as you said, you know him, and he would never murder anyone. Just promise me you won't tell Papa what I'm doing."

The carriage came to a rolling stop before her aunt could answer. Aunt Margaret stepped out of the carriage and turned to Amy. "This still sounds dangerous to me. We will discuss this on the way back from our calls."

Thinking perhaps it had been a mistake to tell her aunt as much as she had and grateful she hadn't told her everything, especially the part about William being shot, Amy trudged behind her up the steps to the front door.

The ladies seemed pleased to have Amy and Aunt Margaret visit, although they did mention that they hadn't been expecting callers. When Amy and her aunt offered to leave, the sisters declined and insisted they stay for tea.

"We missed you at church Sunday," Amy said, once they all had their tea and it was prepared to everyone's liking. No biscuits or other sweets were offered with the tea, which Amy took as an indication that the sisters were not expecting them to stay long.

Or perhaps hoping they wouldn't.

"Yes, sister and I were feeling a bit under the weather. I think we might have caught a chill."

"I hope you are feeling better." Amy could not help but notice that Miss Gertrude wore some sort of face makeup that was doing a poor job of hiding a few scratches on her face.

"It appears you've been injured, Miss Gertrude." Amy smiled, trying to appear sympathetic. "Nothing serious, I hope."

The woman waved her hand. " 'Twas nothing. There is a cat that comes around occasionally. I told sister we should not be feeding the thing. Especially since the last time we did, it scratched my face."

"Oh dear. Well, do be careful, because those sorts of injuries can cause infections," Aunt Margaret said.

Silence fell, and Amy had the feeling the ladies were uncomfortable and wanted them to leave.

They shared some innocuous conversation about the weather, Bath traffic, the conditions of the road, and the Queen's birthday.

As Amy took her last sip of tea, she decided she would try one more question and then depart. "Will we see you at the book club meeting on Thursday?"

Miss Penelope smiled. "Oh yes. We just love the meetings, don't we, sister?"

"Yes. Everyone in the club is so very friendly too."

Silence.

Amy looked over at Aunt Margaret. "I believe we have other calls to make?"

"Yes." Aunt Margaret gathered her gloves and reticule. The four women walked to the door, and Amy couldn't help but think that the sisters were accompanying them to make sure they left.

It had been a strange visit. Short and awkward.

As they shrugged into their coats, air-kissing commenced, along with good-byes and *See you on Thursday.*

Once they were settled in the carriage, Aunt Margaret said, "Well, they certainly weren't welcoming. I'm afraid this was a waste of your time."

"Not at all." Amy glanced out the window, then back over at Aunt Margaret. "I couldn't help but wonder if the 'chill' they caught and the scratches on Miss Gertrude's face had anything to do with William chasing down the person who attempted to escape with the ledger."

She had obviously startled her aunt. "What? I thought you said—or at least I assumed—that it was a man who absconded with the ledger and who William chased through the woods."

"That's what we thought, but since we didn't see the person's face and whoever it was wore a cap of some sort, now that I think about it, it could have been a woman. William mentioned the person stumbled. If it was Miss Gertrude, she could have been scratched by branches."

Amy considered how William had described the thief. A bit taller than medium height, he'd said, and of medium build. Miss Gertrude was certainly tall enough to be a man, and although she was quite thin, a bulky coat could give her a studier appearance.

Aunt Margaret studied her for a minute. "I would suggest the next thing you work on is finding out if Miss Gertrude is capable of climbing out of windows and running through the woods in the dark."

Amy nodded. "It doesn't seem likely, though, does it?"

★   ★   ★

William had just spent the worst three hours of his life. Detectives Carson and Marsh had fired questions at him from every direction. If William hadn't had Mr. Nelson-Graves, the barrister, there with him, he was almost sure he would be looking at the world from behind bars.

Mr. Alfred Lawrence, William's solicitor, had joined in during the questioning also, requesting a copy of the file that contained the incriminating evidence. The detectives seemed reluctant to share a copy but bowed to the man's request when Mr. Nelson-Graves mentioned getting the court involved.

At the end of it all, William's head pounded, and he felt as though he'd been in the interview room for days instead of hours.

"I believe we are finished for now." Detective Carson turned to William. "Do not leave Bath for any reason."

As William breathed a sigh of relief, Mr. Nelson-Graves and Mr. Lawrence gathered notebooks, pencils, and files in preparation to leave.

"Detective, I wish to put you on notice that my client is not guilty of any crime. It appears from this interview and your evidence that crimes have been committed *against him*." Mr. Nelson-Graves looked every bit the well-respected and powerful barrister he was.

"That's your department, barrister. Our job is to find the person who most likely got Mr. James Harding drunk, then enticed him to walk along the river, and then shoved him in." Carson pointed a finger at William. "Your client had every reason to commit the crime."

"I suggest you turn your attention elsewhere, Detective. I would hate to see the department appear foolish to the public by falsely accusing a man of the nobility and member of the House of Lords of a horrendous crime."

As they turned to leave, Detective Marsh spoke, one of the few times he had, since he'd spent most of his time scribbling in his notebook. "I wish to remind you, my lord, that we await the information you intend to provide showing that you were nowhere near the pub in question a day or two before Mr. Harding was found."

William nodded, anxious to get home and check his appointment book to see what he'd been doing that week. Hopefully there was a notation that would jar his memory and provide an alibi. Right now, as frazzled as he was, he could not remember what he'd been doing the night before, let alone the week in question.

The three men reached the outside of the building. Fresh air had never smelled better. Mr. Nelson-Graves addressed William. "I will need you to meet me in my office either tomorrow or the day after."

"Yes. I will send a note around as to the time and day I will be available for you." William then turned to Mr. Lawrence.

"I hope the police provide the copy of the file to you quickly. I need to begin my campaign to restore my good name with the individuals and businesses that Harding lured into false contracts."

"You have a lot of work ahead of you, my lord. If there is anything I can do to assist in that matter, please let me know." Mr. Lawrence gave a slight bow and walked away, heading for his carriage waiting at the end of the pavement.

"I will see you, then, in a couple of days." Mr. Nelson-Graves also took his leave, heading across the street to where his office was located.

William waved his carriage forward and climbed in. He rested his head on the back of the squab and closed his eyes. He'd never been in such a mess in his life. The murder charge hanging over his head was bad enough, but the predicament Harding had created for him in the business community was almost as daunting.

Feeling like he needed to speak with someone who understood his dilemma, he tapped on the ceiling of the carriage and instructed his driver to take him to Amy's house. Hopefully she would be home and could offer some peace of mind just by being herself.

He spent the ride trying to clear his mind of the session he'd just gone through with the police.

Stevens greeted him and opened the door to allow him entrance. "Yes, my lord, Lady Amy is at home and was expecting you. Her ladyship is in the drawing room."

He made his way down the corridor and stepped into the drawing room, feeling a sense of peace just being there. Amy hopped up from the settee and hurried over to him, wrapping her arms around his middle. Startled, he pulled her closer, and his eyes shuttered as he held her, his chin resting on her head.

They said nothing for a full minute, the sound of his heart pounding in his ears, then slowly returning to normal. Finally Amy pulled back, and he immediately missed her warmth and the scent of lavender that always surrounded her.

"Was it terrible?"

He thought of playing the cavalier and making light of it, but then realized he wanted her to know the truth. He didn't want to hide this from her. Or anything else, for that matter. What that meant, he didn't have the energy to analyze right then. He looked down into her deep-green eyes, full of caring and something else warm and inviting, and said, "Yes." He closed his eyes and tucked her against his body, resting his chin on her head again. "It was terrible."

CHAPTER 21

Three days later, William arrived back at Amy's house in the early afternoon to escort her to the Pump Room. She hadn't seen him since the day he'd been interrogated by the police. He'd told her he would be busy for the next few days, gathering whatever information he could to give to his solicitor and barrister.

He'd sent a note to her saying that he needed a break and a distraction and suggested an outing to the Pump Room and then maybe a walk in Victoria Park. While he was busy with his issues, Amy spent her time making a list of all their suspects. She'd added Mrs. Ethel Burrows from the ledger to her original list of Mrs. Whitney, Patrick Whitney, Miss Gertrude O'Neill, and Mr. David Montrose.

Five suspects. All with a reason to kill Mr. Harding. They'd yet to find Mr. Montrose. William had checked his clubs, and he and Amy had attended the Assembly dances since all of this had started, and so far Mr. Montrose had not yet made an appearance.

Although Mr. Lemmon had admitted to William that he'd had issues with Mr. Harding and they'd found his file among those hidden at Harding's home, they hadn't yet decided to add his name to the list, since he'd seemed to be more interested in getting his barrister to straighten out the mess Harding had caused with his finances.

William had stayed away from the book club meeting the night before, and Amy had to admit the gathering had seemed rather dull without him. A few members had asked after him, and she'd only said he was engaged in business matters.

Apparently no one had heard about the police considering William their top suspect, for which she was grateful. It had been difficult for her the year before when the police had assumed she'd killed her ex-fiancé and everyone had inundated her with questions.

Tomorrow was the Assembly again, and maybe they would be lucky this time. Amy had asked around at morning calls—which she viewed as a sacrifice to William's well-being—and finally someone had heard of Mrs. Burrows. She apparently owned a small millinery in the center of Bath.

Maybe before she and William returned home from their trip to town, they could find the millinery shop, the Hat Box, and speak with Mrs. Burrows.

The door to her bedchamber opened. "His lordship has arrived." Lacey walked into the room. "You've done your hair yourself. Why did you not summon me?"

Amy shrugged. "You were busy with something else. Why? Does it look bad?"

Lacey studied her mistress. "It could be worse. Let me adjust your hat so that it might hide part of it."

"I guess that means yes, it does look bad," Amy mumbled, as Lacey directed her to a chair and began to fool with her hair and hat.

"Don't take too long. I don't want to keep Lord Wethington waiting."

"Oh my." Lacey grinned and continued to fuss with her hair.

Amy stood. "I don't know what you mean by *oh my*, but I think you've done enough with my hair."

She grabbed her reticule and left the room. William waited for her at the front door, chatting with Stevens. He turned and gave her a wide smile that set off some strange sensations in her stomach.

"Good afternoon, my lady. You look wonderful." He gave a slight bow.

Amy turned to face Lacey, who was just descending the stairs, and merely raised her eyebrows. Apparently William didn't think she'd made such a mess of her hair.

Once they were settled in the carriage, Amy withdrew the list she'd compiled that morning. "I have names here that we can investigate."

William raised his hand. "I appreciate your work on this, but for this afternoon, I prefer not to speak of anything having to do with Harding's death, my pending arrest, the suspects, and my friends Detective Marsh and Detective Carson. Let us just enjoy the day out."

Although she was anxious to share her information, she understood his need for a respite. He must have spent a great deal of time worrying and searching for information since the last time she'd seen him.

"Yes. You are correct. The sun is shining, it's a beautiful day for February, and we should discuss nothing but happy, joyful things."

William grinned. "I wouldn't go so far as to say only rainbows and unicorns can be discussed, but let's put off any conversation about the murder until we've at least had our tea."

Silence ensued for the rest of the ride, since nothing else seemed worthy of consideration.

Once the carriage arrived close to the Roman Baths, William helped Amy out, and instead of taking her arm, he entwined their fingers, and they strolled along holding hands.

It felt much different than having their arms joined. Again that strange sensation reared itself in her stomach. Strange, yet pleasant.

First they ventured into the Pump Room and had a glass of the beneficial spa waters. Then they made their way to the dining area, which was about half-full. Amy didn't recognize too many people, so chances were visitors and tourists made up the majority of diners.

"Tea for the lady and me," William said to the server who approached them.

"Very good, my lord. I shall be right back."

"How did he know you were a lord?"

William raised his brows. "Don't I look like a lord?"

Amy sat back and studied him. Tall, aristocratic nose, firm chin, well-built body, clothes of the finest cut and fabric, an adeptly tied cravat, and an arrogance about him that only a member of the nobility could pull off. She nodded. "Yes."

They both laughed.

Amy looked around the room while they waited for their tea. "Isn't that Mr. Davidson over there?" She gestured with her head in the direction of two men sitting at a table near the window.

William studied the pair. "I believe it is. And if I am correct, it looks like that gentleman friend of his is with him again. Strange. He introduced Mr. Rawlings to the group for the first time a few weeks ago, but now it seems every time I see Davidson, they are together."

"Most likely he is a new friend." Amy looked back at William. "I can't imagine anyone being his friend, actually.

He is certainly not an amiable man, and I do dislike remarks he's made during book club discussions about women."

William laughed. "Yes. I know a few times the two of you almost came to fisticuffs."

Conversation ceased as the server placed a teapot, cups, saucers, silverware, and a plate of small sandwiches and sweets on the table. "Shall I pour?" the server asked.

"No, but thank you. I will pour."

The server nodded at Amy and headed back to another part of the dining room to stop and chat with two diners.

"Don't pass up the sweets again," William said as she placed a half sandwich on her plate.

Amy looked down at the tarts, biscuits, and scones. "I really do need to watch what I eat."

"Nonsense. You're perfect just the way you are."

The fluttering sensation again.

He really did say such nice things to her. She shrugged and took a small piece of chocolate cake from the tray.

"I know you don't want to talk about the murder investigation, but I need something to occupy my mind. Using the code, I added another name to our list. It turns out one of the blackmailees—is that a word?—is a woman who owns a millinery shop on Union Street called the Hat Box."

"Very imaginative."

"Yes, well, I thought perhaps we could visit with her this afternoon. That is, if you want to. I know you said you prefer to forget about all of it this afternoon."

William reached across the table and covered her hand with his. "I know you're concerned about me. I appreciate that. Once we've refreshed ourselves with tea, we will visit the millinery shop."

"And then we can take a stroll in Victoria Park."

"If you wish."

The millinery shop turned out to be quite exclusive. Based on the women going in and out, it catered to the upper crust.

They strolled outside the store for about fifteen minutes before there was a break in the streams of women patronizing the establishment.

They entered the store, and Amy was immediately impressed. It was clean, well stocked, and brightly lit, with floor-to-ceiling windows. The woman behind the counter walked up to them. "Good afternoon. How may I help you?"

Amy looked over at William. "I believe I would like to try a few hats."

"Please do." He turned and walked to a grouping of chairs with a small marble-topped table in front of them. It had obviously been set up to provide a space for husbands and fiancés to wait while their women selected chapeaus.

"I would like to try that hat on." Amy pointed to a deep-blue, large-brimmed confection with flowers on the crown and pale-blue netting enveloping the whole thing, with enough left in front to cover the face.

She sat on a stool in front of a line of mirrors. The woman placed the hat on her head, adjusted the set of it, and drew the netting down over Amy's face. "This is lovely on you, my lady." She looked over at William. "Don't you agree, my lord?"

"Yes. It does look quite elegant on you, Lady Amy."

Still confused as to how the woman knew them as lord and lady, Amy turned left and right, admiring herself. "Do you own the shop?"

"Yes. I am the owner. My name is Mrs. Ethel Burrows, and I would be honored to be of service to you."

Amy glanced at William through the mirror. His eyebrows rose.

"Your name sounds familiar to me. I feel as though I know you from somewhere." Amy continued to admire herself in the mirror.

"May I ask your name?"

"Yes. Of course. I am Lady Amy Lovell. And that is Lord Wethington."

The store owner gave a quick dip to them both. "It is a pleasure, I am sure."

"I remember now. I believe we have a mutual friend in Mr. James Harding. Although I understand he—"

Mrs. Burrows snatched the hat off Amy's head, taking a bit of her hair with it. "If you will excuse me, my lord, my lady. I just remembered an appointment, and I must close the shop."

She scurried from around the counter, lifted Amy by her arm, and marched her to the door. Amy dug in her heels. "Wait. Wait a minute. Please."

"I do not wish to discuss that man. If you have anything else to say about him, I ask you to please leave."

William stood and walked over to the two women. "If you will humor me, Mrs. Burrows. I believe my companion here would be delighted to purchase one of your hats. We did not mean to upset you."

Mrs. Burrows straightened her shoulders and raised her chin. "*Upset* does not begin to define it. The man was a scoundrel, a criminal, and a rogue. If he were not already dead, I would be purchasing a gun right now to kill him myself."

Well then.

"Mrs. Burrows, I apologize that we have upset you so." William led her over to the cozy corner, where all three of them sat. "I understand your not wishing to discuss the man, but I find myself a main suspect in Harding's murder, and I am trying my best to uncover the true killer."

"As I said, I did not kill him, but given enough time, I would surely have gone completely against everything I believe in and put a hole in the man's heart. Well, actually, he had no heart, so maybe his brain."

"I assume he was blackmailing you."

Mrs. Burrows eyes grew wide, but she clamped her lips shut and nodded.

"I believe you are one of several," Amy said.

"Then if you are looking for his killer, I'm afraid you will have quite a long list of potential suspects."

"Did you know any of the other people he was blackmailing?" Amy reached over and took the woman's hand. "I have absolutely no interest in why he was blackmailing you, so you may ease your mind on that."

Just then the door to the shop opened. Mrs. Burrows hopped up. "Good afternoon, Mrs. Paisley." She waved at William and Amy. "They were just about to leave." She glared at them, leaving them no choice but to gather their things and exit the store.

"Well, that went very well." Amy stared back at the storefront. "I would have liked to buy one of her hats, actually. They were quite pretty."

William took her hand again, and they walked to where his carriage waited behind the store. "It seems there are several people who would have liked to kill Harding. Our problem is, which one of them actually carried through on their threat to do so?" He helped Amy into the carriage.

"Do you still wish to walk in the park?"

"No. Frankly, I am quite rattled by Mrs. Burrows's actions and words. There was a great deal of hatred and malice in her attitude. I honestly believe her. I think if she had the opportunity and the means, she would have killed him."

"So far, Patrick Whitney and Miss Gertrude would have as well. And we have yet to speak with Mr. Montrose."

William looked out the window as the carriage moved into traffic. "We have a few suspects who certainly had a motive to kill him, but we need the person who actually did the deed."

"And are you one of them?" Amy asked.

"With a motive to kill him? Not that I would ever step over that line, but I'm afraid to say, yes. Although I didn't discover I even had a motive until after he was already dead, so we don't need to add my name to our list."

"Not since the police already have you at the very top of theirs."

He shook his head. "They have what they consider conclusive evidence." William reached into his pocket and withdrew a paper. "I forgot about this note my butler handed me as I left earlier today to escort you to tea. I'm afraid I was a bit distracted."

He opened it, read it, and smiled at Amy. "Nick Smith has found Patrick Whitney."

CHAPTER 22

William dropped the knocker on the worn wooden door and stepped back, prepared for anything. Nick Smith had provided this address as belonging to Patrick Whitney. It was not his home, apparently, but for some reason he was living here.

It was eleven o'clock in the morning, and unless Whitney was an early riser, he should be at home. William had been watching the house for the past hour to see if anyone came out, but everything remained quiet.

It was a hoarier section of Bath, the houses mostly eighty to a hundred years old. Not exactly seedy, but the area would not be considered middle class. William dropped the knocker again.

About two minutes later the door opened and a woman stuck her head out. She appeared to be somewhere in her early thirties, and judging by her dishabille, she had just risen from her bed. "Who are you and what do you want?"

"I was told Mr. Patrick Whitney was residing here."

"What if he is?"

"I would like to speak with him. His stepmother is quite concerned about him."

The woman snorted and opened the door wider, allowing William to enter. "If she's so concerned, why isn't she here herself?"

"She was unable to locate him." As he stepped inside, his eyes swept the inside of the residence, which was quite pleasant. Although the furniture and accoutrements were old and worn, the place was clean and tidy, with splashes of color provided by pillows and a vase of flowers. The woman tightened the belt around her dressing gown.

"May I speak with Mr. Whitney?"

"I'll have to get him out of bed first. He's been sick, you know."

"Sick?"

The woman nodded. "He's been suffering from an ague, and I've been caring for him."

"That is very kind of you. How long has he been sick?"

"Aye. About two weeks. He showed up here sick as can be and practically collapsed at my feet."

"You are friends, I assume?"

She narrowed her eyes at him. "It's not what you're thinking. I'm a respectable woman and earn my wages by working in a pub. Serving drinks. Nothing more."

A bell went off in William's head. "At which pub do you work?"

"What's it to you? I just said I only serve drinks."

"No. I apologize; that is not what I meant. I am looking for those who work in the pubs near the river."

"Looking for Patrick, looking for people who work at pubs. What are you, some private investigator?"

"No. I am checking on Patrick on behalf of his stepmother. I would like to speak to those who work at pubs near a certain part of the river for another reason."

The woman sniffed. "Sounds suspicious to me."

Perhaps his title would get him some answers. "I am Lord Wethington. May I ask your name?"

"Millie. Mrs. Millie Johnson." She fisted her hands on her hips. "Why?"

The woman was certainly of the suspicious sort. But then, if she was serving drinks in a pub near the river and allowing men to stay in her house while they recovered from illnesses, she would have to be suspicious in order to stay unharmed. And alive.

Since it appeared he would get nowhere with Mrs. Johnson, he said, "May I speak with Mr. Whitney?"

Millie shrugged and pointed to a room to his left. "You can wait in there. I think he's probably well enough to come downstairs."

William nodded his thanks and entered the drawing room. Whitney had been sick for the past couple of weeks and staying here. Why he wouldn't seek help from his stepmother raised a few questions in William's mind.

About fifteen minutes passed before Whitney entered the room. William had no idea what he had expected the man to look like, but nevertheless he was startled to see a very young man, perhaps little more than eight and twenty years. He had the look of someone who had been sick for a while. Moving slowly, he had pasty skin, dark circles under his eyes, and a slender form, which could be his normal figure. "Why are you looking for me?"

Just the walk to the room and that little bit of speech had left Whitney breathless.

"Why don't we sit?" William waved to a faded olive-green settee.

Whitney nodded and plodded over to the settee. He let out a deep sigh once he was seated. For having been sick for a couple of weeks already, the man was not in good shape. Whatever had gotten hold of him must have brought him close to his death.

He looked over at William with narrowed eyes. "What do you want?"

William leaned forward. "Your stepmother is concerned about you. She wanted me to find you and let her know you are all right." No point in mentioning she was afraid he might be hiding for killing Harding.

"As you can see, I am not all right, but don't tell her that; she worries about everything. Which is why, when I started to feel really sick, I came to Millie's house. We've been friends for years."

"How long were your father and stepmother married?"

"Only about three years when he died last year." He leaned his head back on the settee and closed his eyes. The man was really in poor condition.

"Do you have employment you've been unable to attend to while you've been sick?"

He shook his head. "No. My father left me a tidy sum. I also inherited his two businesses." He remained silent for a bit, then said, "How is Mrs. Whitney? She was distraught the last time I saw her."

Likely she had been distraught because he was making threats. It was time to either cross Patrick off his list of suspects or move him to the top.

"When she spoke with me, she was troubled because she said you had threatened Mr. Harding."

He waved his hand. "I've been sick too long to deal with Harding. But you can be sure I will visit with him to check on Mrs. Whitney's trust."

William was taken aback. "Did you not know that Mr. Harding is dead?"

Patrick sat up, his eyes wide. "Dead?"

"Yes. He drowned a couple of weeks ago. His body was found floating in the River Avon."

Patrick shook his head. "I didn't trust the man, but I'm sorry for his death."

William still had one question to ask, despite the man's reaction to Harding's death. "Did you kill Mr. Harding?"

"I've been sick. Haven't left the house for weeks. Was it not an accident, then?"

"No. Someone apparently got him drunk and pushed him into the river. Right about the time you had a conversation with Mrs. Whitney about seeking Harding out."

Patrick groaned and shook his head. "Are the police looking for me?"

"No. They think they have found the culprit, but I'm sure they have not."

"Why not?"

"Because it's me."

Patrick laughed. "No wonder you were anxious to find me—not so much that my stepmother was concerned as you wanted to pin this thing on me. Well, I can tell you, my lord, I had a bit of whiskey in me and ranted about the man and his stealing from my stepmother, but then I went out and got more drunk. I woke up in an alley feeling like death would soon arrive.

"When I realized my illness was not the result of over-indulging but something else, I managed to get to Millie's house. She's been taking care of me. I'm afraid you will have to look elsewhere for someone to take your place at the swing-ing rope."

Patrick's story made sense, and William was sure Mrs. Johnson would back him up in saying he'd been here in her house, recovering from some illness, since the night he'd left his stepmother.

It seemed young Whitney would have to be removed from their list of suspects.

"What shall I tell your stepmother?"

Patrick sighed. "Tell her I have been ill and am slowly recovering at a friend's house and will be in touch with her when I'm feeling better. She worries far too much about everything. You might sweeten it a little bit by saying I don't want to see her until I am sure I am no longer contagious."

William nodded and then slapped his thighs and stood. "Thank you for seeing me. I appreciate the information."

"Do you?" Patrick's brows rose. "Aren't you a bit sorry that you couldn't lay the blame for Harding's death at my door?"

The young man was sharp.

"No need to walk me to the door. I assume you wish to return to your bed."

"Yes. I have been seen by a doctor, and he believes I should be up and about in another two or three days."

"One more thing before I leave. Mrs. Johnson mentioned she works at a pub near the river. Which pub is that?"

Whitney hesitated slightly. "The King's Garden."

The pub where the man had told them Harding was meeting people every couple of weeks. Perhaps, since he had met Mrs. Johnson, he and Amy could revisit the place and speak with her there.

"Do you know when she works next?"

"Why?"

"I just wondered if she saw anything. Mr. Harding's body was found not too far from that pub."

"She works various times." Patrick gave William a look that told him he wanted to return to his bed.

If William remembered correctly, he and Amy had made their visits to the pubs on a Tuesday afternoon. Since he hadn't recognized Mrs. Johnson when she came to the door, possibly she worked at night.

"Well, thank you again. I will advise your stepmother of your condition. I am sure she will be relieved."

There was no reaction from Whitney.

William left the house without seeing any more of Mrs. Johnson and wondering if there was warmth or absolute coldness between Patrick and Mrs. Whitney. His visit with Patrick had not cleared it up either way.

After leaving the house, he made his way to the public mews for his horse. Since he was alone on this trip, he hadn't bothered with his carriage.

He purposely hadn't told Amy about the visit, because she would have insisted on coming with him, and since he'd had no idea what he was walking into, he hadn't wanted to worry about defending himself and her.

When he picked her up later for the Assembly, he would relate the details of his visit. Hopefully she wouldn't be too mad at him, but even if she was angry, it had been worth it not to have to be anxious about her.

About an hour later, he walked into his house to find his mother pacing in the entryway. "There you are." She hurried to him, threw her arms around him, and burst into tears.

"Mother, what's wrong?"

She kept sobbing and clinging to him. He slowly walked her into the drawing room, where he placed her on a sofa and sat alongside her.

She looked up at him and waved a sodden handkerchief at him. "Those horrible police people were here again."

Uh-oh. That didn't sound good. He wasn't supposed to hear from them until he had a chance to go over the records his solicitor had requested from Harding's files. "What did they want?"

She patted her eyes and took a deep breath. "They wanted to talk to you again."

"What did you tell them?"

"I gave them quite a tongue-lashing—bothering an upstanding citizen of Bath and our wonderful country of England. I sent them on their way and told them to never show their faces here again."

William didn't know whether to laugh or cry—his mother had told police detectives who believed he was guilty of murder to never show their faces again. "Did they say anything about a warrant?"

"A what?"

"A warrant for my arrest?"

She sucked in a breath and glared at him. "Of course not. And they better not dare come here with something like that. I will get a gun and shoot them."

"Mother!" Whatever was it with fine well-bred ladies wanting guns? "You will do no such thing. You have never handled a gun, and if you did, you would most likely shoot your foot off."

She raised her chin. "I can learn."

The devil take it. Didn't he have enough on his hands without worrying about Amy and now his mother purchasing a gun and racing off to do damage to themselves?

"Mother, promise me you will not buy a gun."

"I think it might make me feel secure."

"No. It will not make you feel secure. You will end up shooting me or one of the staff who startle you. I have never felt the need to protect myself in my own home with a gun. Now promise."

Images of his mother hanging out the window, waving a gun and taking shots at the police detectives, had his heartbeat picking up speed.

Mother wiped her nose. "I consulted with your dear father last night, and he knows you will overcome this foolishness, since it grows near the time you should be married and filling your nursery."

William dropped his head in his hands. "Mother, we've been through this before. It is not possible to receive information and advice from dear Papa."

"Nonsense. The link between the two of us does not end with death."

A change of subject was in order. "You didn't answer me. Please promise you will not buy a gun." Just the thought of it made him shudder.

"Very well. But they better not come around here again. I will refuse to receive them."

Well, that would certainly stop the detectives in their path.

"Why don't you take a cooling bath and have dinner sent up to your room? Perhaps you might skip the Assembly tonight."

"No. Not at all. I just love spending time with Lady Amy; she is such a pleasant young woman, and she seems quite fond of you." That look was in her eyes again.

"Yes, Lady Amy is quite pleasant. Now I think you should take a short rest, have your bath and dinner, and then if you still feel up to it, we will attend the Assembly."

She patted his cheek. "You are such a fine son. I am so very proud of you." She stood and kissed him on the head as if he were seven years.

Only a mother would say she was proud of someone who had a murder charge hanging over their head.

It was disturbing that the police had returned so soon. Hopefully it had not been with an arrest warrant. He headed to the sideboard and poured himself a brandy. Were it not for the fact that he would be disappointing Amy and his mother, he would skip socializing for the rest of the day and crawl into bed and drink himself into oblivion.

He downed his drink and trudged upstairs. It didn't bother him at all that he wished Amy was upstairs waiting for him. He could use a bit of consolation right now. Maybe it was time for him to marry. He smiled. The word that had always had him breaking into a sweat no longer seemed so terrifying.

CHAPTER 23

"I don't understand what is wrong with Persephone." Amy settled into William's carriage after wishing Lady Wethington a good evening. "She has been so clingy lately. She doesn't want me to leave her side."

"Hasn't she always been that way? I remember when we . . ." William drifted off, no doubt remembering their foray into Harding's house, where Persephone had barked every time Amy walked two feet from her.

"I would say yes, she is a bit attached to me, but it has certainly gotten worse lately."

"She's getting old."

Amy had a difficult time leaving for the Assembly, one place she could definitely not bring her dog. She hated having to trick her in order to depart with any sense of dignity. Right now Persephone was happily gnawing on a bone from Cook. Once she finished that and looked around to find Amy gone, she might begin to wail.

Lady Wethington seemed distracted and a bit on edge. Whatever was troubling her hadn't kept her from attending the Assembly, though. Amy made a mental note to ask William when they were alone if something was wrong. Men didn't always notice such things, and he might need some prodding to see what was troubling the woman.

Aunt Margaret had left earlier, once more accompanied by Lord Pembroke. He had apparently returned from the business trip she had told Amy about.

Aunt Margaret was closemouthed about his lordship, and Amy allowed her that discretion, even though her aunt had no qualms when it came to offering suggestions and advice about William.

The gathering was well under way when they arrived. Well-dressed couples swirled around the dance floor to the tune of a quartet. It was late February, and though the Assembly was full tonight, many of the families would soon be leaving to travel to London for the Season.

For at least two decades, American heiresses had made up a sizable proportion of the young ladies presented each Season with the idea of snaring a husband. Railroad barons, hoteliers, and industrial giants in America were anxious to secure titles for their daughters to solidify their social standing in the United States.

English estates had long been financed by agriculture, with England being the worldwide leader in grain production. However, once the United States started cultivating grain on its prairies, production in England had begun to suffer. Consequently, aristocrats were more than willing to trade their titles for money.

During the Season in London, families would retire to Bath for a week or so to take a break from the social swirl, but the number of tourists would shrink considerably very soon.

Amy and William and his mother were barely past the front door when Mr. Colbert strode across the room, dodging dancers, heading straight for Lady Wethington, a huge smile of welcome on his face. Amy kept her own smile to herself when she saw William scowl.

Mr. Colbert took Lady Wethington's outstretched hand and bowed over it. "Good evening, my lady. You are looking splendid, as always."

Lady Wethington was not immune to flattery and blushed slightly. "Thank you, Mr. Colbert. It is a pleasure to see you."

"Colbert." William offered a curt nod.

"Good evening to you, Lady Amy."

"You as well, Mr. Colbert." Wishing to distract William so that poor Mr. Colbert could have a word with Lady Wethington, or possibly ask her to dance, Amy took William's arm. "I find myself a bit parched; will you join me in a stroll to the refreshment table?"

He didn't look happy, but being a gentleman, he took her arm, and they moved away. "For goodness' sake, William. You're acting like an overprotective father of a young blushing miss."

"Did you not see my mother blush?"

Amy laughed. "I thought you liked Mr. Colbert."

"I like him as a co-member of the book club. I like him as a well-respected solicitor. I like him when I see him in my club. I like him as the leader of the book club meetings. I don't like him as a man who looks at my mother in that way."

"She's an adult. She's been married. She raised two children and is a grandmother. I'm sure she can handle a mild flirtation with a man."

William snorted. "Mild flirtation." He shook his head as if she were trying to convince him of the truth of a fairy tale. "I wonder what my father will think of this."

"Your father? He is deceased, is he not?"

He waved his hand. "Yes. But Mother 'consults' with him on various things."

"Seriously?"

"Unfortunately, yes. But believe me, she is not crazy, just a little early for old-age eccentricity."

Amy picked up a glass of warm lemonade, and they began to stroll the room. Aunt Margaret twirled by, chatting away with Lord Pembroke.

"I had hoped to see Mr. Montrose tonight," William said. "I know he attends on a somewhat regular basis, but the last few times we were here, he was missing."

Amy scanned the room. "Your Mr. Harding really was involved in despicable behavior. I don't wish ill on anyone, but I can't help but think after speaking to some of his victims that he was lucky to have not been murdered before now."

"That reminds me." William cleared his throat as if to make a formal announcement. "I saw Patrick Whitney today."

Amy drew back and stared at him. "You did? How did that come about?"

"Nick Smith sent me the information."

She raised her chin, and her eyes narrowed. "And why wasn't I asked to go along?"

William ran his fingers through his hair. "I didn't want you there." He held up his hand as she felt her anger growing. "Because I had no idea what I was facing. He could have greeted me with a pointed gun."

"Did he?"

"No."

"Then?"

"But I didn't know that ahead of time. Seriously, Amy, I decided I would rather face your wrath than put you into a position where you might be harmed. I don't think my mind is completely recovered from us being shot at." He shook his head. "I won't put you in danger again. If that riles you up, then so be it."

Well then.

"What did you discover?"

"Patrick Whitney is much younger than I had thought. He seemed to be no older than his late twenties. He is staying with a woman, Mrs. Millie Johnson, that he claims is an old friend.

"Do you doubt that?"

"That they are just friends? I'm not sure. However, it seems the very night Patrick threatened Mr. Harding and left Mrs. Whitney's home, he continued to drink and the next morning found himself lying in an alley somewhere feeling dreadful. He assumed it was merely the results of a night of overconsumption. However, when he got worse instead of better, he made his way to Mrs. Johnson's home, where he has been quite sick with an ague of some sort ever since."

"Do you believe his story?"

"After seeing the man? Yes. Even after a couple of weeks, he looked like he'd come close to knocking on death's door. I didn't get a chance to speak with Mrs. Johnson to back up what Whitney said, but he told me she works at the pub we visited before."

"Which one?"

"The one where the man told us an individual—most likely Harding—had met people every couple of weeks for what looked like an exchange of money. The King's Garden."

"That was quite a sleazy place, if I recall. Yet we did not meet her then?"

"No. Patrick was a bit nebulous about the hours she works, but since you and I we were at the King's Garden in the afternoon, I'm thinking she might work mostly nights."

"I believe another trip to the pub is in order."

"Yes." He looked down at her. "I don't suppose I can convince you to stay safe at home this time?"

"Yes."

"Yes?" His eyebrows shot up. "You will stay safely at home and allow me to go by myself?"

"Wrong, my lord. I said yes, you cannot convince me to stay home."

"I should have known."

They continued their stroll, stopping to speak with various people. Soon a waltz began, and William took her by the hand and led her to the dance floor.

Things were becoming a bit different between her and William. Comfortable. Although at the beginning she had been troubled by her body's reaction to him, she was growing accustomed to it and had started to look forward to it.

"Isn't that Mr. Davidson?" Amy nodded in the direction of two men who seemed to be in the middle of a heated argument.

"Yes. And that's his friend, Mr. Rawlings."

"They don't look too friendly now, do they?"

While keeping up with the music, they continued to watch the men, whose quarrel began to draw attention. Mr. Rawlings threw his hands up in the air and stormed off. After a minute or two, Mr. Davidson followed him out.

"Well, that was certainly interesting," William said.

"Oh, I also forgot to tell you about my visit with Miss Gertrude. Aunt Margaret and I made a call there. We were the only visitors, and while I wouldn't say the ladies were rude in any way, I didn't get the feeling that we were very welcomed. They made it a point to mention that they were not holding morning calls that day."

"Did you learn anything?"

"One thing I thought noteworthy was that Miss Gertrude had scratches on her face. It made me think of the person who attempted to steal the ledger and then ran through the woods and stumbled."

"You think it was Miss Gertrude?" He seemed to think for a minute. "That's fascinating. I never considered that our shooter could have been a woman."

"I'm not saying it was, only that the scratches on her face brought that to my attention."

"Did you ask her about them?"

"Yes. She mentioned a cat that wanders her neighborhood that they feed on occasion. She said the animal scratched her."

The music came to an end, and William walked her to where Aunt Margaret stood with Lord Pembroke, Lady Wethington, and Mr. Colbert.

"Must he stay by her side all night?" William groused.

Amy grinned. "You are by my side most nights." She stumbled and sucked in a breath, heat rising to her face at the image her statement produced. "I mean most nights at the Assembly."

He had the nerve to grin at her discomfort. "That's different."

They had already made it to the group, so Amy did not pursue the conversation and hoped the redness of her face would diminish before anyone noticed.

"Wethington, I just invited your mother to attend the theater with me Friday next," Mr. Colbert said. "Would you and Lady Amy care to join us?"

"As a chaperone?" William muttered under his breath. Amy nudged him in the middle with her elbow.

"I love the theater," Amy said, turning to William.

He sighed, obviously feeling trapped. "Yes. Of course we would love to attend." He looked about as happy as he did each time she brought Persephone with her on one of their jaunts.

"Lady Margaret, would you care to join us as well?" It appeared Mr. Colbert was going to make it a group outing.

Lord Pembroke spoke up. "I'm afraid Lady Margaret and I already have plans for next Friday."

All heads turned toward her aunt, who looked back at them as if daring them to ask questions.

How very odd.

William stiffened as he glanced across the room. "If you will excuse me, there is someone I must speak with." Before Amy could ask a question, he was gone.

She studied him until she saw him stop and begin a conversation with a man she did not recognize.

★   ★   ★

Not having seen Mr. Montrose at the Assembly since he and Amy had started their investigation, William was quite surprised when he glanced across the room to see the man leaning against a wall, speaking with another gentleman.

Not wanting to appear as though he was conducting an interrogation, William slowed his walk and sauntered up to the two men. "Good evening, Montrose. Haven't seen you in a while."

Montrose stuck out his hand, and they shook. "Good to see you too, Wethington."

The man whom Montrose had been speaking with stepped back. "If you will excuse me, I see someone headed for the door that I need to speak with." He made a quick turn and strode toward the exit.

"Did you hear about James Harding's death?" William watched Montrose carefully.

The man's lips tightened, and his face flushed. "The man was a crook, a cheat, and a snake. Drowning was too good for him."

William was a bit taken aback. Harding had truly been a hated man, and what troubled William the most was that he'd worked with the man for a few years and somehow missed all this. He did not consider himself neglectful or stupid, yet his man of business had stolen from so many. "He was my man of business too."

"You would be wise to check your financial records," Montrose said. "He stole quite a bit from me, and it was my fault for not double-checking everything he did." The man shook his head.

"Yes. Well, I have a bit of a problem myself."

"What is that?"

"Harding was stealing from me as well and also forging my name to contracts that have done a bit of damage to my business reputation."

Montrose shook his head and blew out a soft whistle. "He was truly a devil. I am in the process of having my barrister solicit the courts to get back my records, which the police currently have in hand."

William leaned his shoulder against the wall. "How successful have you been?"

"Not very. Since I was out of the country when the man died, I was a couple of weeks behind in the news."

William's ears picked up. "You were out of the country?"

"Yes. Spent a few weeks with my parents in Scotland. Near Aberdeen."

Another suspect to be crossed off their list. It wouldn't take much to have Montrose's parents confirm he'd been visiting them when Harding took his final swim in the river.

"I hope all is well with them?"

"Yes. They are getting on in years, and you know how it goes. I should really make an effort to get out there more often."

Mr. Colbert strode up to the two of them, nodding in Montrose's direction and then turning his attention to William. "I will be escorting your mother home this evening."

"What?"

"Yes. She has agreed, and we will be leaving soon. She said she has a bit of a headache."

Remembering how upset she'd been earlier, William was not surprised. "I can leave now and see her home."

He slapped William on the back. "No need. I'm more than happy to see her home." He turned and walked back to where William's mother stood conversing with Lady Margaret.

William studied his mother for a moment. She didn't look to him as if she was suffering any headache. Before he could march over and demand that he personally see her home, Amy stepped up to his side, a very feminine smile on her face.

"Leave them alone, my lord."

Chapter 24

William looked up as his butler, Madison, entered the library, where he was struggling to make sense of his finances.

"My lord, Mr. Frank Wilson has arrived."

"Send him in." He'd been employing Wilson ever since Harding died. His new man of business came highly recommended by Lord Winchester, among others, and William actually felt sorry for the poor man on account of the financial tangle he was having to unravel for him.

"Good morning, my lord." Wilson strode into the room and extended his arm.

William stood, and they shook hands. "Have a seat."

Wilson settled in and placed a portfolio on the desk in front of him. He took a deep breath and looked him in the eye. "My lord, you are in a mess."

"Tell me something I do not already know." William sighed. "What I'm anxious to find out is, can I recover my good name?"

"Absolutely."

The man's confident assurance went a long way toward easing William's anxiety. "I am happy to hear that and am willing to do whatever you think is necessary to clear up this dilemma."

Wilson pulled a pile of papers out of his portfolio. "One thing I discovered in my efforts to unravel all of this is most likely the reason Mr. Harding went from a reputable man of business to a thief."

That certainly got William's attention. "Pray tell."

"Apparently Mr. Harding chose a very risky investment for a few of his clients."

"Indeed?"

"Yes. You were one of the investors, as were two others."

William had a good idea who those other investors were: Lemmon and Montrose. "He never said anything to me about that."

"Just so." Wilson studied the paper in front of him. "Rather than advising these clients, it seems, in an effort to recoup his losses, he began taking money from other clients and using it to gamble."

"Gamble?"

"Yes. In order to keep it as quiet as possible, he made trips to London for that purpose."

William shook his head. "Only a foolish man attempts to make money on gambling."

"From what I've discovered, he got deeper and deeper into trouble, and dipped once more into your account and then pulled some other shenanigans which are just now coming to light. It was only a matter of time before his nefarious deeds became known."

It crossed William's mind that perhaps Harding had not been pushed into the river but had gotten himself drunk on purpose and taken a dive. It would not be the first time a man had done such a thing to escape a bad situation.

"Thank you very much for that information, Wilson. Now I suggest we look at how bad things are and what we can do to correct it."

★ ★ ★

It was Tuesday evening, and as the carriage made its way to Amy's house, William patted his pocket, where he did, in fact, carry a gun. Even though he'd told his mother he didn't have one and constantly thwarted Amy's intention to buy one, he did have two pistols locked away in his library.

However, unlike the ladies, who thought they could pick up a gun and shoot anyone who threatened them dead center, he had spent years practicing and was quite confident in his skill.

At least he would not shoot himself in the foot.

On the way home from the Assembly Saturday, William had made one final effort to convince Amy not to accompany him to the pub. But she had been stubborn and adamant.

"We can bring a gun," she'd said.

He'd pressed his index finger and thumb to the bridge of his nose. "No gun."

Amy was ready and eager to go when he arrived at her house. However, since fate loved to play little games, Lord Winchester was also home, and invited him in for a drink.

"Where are you off to tonight?" Winchester swirled his brandy and smiled a warm and frightening smile at him.

Well, my lord, I am about to bring your daughter to one of the seedier parts of town. In fact, next to a place where a man was killed. But then, I'm sure you don't mind. No need to worry, since I am carrying a gun, because once before when we were out and about, we were shot at. May I have some more brandy, please?

"We are making a trip to the bookstore."

"The bookstore? Don't you go there every Thursday?" Winchester frowned. "Today is Tuesday."

William cleared this throat. "Yes, very true. However, the book we are to read for this week's meeting was unavailable last week, but the store clerk said it would be in today. Late shipment."

Winchester nodded and then quickly changed the subject, for which William was grateful until he heard the question. "Young man, I would like your support in something."

Amy glared at her papa, and William got a sinking feeling in his stomach. "Yes, my lord?"

"Amy tells me that you are aware of her writing hobby."

"Hobby! Papa, I write well-selling books that I make money on."

Winchester pointed his finger at her. "No matter. A woman has no need to earn money if she has respectable men in her family. Only the lowest of the low must send their wives and daughters out to seek employment." He took a sip of his brandy. "Am I not right, Wethington?"

How the devil was he going to get out of this one? He decided to play the diplomat. "I agree that there is more female employment in the lower classes."

He didn't applaud himself for avoiding the issue, because he knew Amy's father was not finished. The questions were only going to get harder to answer if he wished to maintain his friendship with Amy *and* not vex her father at the same time.

Since William had been considering marriage of late, Lord Winchester would be the man to approve or disapprove when he came with a request for his daughter's hand in marriage. He would have to tread very carefully here.

"Lady Amy tells me her publisher is requiring her to appear at some book fair." Lord Winchester waved his hand around in a sign of dismissal.

Since that was not a question, William merely nodded and looked longingly at his empty brandy glass. He could use a bit more, facing the interrogation.

"I have the perfect solution, but my daughter is not happy with the perfect answer."

"Oh?" *Here it comes.*

"I suggested we hire someone—a man—to appear as this E. D. Burton person at the book fair and make everyone happy."

William groaned inwardly. This would not make Amy happy, and in this case he had to agree with her. There was simply no easy way of getting out of this. Straightening his shoulders, he looked Winchester in the eye. "My lord, I find I cannot agree with you."

Winchester's brows rose. "Indeed?"

"Yes, sir. With all due respect, Lady Amy has worked hard on those books, and while she has abided by your wish to keep her identity private, I cannot support your idea, which would wipe out all her work and hand the accolades and praise for such fine books to an unknown man."

Amy's father stared at him for a few moments while William sweated it out. "Is that right?" Winchester gulped the last of his brandy.

William looked over at Amy, and the glow on her face and happiness in her eyes was worth whatever misfortune he had just brought down on his head.

"I have matters to attend to right now." Lord Winchester stood and placed his glass on the table in front of him. "Enjoy your trip to the bookstore." With those curt words, he strode from the drawing room, leaving Amy and William staring at each other.

"At least he didn't have Stevens throw me out." William stood and took Amy's hand. "Let's go before he changes his mind."

Once they were settled in the carriage and on their way, Amy folded her hands and placed them in her lap. "Thank you."

"You're welcome. While I sympathize with your father in wanting to keep your identity hidden, I don't agree with it."

Her jaw dropped. "You don't?"

William shook his head. "Not at all. There is no reason why you cannot take credit for your work. You are not the first woman to publish dark novels. Mary Shelley's *Frankenstein* comes to mind, along with books by Ann Radcliffe. And look at it this way, you are making inroads for other female authors to delve into the dark and dangerous."

Tears welled in her eyes. "Thank you."

Something deep inside him woke up then, and he knew at that moment that it would never go back to sleep again. He reached over and pulled Amy to his side, put his arm around her, and held her close.

It felt right.

The night was as dark and dreary as the pub looked. When they'd seen it the last time, it had been daylight, and even though the extra light had accentuated the bleakness, now, shrouded in darkness, the place looked downright ominous.

"I think we should have brought a gun." Amy moved the window curtain aside and looked out at the building.

"I did."

She turned back to him, her eyes wide. "You did? I thought you told me no guns."

"No guns for you. Or for my mother, who also mentioned getting one."

"Why can you have a gun and I cannot?"

William stepped out of the carriage and held out his hand for Amy to grasp. "Because I am trained in the use of guns. I keep my skills up by practicing."

Before she could continue the argument, he ushered her down the path and into the pub. It was almost as dark inside as outside. Most tables were full, and William managed to secure one near the middle of the room.

There were small tables in the corners, their occupants not visible in the darkness. "This is sort of spooky." Amy rubbed her palms up and down her arms. "I can't imagine working in a place like this at nighttime."

"I don't want to imagine you working in a place like this at all. Or any place, for that matter. In that I agree with your father. Women should not leave their homes to work unless there is no other way to keep the family housed and fed."

She grinned. "Aha. I notice you danced around that one quite nicely by saying *not leave their homes to work*."

"Just so." He winked at her and then looked around and immediately spotted Mrs. Johnson. He waved his hand, and she nodded that she would be right there. He didn't think she recognized him from that distance; she was just acknowledging another impatient customer.

"What can I get ya?" Although she spoke to them, she looked around the room, no doubt seeing who she needed to take care of next.

"Hello, Mrs. Johnson."

Her head snapped back, and she looked down at them. "Aren't you the man who came to my house to see Patrick?" She didn't look pleased.

"Yes, I am. I wonder if I could speak with you."

She looked around and then said, "What can I get you?"

"Two ales."

She walked off before he could say anything else.

"Was she that unfriendly when you met her earlier?" Amy asked.

"I wouldn't say unfriendly as much as suspicious. But I imagine if I were a woman working in a place like this, it would make me a bit uncomfortable to have someone come into my place of work looking especially for me."

Mrs. Johnson plunked the two glasses down on the table and skirted around the two of them to hurry off before William could say a word.

"I guess we wait to see if she comes back." Amy gingerly picked up the glass and held it to the dim light. "Not very clean."

"I expect not." William eased his glass away.

"I'm glad you brought a gun." Amy looked behind her. "In my books, anyone who feels threatened always sits with their back to the wall, facing the door."

"In *real life*, people who feel threatened sit with their back to the wall, facing the door."

Mrs. Johnson rushed by, ignoring them.

"Do you think she will talk to us?"

"I hope so. The fact that she's avoiding our table makes me wonder if she knows something and is afraid to say anything. I think Whitney might have told her what we discussed when I visited him."

The next time she came near their table, William said, "Madam, may I have a brandy?" If he ordered something, she would have to come to their table.

She reappeared a few minutes later. "Here you are." She slammed the small glass down on the table. She looked around and leaned in. "If you want to talk to me about anything, it won't be here. Too many ears." She looked around again.

"When?"

She leaned closer and wiped the table with a dirty cloth. "Come to the Roman Baths square tomorrow. That's the best I can do." She walked away, then turned back. "Three o'clock."

William nodded, placed some coins on the table, and stood. Amy followed him, and he took her hand in his as they left the pub.

★ ★ ★

The next day William sat behind his desk going over his files again, trying to reconcile his bank statements with the records he had received from Wilson. Hopefully his new man of business—who seemed very efficient—would help to get all of this straightened out, before too long. He'd found himself unable to sleep the past few nights with all the worries on his mind.

Another conundrum—as if he hadn't enough of them in his life—was his missing appointment book. He had left it on his desk and had planned to go over it to see if he could piece together his activities the week James had been killed.

With the way things were in his life right now, there was a good possibility he hadn't left it on his desk but had put it somewhere else. He planned to leave for Amy's house in about an hour so they could proceed to see Mrs. Johnson. He was sure she had wanted to give them some information the night before but had felt uneasy doing so at the pub. Hopefully it would be something that could lead to Harding's killer.

Since his session with his solicitor, his barrister, and the police, he had felt as though he were waiting for an ax to drop.

The fact that the detectives had come to his house to harass his mother and hadn't returned since worried him. If it had been something important enough for them to make the trip to his house, why hadn't he heard from them?

His mother entered the library, pulling on her gloves.

"Are you going out?"

"Yes. I have an appointment with my modiste. I am in dire need of an updated wardrobe."

William leaned back in his chair and studied her. "Why the sudden need for more clothes?" He hadn't spoken to her yet about Mr. Colbert seeing her home the Saturday before. She'd been busy making her morning calls and receiving her own guests. She'd also been out a couple of nights with no indication of where she was going. Although he was very curious, it felt odd asking his own mother to keep him abreast of her comings and goings.

Truth be known, he was a bit reluctant to question her because he was afraid to hear what she'd have to say. He knew that she was a grown woman and had already lived through a marriage, so she certainly knew what was what about male-and-female relationships.

He could not condone any sort of an affair, however. After all, she was his mother. Watching her sneak into the house in the early-morning hours, or worse yet, seeing Colbert creep out the front door, would push him close to calling Colbert out.

"I just feel the need for some new things. Is there a problem with funds, dear?"

William shook his head. "Not at all. You may purchase whatever you like."

"Thank you, son." She kissed the top of his head and proceeded toward the door, almost running into Stevens.

"My lord, the two detectives are here again."

"I thought I told them never to return," his mother huffed.

William stood and walked around the desk. "Mother, one does not forbid the authorities from coming to one's house if they have reason to."

She raised her chin. "They have no reason. This idea of you having anything at all to do with the death of that business manager is preposterous."

"Thank you for your vote of confidence, but nevertheless, the police generally tend to dismiss character references from one's mother."

"The drawing room?" William asked.

"Yes, my lord. They are waiting there."

He would really have preferred to leave his mother out of it, but she appeared unlikely to sail out the door for her appointment, so they both entered the drawing room.

The two detectives stood in the middle of the room. When William entered, Detective Carson moved up to him. "Lord William Wethington, please place your hands behind your back."

"What?"

"You are under arrest for the murder of Mr. James Harding and Mrs. Millie Johnson."

"Mrs. Johnson! I just saw her last night."

"Yes. We know that. She was found behind the Kings Garden with a bullet in her. We had a tip that you met with her last night after she finished her shift."

"That's absurd. I did not meet her after her shift. Who provided this tip?"

"It was anonymous."

Just then, with a soft sigh, his mother slumped to the floor. Somehow he didn't think this swoon was fake.

"Detectives, I cannot leave until I see to my mother." William walked to where she lay on the ground, picked her up, and placed her on a settee. "Get me a maid, please," he said to Stevens. "Then send someone to Lady Amy's house with a message that I need her here as quickly as possible."

A maid entered, and William immediately began to shout instructions at her to tend to his mother.

"I beg you, please, Detectives, to allow me time to see that Lady Amy has arrived."

The two detectives looked at each other and shrugged. "We will give you a half hour, no more."

They both sat in chairs near the door, obviously making sure William could not leave the house.

"Stevens, fetch me some paper and pen. I must write a note to Mr. Nelson-Graves."

William had learned enough from watching the barrister in operation last week as well as last year when he represented Amy to know that he needed to keep quiet and allow Mr. Nelson-Graves to do all the talking.

His mother was finally sitting up and clutching at her maid's arms. "Detectives, you cannot arrest my son. He is a member of the nobility."

"I'm sorry to dispute you, Lady Wethington, but these are serious charges, and yes, we can arrest him."

William's head was still spinning with the news about Mrs. Johnson. Obviously there had been someone in the pub the night before who had heard her tell them to meet her at the square.

That same someone had killed her to keep her from telling him and Amy something important.

At last, close to a half hour later, Amy hurried through the door to the drawing room. "Whatever is going on?"

William walked up to her and took her hands in his. "You must stay here with my mother; she is extremely distraught."

"Why? What's happened?"

"I am being arrested for murder."

CHAPTER 25

"I reiterate one more time, Detectives. I had nothing to do with Mr. Harding's death, nor Mrs. Johnson's." William ran his fingers through his hair, frustrated and angered.

He'd sent word to Mr. Nelson-Graves before being taken to the police station, but so far the man had not arrived. William had been in the interrogation room for only about an hour, but it seemed like all day.

"Let's go back again and tell me why you and Lady Amy were at the King's Garden pub last night, Tuesday, the third of March."

"I've answered that question several times already, and at this point I will answer no further questions until my barrister arrives."

Detective Carson looked over at Detective Marsh. "Sounds guilty to me."

William kept his mouth closed. They were taunting him, trying to get him to say more, but the entire situation was frightening enough without him blundering about and saying something that would only get him in deeper.

"Detective, Lord Wethington's barrister has arrived." A young police officer entered the room after giving a slight knock.

"Send him in."

Mr. Nelson-Graves entered the room and nodded at them. "Good afternoon, Detectives." He took the seat next to William. "Before we go any further, I would like to speak with my client in private."

Without a word, the two detectives stood and left the room.

"Start from the beginning." Mr. Nelson-Graves pulled out a pad of paper and a pencil.

William took the barrister through everything step by step, from the time he had visited with Patrick Whitney to when he had spoken with Mrs. Johnson at the pub and then returned home.

"You are in a mess here, my lord."

"I know."

"Right now we need to get you out of here. I will arrange for bail, but if the detectives insist on continuing their interrogation, I will insist it happens at another time. We need to gather some facts first."

William nodded, hopeful for the first time since he'd been arrested. Mr. Nelson-Graves stood and walked to the door. "Detectives, we are ready."

They both lumbered into the room, taking the same spots they'd occupied when William arrived over an hour before.

"Is you client ready to confess, barrister?"

"No. Of course not, and I find the question ridiculous. We are requesting Lord Wethington be released with a bond."

"No."

William's stomach sank.

Mr. Nelson-Graves didn't flinch. "You are speaking of a peer. Lord Wethington is a viscount and an upstanding member of the community. He has nothing in his background that would suggest he would commit a crime such as murder."

"Nothing in his background would suggest he would be fleecing people, setting up false business, and therefore robbing investors either."

"We've been over this before, Detective. My client denies any knowledge of the information contained in the file you found in Mr. Harding's home."

"His signature is on the papers."

"Again, we've covered this already. Those are forgeries. However, I do not intend to try this case here in the interrogation room."

Try the case? Does Nelson-Graves believe it would go that far? William broke into a sweat.

Nelson-Graves stood. "I have an appointment this morning with the magistrate to release his lordship with a bond."

"Until its granted, *his lordship* will stay here."

It looked as though Nelson-Graves was going to argue the point, but apparently deciding against it, he nodded. "Very well." He turned to William. "I shall be back within the hour." He looked over at the detectives. "Based on his lordship's peerage, I demand he be allowed to wait here. I do not want him subjected to a jail cell."

To William's surprise, the detectives agreed, and they left the room with Mr. Nelson-Graves.

William slumped in the chair and rubbed his forehead. With all that had happened since the detectives stormed his house, he hadn't had a chance to even think about Mrs. Johnson being murdered.

Obviously, someone who had been in the pub the night before had heard her tell him and Amy to meet her today. There were four dark corners in the place, as well as other spots that were poorly lit, so there could have been several people William and Amy hadn't seen who overhead the conversation.

Here the poor woman had done a good deed by taking Whitney in when he was so sick and nursing him, and because of that she had been dragged into a murder investigation and ended up dying for it.

William also wondered if the detectives had gone to Mrs. Johnson's house and notified Patrick of her death. William still hadn't reported back to Mrs. Whitney about her stepson.

First and foremost, he needed to find the person who had already killed two people and attempted to kill him and Amy. With the police focused solely on him, he and Amy had to unravel the mess and find the real killer.

He blanched, imagining the harsh feel of a rope around his neck.

★   ★   ★

Amy rested on the settee and held Lady Wethington's ice-cold hand. The now-cool teapot and half-empty cups sat on the small table in front of them.

"I cannot believe my son was arrested for murder." Lady Wethington had been repeating these words nonstop since the detectives and William left the house. Amy's assurances that of course William would never do such a thing as kill anyone failed to make his mother feel better.

"Perhaps I should escort you to your bedchamber and you can take a tisane to help you sleep for a while," Amy suggested.

Lady Wethington shook her head. "I could not sleep a wink until I know this nonsense has come to an end." She gripped Amy's hand so tight that Amy thought the bones in her hand would snap. "Suppose they keep him in jail? That would be horrible."

"I think we should not worry about that. William has an excellent barrister who would never allow that to happen."

"Why? Why my son?" Lady Wethington wailed, for about the seventieth time since Amy had arrived. Amy knew why, but there was no reason to share her information with her ladyship.

Someone had been at the pub, sitting in darkness, and overheard their exchange with Mrs. Johnson, then decided to kill the woman before she could tell Amy and William what she knew. Since Mrs. Johnson worked in the pub and had seen Harding collecting his blackmail money any number of times, it was quite possible she could have pointed them to the killer.

Now, instead of having that vital information, William was sitting in jail, and Amy was trying to keep Lady Wethington from jumping out the window.

"You know I am fond of you, Amy. You don't mind if I call you Amy, do you?"

"No. Of course not. Why don't you remove your shoes and lie down for a while? I can get you a lavender cloth for your head."

Lady Wethington bent to remove her shoes while Amy rang for a maid and asked to have a cool cloth sprinkled with lavender for William's mother.

Once she was free of her shoes, Lady Wethington shifted so that she was lying on the sofa. Amy placed a pillow under her head, and the woman closed her eyes and was silent for a few minutes. The young maid returned with the cloth and handed it to Amy, who placed it on Lady Wethington's forehead.

The woman sighed. "You are such a lovely young lady. And so very good with my son." She wiped her nose on her soggy handkerchief. "He needs a wife." She opened her eyes and looked pointedly at Amy. "Soon. I am not getting any younger, and I need grandchildren. Grandchildren who live near enough for me to actually hold them and spoil them."

Amy didn't think this was the best time to travel in that direction, so she diverted the conversation. "You are quite young, my lady. I am sure you have many, many years ahead of you to enjoy grandchildren."

She was silent for a few minutes, and Amy thought she had fallen asleep. Then she wailed, "Why?" for the seventy-first time.

The front door opened, and Amy let out a huge sigh of relief when she heard William's voice. She prayed it was all a mistake and he had been released for good.

"How is she?" he asked as he walked over to where Amy sat with his mother.

"I am not well, son. This horrid business has upset me profoundly." She took the cloth off her head and sat up. "Please tell me it was a misunderstanding and life can return to normal."

William sat in the chair across from the sofa, his legs spread, his forearms resting on his thighs. "I'm sorry, Mother, but it is not all over."

When she began to wail, he continued, "However, Mr. Nelson-Graves appeared on my behalf in front of the magistrate today, and I was released on bond."

"My lady, now that you know his lordship is home safe and sound, can I persuade you to retire to your bedchamber for a lie-down? I think it will do you well." Amy looked down at the distraught woman, feeling sympathy for her. It must be a horrible thing to have your child charged with murder.

"I think you are right. Will you accompany me upstairs, Amy?"

"Of course." As she took Lady Wethington's arm and they proceeded up the stairs, William made a beeline for the brandy bottle sitting on the sideboard.

★   ★   ★

William and Amy settled into his carriage, and after a tap on the ceiling, the vehicle moved forward.

They were on their way to the book club meeting. This was the first time he and Amy had been together since he'd been arrested the day before. Once his mother had retired to her room, William had given Amy a brief overview of what happened at the police station. They had decided to take the rest of the day apart so they could calm themselves and ponder what their next steps should be.

As much as he had the strong desire to hide away in his library and consider the chaos his life had become, he felt it was better to carry on with his normal routine until it could all be resolved.

"I am concerned about Persephone," Amy said before the carriage had gone more than a few feet.

Ah, the ghastly dog. "Why is that?"

"She is still extremely clingy. Would you believe I had to fool her into believing I was going to the water closet so I could sneak out of the house today?"

William shook his head. "That, my dear, is ridiculous."

"Maybe so, but I am concerned." She grasped the strap hanging by her head when the vehicle hit a hole in the road. "They need to fix these streets."

"Agreed."

She adjusted her hat, which had slid backward when they hit the gap. "Have you had any ideas?"

There was certainly no reason to pretend he didn't know what she was talking about. "Yes. Right now we have Miss Gertrude and Mrs. Burrows who were being blackmailed and Mrs. Whitney whom Harding was cheating. All women. That is a bit disconcerting. I also find it near impossible to imagine any of them killing two people."

"Why do you dismiss them because they are women?" Amy asked, her brows raised.

"I'm not sure, but I just can't see a woman killing two people."

She grinned. "It's happened before."

Remembering the case last year, he grinned back. "Ah, but it wasn't two deaths attributed to her, only one."

He gathered his thoughts for a minute. "Montrose claimed he was out of town, but I want to check that. He certainly seemed agitated enough with Harding to have done him harm. Patrick was quite sick when the murder took place, and Lemmon seemed more interested in having his solicitor straighten out his finances than in doing anything to Harding." William leaned his head back and took in a deep breath. "I'm scared, Amy."

She reached across and took his hand. "I know."

He opened his eyes and looked at her. "If we can't come up with the true killer, I might spend the rest of my life in prison, or worse yet, swinging from a rope."

"Stop!" She squeezed his hand. "We will find the murderer. We will."

Mr. Colbert hurried up to them as William and Amy entered the room at the back of the bookstore for the meeting. "How is your mother? I heard she had taken ill."

William frowned. "Where did you hear that?"

"We are supposed to attend the theater tomorrow, if you recall, and I received a missive from her today that she was not feeling up to joining me."

"I am sorry, Mr. Colbert. I know Amy and I were to attend also, but I'm afraid we will be unable to join you as well."

Colbert waved them off as if he and Amy were of no importance if his mother couldn't go.

"How ill is she?" Colbert looked concerned.

Mr. Colbert was certainly someone he could trust, but he preferred to keep the bulk of the story to himself. "I had a bit of a legal issue which has caused Lady Wethington undue stress."

"Legal issue? You do know I am a solicitor. Can I help you in any way?"

It depends. Do you know who killed the two people that I am being accused of murdering?

"No, I have my solicitor working on it. I'm sure my mother will be up and about in a few days."

"May I call on her?"

As much as William did not care for Mr. Colbert pursuing his mother, perhaps a visit from him would cheer her up. "Yes. You may call on her. Send a missive around so she will be prepared for your visit."

"Thank you." The glow on the man's face surprised him. Could it be the man really cared for his mother and didn't have nefarious intentions? Life was so topsy-turvy lately that anything was possible.

Not feeling particularly social, he directed Amy to one of the small settees. "Where has Eloise been? I haven't seen her in a while," William said.

"She's off visiting her cousin in London. She does that twice a year."

"Does he ever visit her here?"

"Occasionally, but they find more things to do in London."

The other members slowly drifted in. Miss Sterling and Miss Penelope walked in together, chatting, with Miss Sterling waving her hands around.

Amy stood and wandered over to the two women. William followed her.

"Where is Miss Gertrude tonight?" Amy asked, when there was a break in the women's conversation.

"My sister was not feeling well." Miss Penelope offered a slight smile.

"That is too bad. Have her scratches healed?"

"Scratches?"

"Yes, when I visited with you about a week and a half ago, she had scratches on her face. Remember?"

"Oh, yes," Miss Penelope said. "Those are all cleared up. She is merely suffering from a megrim tonight."

William and Amy glanced at each other as Mr. Colbert called the meeting to order.

Perhaps Miss Gertrude had a megrim after shooting Mrs. Johnson?

Chapter 26

Amy stared at the letter in her hand, vacillating between anger and worry. She was being threatened by her publisher. Either she must sign the enclosed document, agreeing to appear at the Atkinson & Tucker book fair in three weeks, or she would be the defendant in a lawsuit for breach of contract.

She folded the letter and laid it next to her place at the breakfast table. Whatever was she going to do? On the one hand, Papa was adamant that she refuse to appear as E.D. Burton, yet on the other, her publisher was waving lawsuit papers at her.

"Good morning, daughter." Papa walked into the room. "Why so glum?"

She unfolded the letter and handed it to him. He skimmed the contents and handed it back to her. "I have spoken to my solicitor, and he is prepared to take the matter into hand. We can contact Mr. Nelson-Graves if it goes far enough that we require a barrister."

"Papa, I don't want a lawsuit." She placed her hands in her lap and straightened her shoulders. "I think I should go to the book fair as E. D. Burton. It is time I received recognition for my work."

Instead of the explosion she was prepared for, Papa merely shook his head. "It would ruin you, young lady. No gentleman would want to marry a woman so notorious." He shook out his napkin, laid it on his lap, and began to place items from the platters in the center of the table on his plate.

"Papa, we've been over this. I do not want to marry."

"Is that right?" He stopped loading his plate and stared at her. "It appears to me, miss, that your young man is heading in that direction and plans to take you with him."

Amy felt the heat start in her middle and climb to her face. "Even if that were so," she hurried to add, "which I don't acknowledge as true, William is very forward thinking. He doesn't see any reason for me to be hiding my name."

"I don't believe that's true."

"He said so right here in this house."

Papa pointed his fork at her. "He said that because he didn't want to find himself on the other side of the front door. Mark my words, when you two marry, he will take an entirely different stance."

"Who is getting married?" Aunt Margaret asked as she entered the breakfast room. "You, Franklin?" The mirth in her eyes brought a smile to Amy's face.

"Don't be ridiculous, Margaret," Papa huffed. "I am far too old and set in my ways to consider marrying."

"Ah, talk of marriage again." Michael joined them, taking the seat next to Aunt Margaret and across from Amy. "Is a wedding finally planned for my sister?"

"There is to be no wedding!" Amy snapped. Three pairs of eyes swung in her direction—Michael's teasing, Aunt Margaret's sympathetic, and Papa's determined.

Here she was, trying to convince Papa that she deserved the accolades for her books, and he, as usual, was turning it into another attempt to marry her off.

"If you recall, Papa, you tried last year to push me to the altar, and that didn't exactly work out well, did it?"

"I agreed at the time that St. Vincent was not the best candidate for your husband. I acknowledged my mistake."

"Cheers, Father. I never thought to hear you say you made a mistake." Michael held up his coffee cup. Papa growled in his direction.

"However, Amy, there is nothing wrong with Lord Wethington," Michael said. "He is a fine, upstanding man with a good head on his shoulders."

And accused of two murders.

Since Aunt Margaret was around the house much more than her papa and brother, she was up-to-date on the happenings with Harding's—and now Mrs. Johnson's—murder. Amy had told her about the latest murder victim the night before when she returned from the book club meeting.

Papa, on the other hand didn't need to know what was going on, since he'd warned her last year to stay out of the investigation into St. Vincent's death, which of course, hadn't deterred her in the slightest. No need to have him glowering at her again.

"Franklin, leave her alone. If anything develops between Amy and Lord Wethington, that is up to them. They don't need you pushing at them." Aunt Margaret never held back her opinion from Papa.

Since nothing had been settled regarding the threat of a lawsuit from Amy's publisher, she finished her breakfast and retired to her bedchamber to once again tackle the ledger.

Today she was determined to do the best she could to get the name that had been muddied.

Two hours later, she sat back and stared at the name on her pad. It was not quite a guess, since she had been able to decipher some of the letters, and by playing with them, she had come up with one name she recognized.

Mr. George Davidson.

She did not know Mr. Davidson's first name, and there were probably numerous Davidsons in Bath, but her heart pumped a bit harder when she looked at the results of her attempts to use the code on the letters she had been able to make out.

Then she chastised herself, because she had never particularly liked Mr. Davidson, so it was possible she was filling in letters just to make them fit his name. He was very condescending to women and managed to suck the life out of any event.

Despite her misgivings, she had to get this information to William. If it *was* Mr. Davidson, they had to turn their investigation in his direction.

She quickly pulled a piece of paper from her drawer and wrote a note to William.

★　★　★

William sat with his arms crossed over his chest, playing chaperone to his mother and Mr. Colbert. It was ludicrous, given the situation, but he wanted to make sure Mr. Colbert made no untoward suggestions to his mother.

William hoped the man would leave soon, because he had just received a note from Amy telling him she had made an interesting discovery that she did not want to send by way of the missive. She asked for him to call as soon as possible.

William pulled out his timepiece. "My goodness. Look at the time." He shook his head, placed the watch back in his vest pocket, and looked directly at Colbert.

They had already drunk two pots of tea and eaten a tray of sandwiches and sweets, and now William was about to ask the man if he would like to have a bedchamber readied for him. With a lock on the outside.

Mother, on the other hand, seemed to be enjoying herself. She and Colbert laughed and laughed, sharing stories of their youth and the challenges of raising children.

In fact, William had not seen such a glow on Mother's face since she'd taken up residence in his home. Why it bothered him that she was enjoying the company of a man was confusing.

The devil take it, if he ever married and had daughters, he would most likely be a tyrant when it came to their beaux.

Married.

That word had been popping up a great deal lately and had turned from being a disturbing idea to a quite pleasant one. He imagined him and Amy married and in his home in Bath, or even at his estate in Suffolk County. Even, perhaps, with a child or two.

That vision was quickly replaced with a picture of him swinging from the end of a rope and Amy crying at his feet. He shook his head. He needed to keep a positive attitude. It was time to visit with Amy and see what she had come up with.

Luckily, just then Colbert stood. "I believe I will be on my way." He bent over Mother's hand and kissed the air above it. William rolled his eyes.

"I will walk you out, Colbert. I have an appointment myself."

"Your mother is a most charming woman, Wethington," Colbert said as they made their way down the front steps.

William merely nodded.

Colbert put his hand on William's arm to stop him. "I want you to know I have no improper designs on your mother. It is important for me to tell you that, because if anything more develops between us, I don't want you loading your pistol."

"Thank you for that, Colbert. I understand my mother is an adult and has been a wife and mother. But on the other hand, she is under my protection, and I will not tolerate any sort of shenanigans where she is concerned."

Colbert gave him a slight bow. "I admire you for that, Wethington. Have a good day." He turned on his heel and, whistling slightly, continued down the pavement.

William decided to ride his horse to Amy's house instead of taking the carriage. If they needed privacy, perhaps they could go for a walk.

When he arrived, Stevens opened the door and waved him in. "I will notify Lady Amy that you have come, my lord. You may wait in the drawing room."

William thanked him and made his way up to the drawing room; he'd been here so many times that he knew his way around quite well. He wandered the room, too restless to sit.

He thought about the summons he'd received from Nelson-Graves earlier in the day, asking him to visit the next morning to go over some paperwork. The barrister had also mentioned the appointment book that William had yet to locate.

Hopefully Nelson-Graves had received William's business file that the police had been holding. He had requested copies of the documents contained in the file. Since copying papers was a time-consuming and arduous job, William had his doubts that everything in the file would be copied. He assumed Nelson-Graves could subpoena the file, but that thought scared him even more, because such things usually happened in preparation for a trial.

William firmly hoped to have the entire mess straightened out before it went that far.

"Good afternoon, William. How are you today?" Amy entered the room, looking quite pleased with herself.

He grinned, always happy in her presence. "I am as well as can be expected, given the state of my life recently. You, on the other hand, look like the cat who stole the cream."

"Yes. Well, I have something here that might be of interest to you." She waved a paper at him and then moved to the settee and settled there, waving him over. "Do you want tea?"

"No. I just flooded my body with tea while I watched over my mother and Colbert."

"How did that go?"

William shifted and rested his foot on his bent knee. "He really is a nice man. I know I'm just being overprotective because—well, because she is my mother, and I am overprotective."

Just then Persephone raced into the room, jumped up on Amy's lap, looked over at him, and growled.

"Your dog just loves me."

Amy shook her head and sighed. "I don't understand what is wrong with her. I have learned that there is a man who practices veterinary medicine in London. I was thinking of taking her there to have her examined."

"That is quite a trip; is there no one local?"

"I will continue to ask around, because I'm not sure I can take her on the railway. I believe there is accommodation in a special car for horses, but I'm not sure about dogs."

"Well, that is something to consider once we have all of this straightened out."

Amy scooped Persephone off her lap and placed her alongside her on the settee. The dog turned in a circle and then settled right next to Amy's thigh. Between her and William.

"Now I want to share with you what I discovered." She picked up the papers she'd brought into the room with her. "I tried my best to figure out the name of the person on the page that was muddied up."

She shifted so she could show William the paper. "This isn't definite, since I only had a few letters to go by. Probably about every other one was smeared. Here is what I made of the name with our code." She handed the paper to William.

His brows rose. "George Davidson?"

"Yes. Do you know Mr. Davidson's first name?"

William shook his head. "I don't think I do. I never heard him referred to as anything but Mr. Davidson. That should be easy enough to discover, however. If it is our Mr. Davidson, that makes two people in our book club that were being blackmailed by Harding."

Amy nodded. "Who would think quiet book club members would have done something so horrid that they were willing to pay Mr. Harding to keep his mouth closed?"

"You never know, do you?" His thoughts immediately went to Mr. Colbert, who was also a very benign, innocuous sort of man, and was also interested in his mother. It would do well to investigate him too. After they found the murderer. "I think our next step is to see if this man is our Mr. Davidson, and if he is, do some investigation on him."

"I agree, since it appears the police have no intention of doing their job correctly and fairly." Amy tapped her chin. "Davidson is almost always at the Assembly. Since I've never seen him dance with anyone and he's not terribly social, I've often wondered why he attends. But I suggest we spend some time with him tomorrow night." Amy paused. "Were you planning on going?"

"I have no choice. I must conduct my life as if nothing were wrong. If I hide away, it won't help our investigation and may start some talk. I want this kept quiet until we can resolve it. My business reputation has already been smeared, thanks to Mr. Harding. I have hired a new man of business, Mr. Frank Wilson, who was recommended to me by your father. He is working with my solicitor to get things straightened out."

"Then we shall attend the Assembly and see what we can learn."

"Hopefully no one else will be murdered before then, or I may be passing the time tomorrow night in jail."

CHAPTER 27

William had been attending the Saturday night dances for years, but never had he felt so unsure of himself as he did upon entering the well-known Assembly rooms this night.

Almost as if she understood his dilemma, Amy squeezed his arm as they stepped into the room. Everything looked normal, and no one was staring at him or gasping in horror.

"No one knows, William," Amy whispered. For some blessed reason, his arrest had not been in the newspapers. He was certain Mr. Nelson-Graves had something to do with that. Word of a peer's arrest would undoubtedly spread like wildfire around the city, but nothing here seemed out of the ordinary.

He breathed a sigh of relief and walked them both to the small circle of book club friends who always made it to these events. He was pleased to see that Mr. Davidson and his friend Mr. Rawlings were part of the group.

Mr. Colbert had arrived earlier at the Wethington town-house to escort his mother to the dance. William was happy to see them standing with the others. Mr. Colbert had not absconded with William's mother. Then he scolded himself for being so very suspicious of a man he'd known for years as an upstanding member of society and the book club.

But then, William was also considered an upstanding member of society and of the book club. And he had two murder charges as well as some shady business dealings hanging over his head.

"Good evening, everyone." William and Amy both spoke at once. They received return greetings, nods, and welcomes.

The group chatted for a while, giving opinions on the book the club members were currently reading. The music started up, and Amy looked at Mr. Davidson. "Mr. Davidson, I have never seen you on the dance floor. Would you care to partner with me in this dance?"

Davidson looked like he was about to be executed. Or was about to bring up his dinner. Mr. Rawlings, standing next to him, nudged him in his ribs. "Go dance, George."

Amy flicked her eyes at William, who was staring back at her. They had already answered their first question. The chances of there being more than one George Davidson were much lower than the chances of there being more than one Mr. Davidson.

Mr. Davidson ran his finger along the inside of his cravat and nodded. Instead of taking Amy's arm, he turned and walked to the area where the other dancers were gathering. Amy looked over at William and shrugged, then followed the man.

The dance would not allow for much conversation between Amy and Davidson. Even in the few years William had been attending the Assemblies, balls had seen the great variety of dances from the past dwindle to just the waltz and the two-step. The Bath Assembly, however, had kept many of the older dances alive, and this one was a cotillion.

William watched Amy and Mr. Davidson dance and noted that the man was surprisingly adept at the movements. That left him wondering why he never indulged in dancing. He glanced over at Mr. Rawlings, who watched every move Davidson made.

Theirs seemed to be a strange relationship.

"William, I heard from Atkinson and Tucker that there seems to be a problem with E. D. Burton appearing at our book fair," Mr. Colbert said.

"Indeed?" William thought back on Lord Winchester's attempt to get him to agree to hire someone to take Amy's place at the book event. He hoped it would be resolved and Amy would be granted her due.

"Did they say what the problem was?"

Mr. Colbert shook his head. "No. They only said there was an issue with the author. It's quite possible the man is elderly and doesn't possess the stamina to deal with such an event. As far as I know, no one has ever seen him."

William merely nodded, since there was nothing he could contribute to the conversation. Once the dance ended, Davidson walked with Amy back to the group and mumbled, "Excuse me, my lady, I need some fresh air," and made a beeline for the front door, leaving Amy behind, and moving so quickly that one would think he was being pursued by wild animals.

"That was fun," she said. "I believe I would enjoy a glass of lemonade, my lord. Would you care to accompany me?"

William took her arm, and they both moved away from the circle and headed toward the refreshment table. "It appears Davidson is a fairly good dancer," Amy said.

"Yes, I noticed. I also noticed that Mr. Rawlings seemed to watch Davidson quite a bit."

"Do you think he was jealous of his friend?" She grinned. Then the smile faded from her lips. "Do you suppose . . ." Then she shook her head. "No. That's ridiculous."

"What?"

"Nothing. Just ignore me, I had a silly idea for a moment."

They finished their lemonade and then strolled the room, speaking with various friends and acquaintances.

"At least we now know the chances are good that our Mr. Davidson is the same Mr. Davidson in Harding's ledger," Amy said.

"Yes, most likely so. What we need to do now is uncover why he was being blackmailed and then trace his movements at the time of the two murders."

"We still don't know why Miss Gertrude and Mrs. Barrows were being blackmailed."

"Yes, that's true. I wonder if there is a way to find out."

Amy smiled as Aunt Margaret and Lord Pembroke passed by, dipping and swirling to the waltz the musicians played. "My lord, we have not danced all evening."

William took her by the hand and led her to the dance area. The number was probably halfway over, but if Amy wanted to dance, they would dance.

A few hours later, having had his fill of dancing and socializing, William happily escorted Amy out of the Assembly building. Mr. Davidson and Mr. Rawlings had exited just before them. The four conversed as they awaited the arrival of their carriages.

It was the first time William had actually spoken to Mr. Rawlings, who had always kept his thoughts to himself at the meetings. "How are you enjoying our book club, Rawlings?"

"I do enjoy it. I realize I don't contribute much, but I listen to what everyone else is saying. I find it quite interesting." He paused for a moment. "I am looking forward to E. D. Burton's appearance." He looked directly at Amy. "I'm sure his arrival will be quite a surprise for everyone. Don't you agree, Lady Amy?"

William's eyes grew wide and he looked at Amy, who appeared to be stunned. She quickly recovered herself, however, and said, "Yes. I imagine it will be interesting to meet the author."

Rawlings threw his head back and laughed. The other three just stared at him.

Just then Davidson's carriage drew up. Rawlings entered first and Davidson followed. "Well, good night," he said, and closed the door.

William's carriage was next in line. He opened the door for Amy and climbed in after her. Once they were settled, the vehicle rolled forward. "What did Mr. Rawlings mean?" she asked.

"I have no idea. It was almost as if he knew you were E. D. Burton."

"I know. How very strange. I don't see how he would have that information."

"Actually, we know so little about Mr. Rawlings. It's possible he might know your identity. He might have some contact with your publisher for one reason or another."

They continued on their way and soon were stopped in traffic. William glanced out the window and nodded. "I believe that is Davidson's carriage right next to us."

Amy turned her head to look. A gaslight on the other side of the street briefly lit the carriage before it rolled forward. A couple came into view, kissing. Amy sucked in a deep breath and covered her mouth. "That can't be Mr. Davidson's carriage!"

The vehicles began to move again, and William's fell behind. He thought about what they'd seen and suddenly realized why Davidson had been blackmailed.

"Amy, I am not sure I should even be discussing this with you, but do you know anything about the book *The Picture of Dorian Gray* by Mr. Oscar Wilde?"

"Yes. I've read it."

William ran his hand down his face. "Of course you have."

"I am an enlightened woman, William. As an author, I must read everything. I cannot shield myself from any subject, no matter how displeasing society finds certain topics."

"Well, if that's the case, then you must realize what we just saw could very well have been Mr. Davidson's carriage. In fact, that explains a lot."

"Oh." Despite her ramblings alluding to her sophistication and knowledge, even in the dark carriage he could see her blush. "Then that means . . ."

"Yes. It means precisely what we're thinking. And it certainly answers some questions and raises a few more. After all the time Davidson has been a member of the club, why did Rawlings show up at the book club when he did? In fact, if memory serves, he appeared with Mr. Davidson right after Harding was killed."

He leaned forward, excited by this new idea. "That is probably the reason Davidson was being blackmailed. Such acts are illegal and not only can destroy a man's reputation but send him to prison. If Harding stumbled upon that information, it would be worth it to Mr. Davidson to pay him to keep it quiet."

"And perhaps a reason to kill him so he no longer had to pay."

"Yes." William leaned back. "But that is true of everyone he was blackmailing and cheating."

"I never thought I would say this, but poor Mr. Davidson. I don't understand why, or approve of, the way the government interferes in people's private lives." Amy shook her head.

"I agree, but as long as it is against the law, Davidson must be very careful."

"I think it would be worth our time to learn where Mr. Davidson was the night Harding was murdered," Amy said.

William gave her a curt nod. "I agree. And then moving along to another matter, what about Mrs. Johnson? We need a sketch of Mr. Davidson to show to people at the pub. If he was there the night she was killed, we might have our man."

Amy scooted forward until their knees touched. "And also find out if he has a gun. If it is Mr. Davidson, he was most likely the one who tried to find the ledger and then shot at us."

"It appears we have a lot to consider with this new suspect."

Once again they were stopped in traffic and found their carriage next to Mr. Davidson's. This time the curtain was pulled across the window. Amy and William looked over at each other and nodded.

★ ★ ★

The following Tuesday, Amy rested on the settee with Persephone sprawled on top of her. She studied the little animal's face with concern. "What is wrong with you, little doggy?"

Not only was she very clingy, but she was ill-tempered and had put on weight. "Too much eating and lying around and not enough exercise. We must go for a walk today." Amy sat up and ran her palm over the animal's soft fur.

William had spent time with his barrister yesterday and this morning, but Amy expected him any minute. They would take Persephone for a walk and while they were out and about discuss the next steps in their investigation.

The sound of footsteps coming up to the first floor drew Amy's attention. Aunt Margaret walked into the drawing room, tugging on her gloves. "It is quite chilly out there today."

"Is it really? I was hoping to take Persephone for a walk."

Her aunt looked at the dog. "She looks far too comfortable to me to rally herself for a walk."

"Aunt Margaret, I have a favor to ask of you."

She sat on the settee across from Amy. "I assume this has to do with James's murder?"

"Yes."

"I will be happy to oblige. What do you need?"

"I would like you to accompany me to the book club meeting this Thursday."

Her aunt closed her eyes. "Oh Amy, my dear. Anything but that."

"Oh, please, aunt. It's very important, and it's not so bad."

"Sitting around listening to you and your cohorts discussing murder, mayhem, and dead bodies?" She shuddered. "I prefer sunshine and happiness."

Amy smirked. "Well. . . . I did attend some morning calls with you. Besides, you can stuff cotton into your ears if you like. I only need you to do a sketch for me. You are so very good at drawing, I know you can capture one of our members on paper."

Aunt Margaret sighed as if she were being asked to take her place at the guillotine. "I will do it for you. And for poor William, who is in a very difficult place right now."

"Thank you so much. With your sketch, we might be able to establish that Mr. Davidson was at the pub the night Mrs. Johnson was killed. Then we would be one step closer to solving Mr. Harding's murder too."

"Mr. Davidson from the Assembly dances?"

"Yes. Do you know him?"

"I remember meeting him a few times at the dances. He's an odd man. Very quiet, always seems to be studying everyone."

Just then Stevens stepped into the drawing room. "My lady, Lord Wethington awaits you downstairs."

"Thank you." Amy looked down at Persephone, who looked so very comfortable, and sighed. "I guess I won't take her for a walk today after all." Amazingly enough, the dog shifted and closed her eyes, and made no effort to bark when Amy left the room.

Once she and William began their walk, she told him about Aunt Margaret accompanying them on Thursday for the purpose of sketching Mr. Davidson.

"I didn't know your aunt had such talent."

"Yes. She does. She paints a little bit too, but drawing is really where her talent lies. I just wish she would do more with it, but she always just considered it a hobby."

"Unlike you, who turned your hobby into a career."

"Thank you for that, William. Yes, it is my career."

The wind picked up, and it grew quite cold for walking. "I think we should go back to your house. I'll get my carriage and we can ride to a tea shop."

Amy nodded, beginning to shiver. "Yes. A very good idea."

The walk back was much quicker, and the wind was at their back. William retrieved his carriage from the mews, and his driver soon had them on the road and heading to the center of Bath, where most of the stores and shops were.

"Can we go to Sally Lunn's? I haven't had one of her buns in a long time."

"An excellent idea," William said. "I haven't been there for a while myself."

Sally Lunn's was housed in one of the oldest buildings in Bath. The secret recipe for its famous buns had been handed down for ages and had earned the tea shop many returning customers. The place was also a favorite spot for tourists.

"How was your meeting with Mr. Nelson-Graves?"

William's demeanor immediately grew more serious. "It's not looking good, unfortunately. It appears a date for a trial is being worked out with the House of Lords. Since I am a peer, I must be tried there."

"Then everyone knows about your charges?"

"No. Not yet, anyway. Mr. Nelson-Graves is keeping my name out of it until he has no choice but to reveal it. I am hoping to have the true killer behind bars before it gets that far."

They settled in a seat near the window, watching those brave enough to walk around in the chilly air.

"I must make a visit to Mrs. Carol Whitney," William said as they waited for their tea. "With all that has happened, I forgot to report back to her that I found her stepson—that he has been ill but is now on the mend."

"I wonder how he's getting on with Mrs. Johnson dead. It was her house he was living in, isn't that so?"

"Yes. He went there when he began to feel sick, and she took care of him."

"That was very nice of her. He must feel terrible about her death."

"Yes. I'm sure he was notified by the police."

"He might not even still be there."

William shrugged. "That is a possibility. But first we must visit with Mrs. Whitney and let her know her stepson is all right."

"Have we removed her from our list, then?"

William lips tightened. "No one is being removed from our list until this is over. The only person who I know for a fact is innocent is me."

CHAPTER 28

"Have you seen my copy of *The Woman in White*? I know I left it here in the drawing room." Lady Wethington wandered around the room, looking under chairs and tables.

William looked up from his comfortable chair in the drawing room, where he was reading his morning newspaper. "I believe I saw the book in the kitchen, of all places. I thought perhaps Cook had decided to join our book club too."

"Oh dear. That is correct. I remember having it in my hands when I went to visit Cook yesterday to arrange for my dinner party."

"Dinner party?" He lowered his newspaper and watched his mother blush prettily.

"Yes." She raised her chin. "I decided it was time we held a social affair or two."

"If I remember correctly, we had Lady Amy's family for dinner less than a month past."

"My dear son. Having guests for dinner once a month hardly signifies entertaining. Once you marry, you know Lady Amy will want socializing."

"Wait. What makes you think Lady Amy and I will marry?"

He grew uneasy when she merely stared at him with raised brows and a *you don't fool me* look. He picked up his newspaper, shook it to straighten it out, and continued to read.

"I am planning a dinner party for a week from Friday."

He lowered the newspaper again. "Mother, with murder charges hanging over my head, I don't think this is the best time to plan any sort of entertainment."

She waved her hand as if murder charges were something any dimwit could deal with. "That will all be cleared up any day now. There is no need to avoid normal life."

"Madam, I just indicated that dinner parties were not part of my normal life to begin with."

"You worry too much, my dear. All will be fine." She did that awful pat-on-the-head thing again.

"I wish I had your optimism," he mumbled to his newspaper.

But alas, she was not going to permit him his morning indulgence. "I have the list here of guests, which I would like you to approve."

"Me? Why would I need to approve? It appears you have everything in hand."

Instead of answering him, she slid the guest list between him and his newspaper. He lowered the paper again. "Very well. Since I will have no peace until I do this, let me look it over.

"Mr. Colbert! Why is he invited? I have never socialized with the man." When no answer was forthcoming, he continued to peruse the list: Mr. Charles Colbert, Miss Gertrude O'Neill, Miss Penelope O'Neill, Mr. George (how had she gotten his name?) Davidson, Mr. Christopher Rawlings, Lady Amy Lovell, Lady Margaret Lovell, Lord Franklin Winchester, Lord Michael Davenport.

"Some are book club members, along with all of Lady Amy's family. What are you planning, Mother?"

She looked very innocent. "A dinner party. I just told you."

Knowing his mother as he did, he would get no further information from her, but a sinking feeling in his stomach told him he had a good idea of what she was planning. Perhaps he should visit a jeweler in town before the dinner.

On the other hand, three of the intended guests were on their suspect list: Miss Gertrude, Mr. Davidson, and Mr. Christopher Rawlings, whom he had mentally added after witnessing the embrace in Davidson's carriage the other night. It was apparent that Mr. Davidson and Mr. Rawlings were lovers, and since that was illegal and punishable by law, they would both want to keep Harding silenced.

"Do you care to see the menu?"

He shook his newspaper, which would have been a signal to anyone else that he was irritated with the constant inter-ruptions. Mother had always been an exception to normal rules. "No. I am certain whatever you work out with Cook will be excellent."

"We do want to make it special."

He ignored that statement.

"Certain events require a special menu."

When he remained silent, she said, "Don't you agree, William?"

He pinched the bridge of his nose. Perhaps he could wait until this afternoon and read the morning paper along with the evening paper.

"Yes. I agree, Mother. However, now I must leave for an appointment. I am sure whatever you plan will be wonderful. I await the festivities with great fervor." He stood, placed his newspaper on the table next to his chair, gave her a slight bow, and left the room.

★   ★   ★

If Amy was surprised at his early arrival, she didn't show it. Instead, she greeted him with a huge smile. "Good morning, my lord. I didn't expect you so early, but I am happy to see you."

"Things were a bit uncomfortable at home."

She led him to a sofa in the drawing room. "Why is that?"

How much to tell Amy? Should he share his suspicions? She continued to stare at him.

"Mother is planning a dinner and wanted my advice on it, and you know how little I know about such things."

"Yes, we all received invitations."

He said, "She's invited Mr. Colbert as well."

"That is quite interesting. It appears they are becoming a couple."

William grunted. "As long as his ideas of a *couple* don't encompass anything untoward."

"Oh, for heaven's sake, William, you sound like an old shriveled-up spinster."

He was gentleman enough not to mention that, given her age, she could herself be considered a spinster. Except Amy was much too lively, intelligent, and bold to hold that moniker.

"I was preparing to have luncheon soon. Papa, Michael, and Aunt Margaret will be joining me. I hope you will stay as well?"

A meal with another parent staring him down with that expression so evident in his mother's eyes these days. "Yes. I would be honored. Then I think we should go as planned to

Mrs. Whitney's house and let her know her stepson has been ill but now seems to be on the road to recovery."

"After all this time, she must be quite anxious."

"I know. I feel bad about that. I would also like to visit with Patrick Whitney. I'm almost sure the police would have visited Mrs. Johnson's house when her body was found, so he should already know about her death. But I do want to ask him a couple of questions about her and offer my condolences."

"Wethington, good to see you." Amy's father strode across the room, his hand outstretched. William shook hands with him, and then Winchester slapped him on the back, almost sending him to the floor. "Joining us for luncheon, I hope?"

William straightened his jacket and smoothed back his hair. "Yes, sir. Lady Amy was gracious enough to invite me."

Winchester rubbed his hands. "Good, good. How about a small drink?" He strode to the sideboard, poured two glasses, and brought one over. William rarely drank spirits before the sun set, but not wanting to seem ungracious—or possibly judgmental—he accepted the glass.

Amy's father waved to one of the chairs. "Have a seat, son. Haven't seen you in a while."

Both of them settled with their glasses of brandy.

Isn't this cozy?

"Lady Amy tells me you're still having some issues with the police."

Issues with the police. That's an interesting way to refer to two murder charges. The man must be taking lessons from my mother.

"Yes. Mr. Nelson-Graves is being most helpful. I hope to have them cleared up directly."

"Good, good."

"Company, how lovely." Aunt Margaret sailed into the room. "And we're drinking so early?" Her raised eyebrows were directed at Amy's father.

"Would you care for a sherry, sister? Amy?"

Both refused.

"Are we having a party, then?" Amy's brother, Michael, entered the drawing room. "I'll have a brandy." He walked to the sideboard and poured himself a drink.

They all chatted amiably until Stevens announced that luncheon was ready.

It was a pleasant lunch—white soup, salmon with a dill sauce, potatoes, and a mix of carrots and turnips. The conversation was lively, and Lord Winchester kept them laughing with stories about his travels when he was a young man.

It was obvious the family got along well, even though Lord Winchester chided his sister about not marrying. Once or twice he directed his comments about the married state to Michael, but the earl never took the bait. Smart man.

'Twas interesting that Winchester never mentioned Amy and a potential match for her, although he looked at William more than once with a speculative eye.

Soon the meal ended and he and Amy were on their way to Mrs. Whitney's house.

★ ★ ★

Amy breathed a sigh of relief when she and William were ensconced in his carriage and on their way to visit Carol Whitney. With all the comments Papa had directed toward Aunt Margaret and Michael regarding the state of matrimony, Amy had waited for him to start in on her and William.

She was truly amazed he had not. Strange, that.

"Do you know if Mr. Whitney normally lives with his stepmother?"

"I don't know. I assume he has his own rooms somewhere and that's the reason he sought help in his illness. He told me Mrs. Whitney worried too much about everything, and I imagine that's why he sought Mrs. Johnson's assistance when he fell ill."

"Do you find his relationship with his stepmother a bit odd?"

"What do you mean?" William asked.

"She apparently hadn't been married very long to his father, and yet she and Patrick seem to have a close friendship. Also, even though I never met Patrick Whitney, you haven't mentioned his relationship with his father. For example, was he upset by his death? From what you've told me, he seemed more concerned with Mrs. Whitney's finances than his father's death."

"Perhaps he feels he must support her in the event the money is gone."

"Perhaps." The carriage pulled up to a modest townhouse in an excellent section of Bath. It appeared that Mrs. Whitney's husband had provided well for his wife upon his death.

"Is she expecting us?" Amy asked as they climbed the steps to the front door.

"Yes. I sent a note around advising her we would be calling this afternoon with word about Patrick."

A butler opened the door to them. He was an elderly man, tall and distinguished, a member of the old class of servants.

William held out his card. "Lord Wethington and Lady Amy Lovell calling on Mrs. Whitney. I believe we are expected."

"Very good, my lord, my lady. Allow me to take your coats." They shrugged out of their outerwear and then followed the servant upstairs to the drawing room. "Mrs. Whitney will be with you shortly." He bowed and left the room.

It was a cozy space, small for a drawing room but tastefully decorated. It also didn't contain all the little trinkets and whatnot that were so popular in most homes.

Mrs. Whitney made her entrance with a bright smile. "Lord Wethington and Lady Amy, how pleasant to see you."

They both stood and offered greetings.

"Please, have a seat."

They all settled in, and she folded her hands in her lap. "What news can you give me of my stepson? I am very concerned about his disappearance."

"I am happy to report that your stepson is well. He was ill for a while, but he is on his way to recovery."

"Oh dear. What happened? Why didn't he come to me to take care of him?"

"Apparently he developed an illness and went to the home of a woman he had been friendly with for years."

"Had been?"

William looked as though he wanted to call back the words he had just said. "Yes, unfortunately, the woman— Mrs. Johnson—passed away a few days ago."

"Oh, how sad."

William nodded. "Yes, very sad."

Amy was grateful he didn't add that she had been shot and left behind the pub where she worked.

Mrs. Whitney grasped her throat. "She didn't die from what Patrick was suffering, did she?"

"No."

William jumped in to avert any more questions about Mrs. Johnson and her death. "When I visited with Mr. Whitney, he mentioned he would contact you as soon as he was feeling better."

Something flickered in her eyes. Maybe her relationship with Patrick was not as wonderful as she would have them believe. "Thank you for that. I was most concerned."

Since there didn't seem to be much more to say, they stood and wished her a good day and left the house.

"What do you make of that?" Amy asked.

"You mean in relation to Harding's murder?"

"Yes."

"She seemed genuinely surprised by Mrs. Johnson's death, and since we are convinced whoever killed her also killed Harding, I would say she falls farther down on our suspect list."

"But not off?"

"No one is off." William checked his timepiece as they settled into the carriage. "I believe we have time to visit with Patrick Whitney. I am curious to see if he is still at Mrs. Johnson's." He slid the panel in the roof. "Please take us to Millie Johnson's house. I believe you remember where it is?"

"Yes, my lord."

William slid the panel closed, and the carriage moved forward. "I sense we are at a stalemate. I also have a feeling that we are looking at something and not seeing the entire picture."

"A missing piece?"

"Yes. Either a missing piece or something not aligned. There is also the fact that Mrs. Johnson had something to tell us that probably caused her death."

They continued to the woman's house, both quiet with their thoughts.

It took a while for anyone to answer their knock. They were about to leave when the door opened to a very disheveled Patrick. "Oh, it's you." He opened the door wider and stepped back. "Please, come in."

William looked over at Amy as they entered. Patrick looked terrible.

"May I present Lady Amy Lovell?" He turned to Amy. "This is Mr. Patrick Whitney."

The two merely nodded at each other.

"Are you still ill, Whitney?" William asked.

"No. Just grieving." He led them to the drawing room, and they all sat. He shook his head and ran his fingers through his hair. "A terrible thing."

Although he didn't look sick this time, he had dark circles under his bloodshot eyes, and his hand shook as he picked up a newspaper from the sofa and placed it on the table.

"I am so sorry about Mrs. Johnson."

He merely dipped his head and sighed. "Thank you. I have not been able to sleep or eat since she passed away."

Amy was growing more uncomfortable as they remained. Patrick just sat there, staring into space.

Finally, William said, "We stopped in to see how you were doing and also to tell you your stepmother has been advised of your illness."

He looked over at William. "She is not worried, is she?"

"No. I told her you were on the way to recovery."

"Good, good." He continued to stare, giving a slight sigh every once in a while.

Amy caught William's eye and gestured with her head toward the door. In unison, they both stood.

"We will leave you now, Whitney. If there is anything we can do to help, please let us know."

"Thank you." He climbed from the sofa and walked them to the door. "I appreciate you stopping in."

"Will you be staying here for a while, then?"

"Not for long. I expect to return to my own rooms shortly."

"Well, we'll be off, then." William took Amy's arm, and they descended the steps and climbed into in the carriage.

"The poor man is a mess," Amy said.

"Yes." William stared at the house as they left, his brows furrowed.

CHAPTER 29

Amy and William entered the bookstore for the weekly meeting. Aunt Margaret had agreed to come with them but said she would browse the bookshelves for a while, then join them in the meeting and do a quick sketch of Mr. Davidson before the gathering broke up.

Miss Gertrude and Miss Penelope were standing in a circle with Lady Wethington and Mr. Colbert when they arrived. Amy noted that Mr. Colbert stood closer to Lady Wethington than anyone else.

Miss Gertrude hurried over to Amy, took her by the arm, and led her to one of the settees. "I am very upset, my lady, and I can't think of anyone else I can speak to about this."

"What is the matter, Miss Gertrude?

With shaky hands, the woman patted her upper lip with the handkerchief she clutched in her hands. "You know that horrible Mr. Harding was blackmailing me?"

"Yes. I agree, he is horrible, and yes, you told me he was blackmailing you. Does your upset have something to do with that?"

"Yes."

Amy took Miss Gertrude's ice-cold hands in hers. "What is the problem?"

The poor woman attempted to pull herself together. She straightened her shoulders and took a deep breath. "I received a letter in today's post. The writer of the missive claims to be in possession of the information Mr. Harding had and said he intended to continue with the blackmail." Her hurried words ran together.

Amy was shocked. Since she had the ledger, how did the author of the letter know whom Mr. Harding was blackmailing? Did Harding have a partner?

"I know you and Lord Wethington have been doing a search for Mr. Harding's killer, so I thought maybe you would know who this person is." She continued to wring her hands around the handkerchief.

Amy shook her head. "No, I am afraid not. However, let me speak with Lord Wethington about this and see if we can help in any way. In the meantime, do not agree to meet this person."

"But what am I to do?"

She studied the woman for a minute. "Is your secret so very terrible that it is better to continue paying someone than have it come to light?"

"Oh, yes!" Miss Gertrude reared back, her eyes wide. "It was something I had no control over, but if it is discovered, I would lose my position in society, church, and even here in the book club." She shook her head furiously. "No. I could never let that come to light."

From Miss Gertrude's demeanor and words, Amy suspected they could cross her off their list of suspects. She was much too distraught. Unless, of course, she was upset at the idea of having to kill another person. Two down and one more to go?

One would think that picking up where Mr. Harding left off in blackmailing his victims could be risky, since the man had been murdered. Amy squeezed the woman's hands. "Lord Wethington and I will do everything possible to help. But I wish to restate, do not agree to meet anyone, anywhere. The situation is much too dangerous."

Miss Gertrude slumped. "Thank you. I feel better just knowing the two of you might be able to help. I can't continue to pay. I've been taking the money from the inheritance our father left me and sister. It was supposed to last the rest of our lives. If I keep paying, the rest of our lives would not be more than a few more years." She shook her head. "That is so unfair to Penelope."

Amy wasn't sure if Miss Gertrude was attempting humor or if she was serious about how dire their money situation had grown.

"I will be in touch with you. Please try to calm yourself. You have a friend in me and Lord Wethington."

A lone tear tracked down Miss Gertrude's cheek. "Thank you so much. I can't tell you how wonderful it is to have you and Lord Wethington as friends."

Mr. Colbert called the meeting to order, and the members took their seats. Lady Wethington had come with Mr. Colbert, and she sat right at the front no more than five feet from him.

Mr. Davidson and Mr. Rawlings entered and took seats together on one of the settees.

Amy considered herself a sophisticated woman of the world, so she tried very hard not to stare at the two men. She had no feelings one way or the other about their sort of relationship; she just wished she didn't know quite so much about them as she did now.

"Friends, this week our discussion is on *The Lady in White*. I hope the ladies did not find it too strong for their nerves."

The women all shook their heads.

"In that case, let us start our discussion."

Mr. Davidson raised his hand. "Before we begin, Mr. Colbert, have you received any more information on Mr. Burton? Will he or will he not appear?"

"The latest news is the publisher is certain he will appear."

Several people smiled and nodded to each other. Amy felt her stomach sink to her feet. Papa had not said anything more about her appearance at the book fair since she handed him the last letter from the publisher threatening a lawsuit.

She'd been so thrilled when William disagreed with her papa in suggesting that they find a man to take her place. William was truly a remarkable man. If she ever were to consider marriage—she gulped at the thought—William would be her choice.

The meeting seemed to drag on forever, since Amy was anxious to speak to William about Miss Gertrude's revelation regarding her blackmailer. She was also eager to find the ledger in her room to make sure she still had it. How it would have disappeared was questionable, since she had servants in the house at all times. However, common sense said there must be some way the author of the letter to Miss Gertrude had gotten her name.

Near the end of the discussion, Aunt Margaret took a seat at the back of the room and was mostly ignored by everyone as she sketched her drawing. She'd managed to angle herself so she could see Mr. Davidson's face clearly.

Eventually, Mr. Colbert closed the meeting, and Amy, William, and Aunt Margaret left the room. Since Amy didn't want Aunt Margaret to know too much about what she and William were up to, she decided not to speak about Miss Gertrude while in Aunt Margaret's presence.

As their carriage pulled away, Mr. Colbert was helping William's mother into his carriage. William noticed and snorted.

"Here is your sketch of Mr. Davidson," Aunt Margaret said as she handed the drawing to Amy. "I just hope you aren't going to use this to get yourselves into more trouble."

Amy held it up to the lamp hanging on the wall of the carriage. "This is wonderful, Aunt Margaret." She passed it off to William, who also viewed it.

"Yes. You are a very good artist, Lady Margaret. It appears your family is quite talented." They chatted about the book they had discussed that night and would continue to read the coming week. Some books took two or three weeks to discuss to everyone's satisfaction, whereas others required only a week. Since this book was more complicated than some of the other tomes they had read, it would most likely take three weeks.

Silence fell as the carriage made its way through the Bath traffic and onto the quieter streets where Amy and Margaret's house lay.

"You are both so quiet," Aunt Margaret said. "Is something going on that I don't know about?"

Amy shook her head. "No. I don't know about his lordship, but I'm just a bit tired."

Just a few minutes later, they arrived. William helped Aunt Margaret out of the carriage, and when she waved him off, he climbed back in. "I have the feeling there is something you want to tell me."

"Yes. I spoke with Miss Gertrude tonight—you might have seen us when we first arrived at the bookstore."

"I did. She seemed upset, and I didn't want to interfere. What happened?"

"What happened is something I do not understand. She said she received a letter earlier today from someone who claimed he knew about her secret and intended to keep accepting the money Mr. Harding was taking."

William let out a low whistle. "That doesn't seem possible. Unless Harding had a partner."

"Either that or the ledger has been stolen."

"Then let's check." He helped Amy out of the vehicle, and they both made their way to the front door.

Stevens opened it for them. "Good evening, my lady, my lord."

Distracted, they both nodded and, without removing their coats, walked upstairs to the drawing room, where William waited as Amy took the stairs to the bedchambers floor.

Out of breath from hurrying and nervousness, Amy headed straight for her small office right outside her bedroom. She took a quick look around. Nothing seemed to be out of place.

She went directly to the drawer in her desk where she kept the ledger and gasped.

The ledger was gone.

William was pacing the drawing room, his hands behind his back, when she returned.

"It's gone." Amy flew through the doorway, panting. "I can't believe it, but it's gone."

"How is that possible? There are servants here all the time."

She shook her head, sat on the sofa, and placed her hand over her thumping heart. "I know. But there are times when the few servants we have might be out of the house, or in their rooms resting while on a break. Any number of things."

"Which means someone's been watching your house."

"Correct. But how did they know it was here? It could have just as likely been at your house. I'm assuming it's the same person who tried to get the ledger from Harding's house, then went through the window and dropped it in the mud."

"And shot at us." William ran his fingers through his hair.

Amy rubbed her palms up and down her arms. "I don't like the idea of someone being in my house." She shuddered. "In my room."

William reached out and pulled her to him. Wrapping his arms around her, he said, "Make sure you lock the door to your room every night."

She nodded.

"And the windows." He placed his finger under her chin and raised her head. "Who is at home now?"

"Aunt Margaret, of course, and I believe Papa. He said at dinner that he was going to stay in and spend a quiet night at home. Michael, however, is out somewhere." Amy leaned back. "I can't tell Papa about the break-in. He would be furious with me for getting involved in this."

"I never should have let you keep the ledger here. I should have taken it to my house."

"How do you know whoever it was didn't search your house first?"

"I don't know, and now I have reason to believe I did not misplace my appointment book after all and someone has been to my house as well. Maybe looking for both the ledger and the appointment book.

"I will do a thorough check of my house when I return tonight. However, I can't risk you getting hurt. I will ask Stevens to summon your father, and I will tell him everything."

"No! He will probably confine me to my room for the rest of the year."

"Amy." He viewed her with raised brows. "This has gone on long enough. This is my problem, not yours. Harding was my man of business. I am the one charged with his murder."

She pulled away and rested her hands on her hips. "I thought we were partners."

"We are. Or I should say we were. Things have changed. I should have stopped this when we were shot at."

She plopped onto the sofa. "I feel like we're so close."

He joined her. "I've been feeling for a while now that there is something right in front of me that I should be seeing, but I'm not." He pounded his fist on his thigh. "The problem is, there are several people who have stated that they were either very happy that Harding is dead or would have killed him, given the chance."

"People say those things, but rarely do they follow through. Whoever did this was able to perform a second murder as well. We're looking for someone who not only had a reason to kill him but the temperament to actually do it. Which I can't help but think leaves out Miss Gertrude, I'm sure."

"No one is left out until this is over."

"But she came to me so distressed that she received that letter."

William stood. "I will not speak with your father tonight, but you must promise me you will go nowhere outside this house alone. Preferably, if you do go somewhere, you will go with me."

"Actually, I could use a day to work on my book."

"Good. Stay in tomorrow. If you need to go anywhere, send me a missive. Either I will be at home working on my finances or my butler will know where I am to send word."

★ ★ ★

The next day William pulled out the bottom drawer of his desk, still searching for his appointment book, and groaned. The drawer was piled high with discarded newspapers, loose papers that he had thought at one time were important, and receipts that should have been filed away. No wonder his finances were a mess. He really needed to be more organized. Depending on his man of business had landed him in a dangerous spot.

He pulled out the stack and began to go through them, placing them in piles: some to be burned, some to be saved, and some to be given to his new man of business.

"William, I am taking a short trip into town, so I will be using the carriage. Have you need of it?" His mother entered the room, full of life and enthusiasm as usual.

"No. I plan to organize myself this morning. If I decide to go out this afternoon, I can take my horse, so keep the carriage for as long as you need it."

She stared at his desk. "Oh my, you do have quite a pile there. When was the last time you sorted through that?"

"Too long, to be sure."

He placed an old, folded newspaper on the desk, and it caught his mother's eye.

She picked it up. "Oh, I loved this play." Her eyes moved back and forth as she read the advert for a Drury Lane theater in London. "I saw it with your father many years ago." She hugged the newspaper to her chest.

"What play is that?" She seemed to want to talk about it, and he could certainly give her a few minutes of his time.

"*Othello*. It was well performed when your father and I saw it. However, years later I saw the play again with your sister before she moved to France. Iago in that performance was played by Patrick Whitney, one of the best actors ever."

William's head snapped up, and his hand stilled as he was reaching for a paper. "Did you say Patrick Whitney?"

"Yes. A very well-known actor. First in Dublin and then in London. However, he disappeared off the stage a few years ago."

William told himself to calm down. Patrick Whitney was not an unusual name.

"Mother, what did Patrick Whitney look like?"

She thought for a minute and then described his Patrick Whitney perfectly.

"And you say he no longer appears on the stage?"

"No. Not that I've heard. I still visited the theater quite a bit when I lived in London, but he hasn't done a play for at least two years that I know of. I wonder what happened to him?"

William sat and let out a huge breath. "I think he is right here in Bath."

"Indeed? Is he still acting? I would love to see him in a play once again. He had such a talent for bringing his character to life."

William studied his hands for a minute, his mind in a whirl, then looked up at his mother. "He may very well be acting again. Yes, perhaps he is, but not on the stage." He stood and walked around the desk. "If you will excuse me, Mother, I think I will take that ride now instead of later. Enjoy your shopping trip."

"Wait! What about this stack of papers?"

He waved as he left the room. "I will deal with them later."

CHAPTER 30

A my lifted Persephone and stared at her very rounded body. "We need to take more walks, my love. You are getting quite chubby."

"She's probably breeding." Aunt Margaret walked into the breakfast room and pulled out the chair across from Amy.

"Breeding?"

"Yes. Increasing, pregnant, expecting, gravid, with child—or rather, with puppy." She shook out her napkin and placed it on her lap. "You are going to be a grandmother."

Amy looked wide-eyed back and forth between Aunt Margaret and Persephone. "How did that happen?"

Aunt Margaret took a sip of her tea. "I know you are an unmarried, gently bred woman, Amy, but I am quite sure you have some knowledge of the workings of reproduction."

"Of course I do." She raised her chin. "However, Persephone is never out of the house."

"Given how strange she's been acting lately and her 'chubbiness,' I would say she did manage to escape her confines at some point."

"Persephone, you have been a naughty girl." Amy shook her head. "I have no idea how to deal with a dog giving birth."

"My dear, dogs have been giving birth since the beginning of time with no help from humans. When the time comes, she'll let you know."

Amy continued to look at Persephone. "I think I shall go to the bookstore and see if I can find any books on dogs' breeding."

"How goes your investigation into James's murder?"

"Not well, I'm afraid. We have a few suspects, but no one who really stands out. What is troubling is that just about everyone we've spoken to has indicated that, given the opportunity, they would have done away with the man. He certainly made a lot of enemies in his life."

"Strange. James had been doing business here in Bath for years. I wonder what made him turn to crime only recently?"

"William shared some confidential information with me that explained what happened. All I can tell you is he made some bad decisions and choices starting not too long after William hired him.

"This morning I am taking a trip into town to see a woman whom we've questioned once before. Mrs. Edith Burrows owns a hat shop, and she was also being blackmailed by Mr. Harding. She was not anxious to speak with us when William and I visited her before."

"Why do you think she will speak to you now?"

"I'm not sure she will, but she does have some lovely hats, and one in particular I might purchase. I'm hoping to work in a few questions while I shop." Amy took one more look at Persephone, shook her head, and left the room to the dog's wails.

★ ★ ★

When Amy arrived at the store, two women sat in front of small mirrors at a long table, trying on hats. Mrs. Burrows's lips tightened when she saw Amy, but then she offered a slight smile. "Lady Amy, how pleasant to see you again."

"And you as well, Mrs. Burrows." She walked up to the table that the store owner stood behind. "I would like to try on a few hats."

Mrs. Burrows relaxed her stiff stance and offered an even brighter smile. "That's wonderful. Please have a seat and tell me the hat for which you have a fancy."

Amy chatted easily with the other customers while she tried on a number of lovely hats. Once the store emptied out, she said, "I think I would like to purchase these." She pointed to the two lovely confections sitting on the table in front of her.

"Splendid choices, my lady. They both looked exquisite on you."

As Mrs. Burrows commenced wrapping up the hats, Amy said, "It must be nice to no longer have to pay Mr. Harding." She quickly smiled at the woman in sympathy, hoping she wouldn't throw her two hats at her.

Mrs. Burrows looked up at Amy, and her eyes filled with tears. "I'm afraid not." She began to wring her hands, and her lip quivered. "I received a letter from someone just two days ago who said he had Mr. Harding's records and he was going to continue to collect the blackmail money."

Amy leaned forward and took the woman's hand. "How terrible. Do you have any idea who this person is?"

Mrs. Burrows shook her head. "No. Mr. Harding never had anyone else with him each time I met with him. What is so distressing is what I'm being blackmailed for is something I had no control over. I'm just glad I was able to escape without having it held over my head."

"Mrs. Burrows, I would like you to know that we ask these questions of you not out of some sort of morbid curiosity or because we want to do you some harm, but as my friend Lord Wethington mentioned during our last visit, he is the one the police are convinced was Mr. Harding's killer."

Mrs. Burrows drew in a deep breath. "How terrible for him." She shook her head. "I can tell just by looking at his lordship that he would never do something like that."

Although Amy enjoyed the woman's confidence in William's innocence, her statement was borne more out of emotion than fact, since she knew nothing about William.

"I appreciate your faith in Lord Wethington. However, the police don't seem to agree."

Mrs. Burrows handed the two hats to Amy along with a slip of paper stating the total price for the merchandise. Usually Amy had bills sent to her house for payment, but since she had not set up an account with this store, she fumbled in her reticule to come up with the needed money.

Almost as if reading her mind, Mrs. Burrows said, "I will be happy to open an account for you and send a bill."

"I would like to set up an account, actually—I really do love your work. But I have the money with me today to pay." Amy placed the coins on the table.

She rose to leave, happy, both with her hats and with the friendship she'd made with the woman. "Have a pleasant day, Mrs. Burrows, and I will be back to buy more hats and hopefully let you know Lord Wethington and I have been successful and your concerns about blackmailing have ended." She moved toward the door.

What I'm being blackmailed for I had no control over.

The words kept repeating in her mind. If Amy could find out why the two women were being blackmailed, it might help in their investigation. Especially now that someone had the records and knew their secrets.

"God bless you," Mrs. Burrows said, as Amy opened the door, the light tinkle of the bell ringing in her ears.

After a slight pause, Amy said, "Mrs. Burrows, do you by chance know a Miss Gertrude O'Neill?"

Mrs. Burrows's eyes grew wide. "Gertie? Oh goodness, don't tell me she's being blackmailed too."

★ ★ ★

William rose in the morning with a sense of excitement, feeling that very shortly something great would happen in their investigation. The ride he'd taken the day before on Major had done a lot to clear his mind. He'd purposely avoided places he would meet people he knew, as he wanted time to think and see if he could make sense of what they had so far.

His first order of business after his valet shaved and prepared him for the day was a hearty breakfast to begin what he hoped would be the last of the investigation into Harding's death.

The clue he'd received from his own mother that Patrick Whitney was an actor, and a fine one at that, had immediately given him hope that the illness and grieving Patrick had presented were an act, merely his way of giving himself an alibi for when Harding was killed.

His acting might also have been a way for him to pass himself off as a messenger or some other sort of daily worker in order to gain access to his house and Amy's house.

William hated to think so, but it was conceivable that Patrick had killed Mrs. Johnson also, if he'd thought she was going to hinder his alibi. He must have been one of the people sitting in the corner at the pub the night he and Amy visited and Mrs. Johnson told them to meet her the next day.

It was possible that Patrick had indeed been enraged at the thievery committed by Harding with his stepmother's trust. However, since he was friends with Mrs. Johnson, it wouldn't have been too difficult for him to learn about Harding's other nefarious activities and his habit of collecting from his victims at the King's Garden. Kill the man; step into his shoes as a blackmailer. To do that, he would have needed to get his hands on the ledger.

If what William had begun to put together was true, it would have been Patrick who broke into Harding's home before them and attempted to steal the ledger, then shot at them.

William greeted his mother with a kiss on her cheek and took a seat across from her. "You are looking lovely this morning." He added toast, eggs, kippers, bacon, and beans to his plate. Excitement at the possibility that he would soon hand the true killer over to the police had spurred his mood and appetite.

"And you are quite cheerful yourself." She beamed at him. "I have the menu worked out for our dinner party. I would be pleased to have you review it to make sure there isn't anything that our guests would not enjoy."

The dinner party.

The devil take it. He'd been so busy the last few days meeting with his barrister, solicitor, and man of business as well as trying to clear his name as a suspect that he'd forgotten about the blasted dinner party.

"If you will place it on my desk, I promise upon my return later today I will look it over. As soon as I finish breakfast, I am off again."

"My, you are certainly busy these days. I hope you can clear up that murder nonsense before the dinner party."

William almost laughed. His mother wasn't concerned that he was a suspect in two murders—only in how it would affect her dinner party. "I am trying my best, Mother."

She patted his hand. "That's good, dear. And thank you so much for the extra gardener you sent. He did a wonderful job with that part of the flower garden that was looking quite sad."

"Extra gardener?"

"Yes. A lovely man—even did some arrangements in the house for us."

He had no idea what Mother was talking about, but with more important issues to deal with, he dismissed her words.

His first trip of the day would be to the Principal Probate Registry, which had copies of every will proved in Somerset County. He wanted to see for himself if Patrick Whitney had in fact received a great deal of money from his father, as he had stated.

The clerk at the Registry was a pleasant young man. He handed William a paper to fill out to see a copy of the pro-bated will. Within minutes the will was placed in front of him.

He flipped through the pages, taking notes. When he was finished, he thanked the clerk and left the building with very interesting information.

Patrick had inherited one pound from his father. There had been a notation in the will that Mr. John Willingham Whitney, being of sound mind and body, was leaving his son one pound because that was all he was worth.

Apparently there had been no love lost between father and son. The next thing of note was that Mr. Whitney had left his entire estate to his wife, Mrs. Carol Swain Whitney, in trust, with Mr. James Harding acting as trustee.

Feeling more confident than he had in weeks, William made his way to Mrs. Johnson's house for a bit of surveillance.

There was a tea shop across the street from the house. William checked his timepiece. Two o'clock in the afternoon. He ordered tea and a sandwich and was fortunate enough to find a table at the front of the store, with a full view of Mrs. Johnson's house.

He took his time eating his food and drinking his tea. When nothing happened after about an hour, he paid his bill and left. He then entered an ale house three stores down. The window in the pub was small, but if William stood against the wall, he could watch the house.

After another two hours and one more watered-down ale, he left the pub and headed for home. As he slowly rode his horse back to the townhouse, his thoughts were in a jumble. If Patrick was indeed the talented actor Mother seemed to think he was, he was certainly capable of convincing William that he was ill, then grieving, the two times William had seen him.

He decided to stop at his club and have a decent drink before he returned home and was again subjected to his mother's enthusiasm about the dinner party. Also, there was a good chance one of the members who was familiar with the law might be able to answer a few questions for him.

The club was more than half-full. He viewed the area and walked toward Mr. Adam Richards. The man was a solicitor. William had sought his advice before when his own solicitor was unavailable.

"Wethington, haven't seen you in a while." Richards stood, and they shook hands.

"Yes. I've been busy." William waved at a footman to bring him his favorite brandy.

Richards lowered his voice. "I heard some rumors that you are being looked at by the police as a suspect in a murder? That can't possibly be true."

William nodded his thanks at the footman and poured brandy into the glass. "I'm afraid it is true. My man of business, Mr. James Harding, was found floating in the River Avon. For some bizarre reason, they have placed their focus on me."

"Whyever would they have come to that conclusion?"

"They have confiscated the man's files, and unfortunately, Harding was doing some finagling with various businesses and forged my name on some documents that made it look as though I was involved."

Richards let out a low whistle. "That's not good."

"Not at all. That leaves me with another mess to clean up, even after the murder charges are dropped. Based on that, the police have foolishly assumed we were partners in crime and I killed him to take over the businesses."

The man's brows rose. "That is the best they can do?"

There was no reason for William to share that their suspicion had been furthered when he'd been caught twice trying to get his files. "They have refused to look at other suspects and are spending their time trying to build a case against me."

"If there is anything I can do to help, let me know. It's a very bad position they've put you in."

"Yes. However, there is one thing I wanted to ask you." He paused. "If a man is a trustee for an estate, is it possible to transfer the trust to another person?"

"Yes." He nodded. "Given that it is quite hard to come by trustees because it involves a lot of work, transfers occur all the time. Considering the age of the beneficiaries of the trust, the responsibility could last a considerable length of time."

"How is a transfer done?"

"As soon as the trustee has the consent of another person willing to step into his place, he merely files papers with the court transferring the trust."

"Does it involve an in-person interview?"

"It may, depending on the court. Not usually, though, since as I said, it is hard to find trustees, so they generally just accept a notarized document."

"Thank you. That does help."

"You're very welcome, and I hope you are able to clear up this mess soon. I take it you are doing your own investigation, since the police seem to have fallen short on their duties?"

"I am. After a few weeks of stumbling around, I think I might have a solid suspect."

"Good for you. It's a shame we pay the police to protect us, and then we find ourselves in a position such as yours where you are forced to do their work." He took another sip of his brandy and shook his head.

William nursed his own brandy, going over the facts in his head. He now needed to learn if a new trustee had been named on Whitney's estate trust and when that had happened.

Before or after Harding's death.

CHAPTER 31

Amy yawned as she padded over to the cushioned box on the floor in the corner of her bedchamber. Persephone's bed had always been at the foot of Amy's bed, but the dog had been dragging it each day until it sat where it did now. When Amy had tried to move it back, her darling little Pomeranian had growled at her.

She bent down to pet the animal and reared back. From what she could see, it appeared Persephone was going to give birth very shortly.

Amy had scoured the Bath Public Library as well as the bookstore for books on dogs giving birth. One of the early stages of labor was the dog pacing and shaking. Persephone was just climbing out of her box, shaking like a leaf. She began to pace.

Amy panicked.

"Aunt Margaret!" She went flying out of her bedchamber and banged on her aunt's door.

After a minute or so, Aunt Margaret opened the door, tying the belt to her dressing gown. "For heaven's sake, Amy, whatever is going on?"

"I think Persephone is about to give birth." She tried to keep the panic out of her voice, but she was afraid she hadn't succeeded.

Her aunt leaned against the doorjamb, smiling. "These are very natural things, darling. Don't worry yourself. Persephone will be fine."

Amy shook her head. "No! She won't. We have to do something."

"I am going to do something. Get dressed, eat my breakfast, and meet with my man of business."

Amy frowned. "You have a man of business?"

"Yes." She tapped Amy on the nose. "And I do not wish to be late, so I must get washed and dressed. Don't be afraid; your little dog knew how to get herself into this situation without your help, so I'm sure she will know how to complete the rest of it." With those words and a bright smile, she closed the door in Amy's face.

Aunt Margaret had a man of business. Perhaps Amy should have one too. Right now all her royalties went into the family coffers that her brother managed. It was time for her to be a grown-up and handle her own affairs. Or hire someone to handle her affairs.

Panic again seized her when she realized Aunt Margaret was not going to help. She flew down the stairs and made her way to the kitchen. There was no point in attempting to get her papa or brother to assist her. Perhaps Cook or one of the few maids they employed would be able to help.

"Mrs. Stover, I need your help." Amy came to a sliding halt at the sight of Cook, busy assembling the family's breakfast.

The woman offered a cheerful smile. "Good morning, my lady. What is it you need?"

"I need help for Persephone."

She scowled. "What has that animal done now?" She wiped her forehead with the sleeve of her dress.

"She's giving birth."

"Ah. Well, as you can see, I am a tad busy right now. Your father would not be pleased if his breakfast isn't ready because your dog is giving birth."

Amy wrung her hands—something she never did. "I don't know what to do."

"I thought you loaded up your room with books on dogs giving birth." Michael shook his head as he entered the kitchen and poured himself a cup of coffee. He was dressed for a day of doing whatever it was businessmen did.

"I did. But reading about it and seeing it are quite different things."

Michael patted her on the head. "The dog knows what to do." He left the room.

Whatever was it with this family that they patted her on the head and tapped her nose like she was an urchin? It was becoming mighty tiresome.

"Are any of the maids available, Mrs. Stover? Lacey, perhaps?"

"I'm so sorry, my lady, but I sent Lacey to the marketplace and don't expect to see her for a few hours. The two others have morning chores to see to."

Frustrated, Amy headed back to her room and examined Persephone. She was lying in the box now but still shaking. She needed someone to suffer through this with her.

William.

Back down the steps, she asked for the carriage to be brought around. She hurried to the breakfast room, where Aunt Margaret, Papa, and Michael had gathered.

"I am off to see Lord Wethington." She reached for a slice of toast.

Papa lowered his newspaper. "So early in the morning? I'm not sure that is proper, daughter."

Amy scooped some jam on her toast. "I need someone to help me with Persephone."

Her papa raised his brows. "Help your dog?"

"Yes. She is giving birth."

"And why do you need to help her?"

"She won't know what to do."

"And you do?"

"No. That is precisely why I need William's help."

"William has given birth to puppies before?"

Amy shook her head and left the room still chewing on her toast, scowling at the sound of Aunt Margaret's laughter.

She waited about another ten minutes before the carriage arrived in front of her house from the mews behind it. With the driver's help, she climbed in. "Lord Wethington's house, please."

The man tugged on the brim of his hat. "Yes, my lady."

Of course William didn't know any more about dogs giving birth than she did, and he didn't even like Persephone, but just having him there would calm her. When this murder investigation was over and Persephone was the proud mama of new little Persephones, Amy was going to have to give this situation between her and William some thought.

They seemed to be heading in a direction she never would have thought was a good idea. Yet it seemed to grow closer every day.

Once the carriage came to a rolling stop, she hopped out before the driver could help her and paid for her impatience by almost landing on her bum. Straightening herself, she took a calming breath, raised her head, and with as much dignity as she could muster made her way up the steps to William's townhouse.

"Good morning, my lady. How pleasant to see you."

"Good morning, Weston. Please tell his lordship I am here."

He frowned. "Oh, I am so sorry, Lady Amy. His lordship left a little while ago."

Amy's shoulders slumped. "Do you know where he went, or how long he will be?"

He reached in his breast pocket. "I have the information on where he is. He asked to have one of our footmen go to the police station and ask those two detectives to meet him at this residence." He handed her a piece of paper with a direction written on it.

The police detectives?

She studied the paper for a minute. The location looked familiar. She sucked in a breath. It was Mrs. Johnson's house.

★   ★   ★

William had spent a good part of Friday afternoon at Mr. Nelson-Graves's office convincing the man to give him permission to visit the Chancery Court offices to view the trust for Mrs. Carol Whitney.

Since William did not want the barrister to become too suspicious about precisely what he was doing, it took some verbal maneuvering, but eventually Nelson-Graves agreed and gave written permission for William to access the trust papers.

It didn't take long for William to read through the document and see that Mr. Patrick Whitney had replaced Mr. James Harding as the trustee set up for the benefit of Mrs. Carol Swain Whitney.

The week *before* Harding was found floating in the river.

There was apparently no difficulty in forging signatures. First Harding had done it to him in his business matters, and then Patrick had forged Harding's name on the trust papers, turning over the trust to himself.

This morning he'd risen early, washed, dressed, and downed a bit of breakfast. After checking his pistol resting in the locked case in the lower drawer of his desk, he slid it into his right trouser pocket and left for Mrs. Johnson's house.

He'd given Weston instructions to have one of the footmen deliver Mrs. Johnson's address to Detectives Carson and Marsh and request that they meet him there.

With the information he'd gotten recently, it had all come together, and William was certain Patrick was the man who had killed Harding and Mrs. Johnson. His acting abilities and stage makeup had convinced William he was ill and then grieving. William was certain Whitney had switched the trust by forging Harding's name to the document replacing the trustee, then killed Harding before he could learn of his perfidy.

William approached the house carefully. If he was correct in his assumptions, Patrick was the owner of the gun that had been used to shoot at him and Amy the night they broke into Harding's house. He was also the person who had stolen the ledger from Amy to continue with Harding's blackmailing scheme and had most likely taken William's appointment book, which might have supplied an alibi.

He wanted to make this seem like a friendly visit and ensure that Whitney was unaware of his intentions before he pulled out his gun and tied the man up in preparation for the police to arrive.

He planned to offer a smug smile to the two detectives when he told them their concentration on him as the murderer had once again proved their incompetence.

William paced outside the house, hoping Marsh and Carson would catch up to him so he wouldn't have to face

Patrick alone. Eventually, afraid Patrick might see him and try to leave out the back way and disappear again, he climbed the steps to the front door.

It took a few minutes for Patrick to answer. He wasn't wearing any stage makeup and looked quite fit and hardy. "Good morning, Patrick. I just came by to see how you were doing." William edged his way into the house.

"Nice of you to stop by, Wethington, but as you can see, I am quite well." Patrick did not look inviting and frowned as William stepped past him and headed to the drawing room.

William turned as Patrick followed him in. "You look as though you've recovered nicely from your illness. And the grief of Mrs. Johnson's death."

Patrick scowled. "Yes. I just told you. I am doing quite well."

It might have been wiser to wait for the detectives to arrive, but since he had no way of knowing how long it would take, he didn't want to give Patrick the chance to abscond.

"Have you seen your stepmother? She was concerned about you."

Patrick snorted. "No. I haven't seen her yet."

William took a seat, looking as though he intended to make this a lengthy visit. Patrick sighed and sat across from him. After a few minutes of banal bantering, Patrick stood. "If you will excuse me, I need to retrieve something from my bedchamber."

William also stood and took out his gun. "No. I don't think so."

"What's this about, Wethington?" Patrick asked. "Is there a reason you are pointing a gun at me in my own home?"

"I know you killed Harding, Patrick. The police are on their way. I have evidence that you changed the trustee on your stepmother's trust to your name the week before Harding died."

Patrick shrugged. "So? He asked me if I would take over because it had become too burdensome for him."

William needed to remember that the man was an actor. "I don't believe you. Also, you told me your father left you a considerable amount of money as well as two businesses. I saw the will, Patrick. He left you one pound."

"Yes, he did, the bastard!" Patrick slammed his fist into his hand. "He left it all to Carol, but then tied it up in a trust so she couldn't get at the money either."

"You were in the King's Garden the night Lady Amy and I spoke with Mrs. Johnson, weren't you? You killed the woman who took you in and provided you with an alibi."

"No. He didn't."

William's head whipped around at the female voice coming from the doorway. Carol Whitney pushed Amy into the room, a gun at her back. "I killed Millie Johnson, because this sneaky bastard was having an affair with her."

She narrowed her eyes at William. "Drop the gun, or your lover here will get a bullet in her sweet little head."

William felt all the blood drain from his face, almost to the point of making him dizzy. This woman who had just admitted to killing another woman in cold blood had a gun pointed at Amy's head.

He immediately placed the gun on the table in front of him. "Let her go, Mrs. Whitney." William raised his hands and stepped back from the table. He could feel the sweat trickling down his back. "I will not touch the gun or move in any way toward you or Patrick."

"Patrick?" She snarled. "Ha! That snake betrayed me." She swung around and aimed the gun at her stepson. "I killed my husband for you! We were supposed to be together, with all his money. Yet after Harding died, you disappeared. I had to act the fretting, nervous stepmother and ask these people to find you."

It appeared that both Carol Whitney and her stepson possessed acting skills. And she had killed not only Mrs. Johnson but also her own husband—Patrick's father? The woman was deranged, and he had to get Amy out of here. Fast.

"Mrs. Whitney. I ask you once more. Please let Lady Amy leave."

"Cease!" She pointed the gun away from Patrick and aimed it at William. "I will decide who leaves and who stays."

If he could keep her talking and if the detectives arrived soon, they might get out of this mess. A couple of *if*s, but it was all he had. Keeping Patrick in his view, he turned to Mrs. Whitney. "I doubt they were having an affair, Mrs. Whitney. Mrs. Johnson made an appointment with Lady Amy and me. I'm sure she was going to tell us Patrick killed Harding."

Mrs. Whitney waved the gun around, taking all of William's breath from his body. "I don't believe that for one minute. I saw her whisper to you two at the pub to meet her the next day. I was right there in the corner, watching her, knowing she would meet this scoundrel." She directed the gun at Patrick. "I'm sure she wanted to tell you two busybodies that I killed my husband. Get me out of the way so they could have all my money and run off together."

"I don't think he was running anywhere, since I am sure he stole the ledger with Harding's blackmailing information in it. He intended to pick up where Harding left off."

Mrs. Whitney shrugged. "No matter. If I was in jail for murder, they could stay right here in Bath, enjoying my money." Once again she took dead aim at Patrick's heart.

Her stepson blanched. "Carol, sweetheart, please put the gun away. You might hurt someone." Patrick moved slowly toward her as he spoke.

"Stop!" She narrowed her eyes, her hand steady on the trigger of the gun. "When his lordship here didn't return right away to give me the information on your whereabouts, I decided to act on my suspicions. It only took me one day of spying to find you. Right here—with her!"

Patrick held his arms out. Pleading. "I was feeling ill and needed a place to recover."

While Mrs. Whitney and Patrick conversed, Amy edged toward William. He took her hand, and they stood together. He gently eased her behind him. Between them and the exit stood a crazy woman waving a gun. He could feel Amy shaking, her hands ice-cold. He had no idea how she had ended up here, but if they got out of this alive, he would throttle her for not doing exactly what he had told her to do—not leave the house by herself.

And then kiss her senseless.

"Don't think you can fool me again, Patrick." Mrs. Whitney moaned. "I thought you loved me."

"I do." Patrick ran his tongue over his lips, flexing his hands and taking deep breaths, his eyes riveted on the gun.

"No. You don't. Once you got your hands on my money, you would be done with me."

He shook his head. "No. That's not true."

In a matter of seconds, Patrick had leaped toward Mrs. Whitney, and a shot rang out. His hands grasped his chest, and he looked down at the blood running through his fingers. "You shot me." His eyes closed and he fell to his knees, then forward, facedown.

"Patrick!" The gun slid from Mrs. Whitney's hand, and she raced toward him. William picked it up with two fingers and turned to Amy. "Get the bloody hell out of here. Now."

"Take it easy, your lordship." Detectives Carson and Marsh walked into the room, both of them holding pistols. "We have it all under control."

William closed his eyes in relief and pulled Amy toward him. He wrapped his arms around her, resting his chin on her head. "Are you all right, sweeting?"

She leaned back and looked him in the eye. "Persephone is having puppies."

CHAPTER 32

Amy gazed down and once again marveled at the tiny puppies nestling close to Persephone. Four little bodies snuggled up to their mum. Seeing her beloved dog act like a mama brought tears to Amy's eyes.

And a sense of longing to her breast. Perhaps she wasn't quite so adamant about never marrying. She could have a child or two. And, married to the right man, she could still do her writing.

The right man? Hadn't he already presented himself?

It had been almost a week since Patrick Whitney had admitted to killing Mr. Harding and Mrs. Whitney had shocked them all by stating that she'd killed Mrs. Johnson. As well as her husband, whom she'd said she had poisoned with arsenic.

The last Amy had heard, Patrick Whitney was recovering in hospital, under arrest, and Mrs. Whitney was behind bars. The best part, of course, was that William was freed of all charges. Since the detectives had released his files to him, he had spent most of his time working with his barrister, solicitor, and man of business to get his finances straightened out.

She'd seen very little of him.

On the way back from the Johnson home the day the killers were arrested, she'd told William that Mrs. Burrows had admitted that she and Miss Gertrude had been kidnapped and sold to a brothel in London many years before. When the place burned down, they'd both escaped and moved to Bath, where Miss Penelope was already living, distraught at her sister's disappearance but unable to get the police to listen to her.

Mrs. Burrows had found a good man to marry, and the two women had decided to go their separate ways, putting the horrible experience behind them.

Until Harding had uncovered their disgrace and used it for nefarious purposes.

After much consideration and musing, Amy and William had decided that since Mrs. Johnson had worked at the King's Garden, where Harding met with his victims, she must have been the one to tell Patrick about the journal, which then began his search for it, first by breaking into Harding's home and then by entering Amy's and William's houses. Although in those two cases, he had most likely used his acting abilities to gain access to their homes.

But tonight was Lady Wethington's dinner party. With all the goings-on, she'd had to postpone it for a week. Amy was looking forward to the event—if for no other reason than to get the sense of a normal life returning to her. She was happy to be free of investigations. The only way she planned to consider suspects and killers in the future was in writing her next book.

"Are you ready?" Aunt Margaret entered Amy's bedchamber after a slight knock.

"Yes, almost." Amy still gazed down at the puppies.

"My goodness, every time I come into this room, you are fussing with those puppies." Aunt Margaret bent over the box. "They are cute little things, aren't they?"

"Mm-hmm." Amy kept running her finger over their soft fur.

"I think perhaps you are feeling the lack of something in your life, Amy." Aunt Margaret straightened and reached out her hand. "However, it is time for us to leave for Lady Wethington's dinner party."

Amy accepted her aunt's hand and climbed to her feet. She turned and blew a kiss at the box. "Sleep well, little family."

When they arrived at the entrance hall, Stevens was helping Papa and Michael into their greatcoats. He performed the same service for Amy and Aunt Margaret.

Once they were all settled in the carriage and on their way, Papa looked over at Amy. "Michael and I will be leaving Monday morning for our return to London."

Amy was surprised to realize she would miss having them living with her. Although Papa was a little annoying about what he would and would not allow her to do, it had been nice having the entire family there for breakfast and most dinners.

"Have you completed your work, then?" Aunt Margaret asked.

"Yes. We have put in the paperwork to purchase two small businesses here in Bath. We both feel they are excellent choices for our portfolio."

"I will miss you, Papa." For heaven's sake, Amy could hear the wistfulness in her voice. She hadn't lived under the same roof as her papa and brother for more than a couple of weeks at a time in her whole life.

He reached over and patted her hand. At least it wasn't her head again. "Well, daughter, there is the possibility that we will be returning to Bath in the future."

"What do you mean?"

"As I get older, I find the hustle and bustle of London doesn't appeal to me so much anymore."

Amy straightened. "You mean you might move here permanently?"

"Do I hear a bit of fright in your voice, daughter?" Papa grinned at her.

"Um, maybe a tad. But I would love to have you here in Bath." Amy turned to Michael. "Are you moving too?"

"I've not decided yet. Since I'm not old and tired"—he grinned at Papa—"I'm not ready to abandon the life, but there is always the possibility. If I find something worth moving for."

"Or perhaps some*one* worth moving for?" Aunt Margaret said.

The rest of the ride was taken up with ideas for homes to purchase, since Papa didn't want to permanently move into the townhouse Amy and Aunt Margaret called home, though he actually owned the dwelling.

Michael glanced out the window. "It appears we've arrived."

The four of them reached the front door just as Weston opened the door. "Good evening, my lords, my ladies. Allow me to take your garments."

He helped them all out of their coats and directed them to the drawing room. "The rest of the group has gathered there."

When Amy entered the room, the first person she saw was William. He looked especially splendid in dark trousers, a stark-white shirt and cravat, and a colorful waistcoat under his dark-blue jacket. He broke away from the O'Neill sisters and Mr. Davidson and Mr. Rawlings. She noticed that Mr. Colbert and Lady Wethington were deep in conversation separate from the group.

It appeared they were the last of the guests to arrive.

"Good evening, Amy, Lord Winchester, Lord Davenport, Lady Margaret." William reached out for Amy's hand and squeezed it. "I would like to speak with you for a moment." He looked up at Papa. "May I have your permission to escort Lady Amy to the library for a moment?"

Papa's face lit up. "Yes, yes. Of course."

Amy's heart began to thump as William led her out of the room and down the corridor to the library. "What do you want?" She licked her dry lips.

"This will only take a moment."

"Is there something you want to show me?" She was becoming more nervous by the second.

"Um, perhaps." He grinned at her as he opened the door. He bowed and waved toward the room. "My lady?"

"Is this about the murder investigation?" Lord, was that her voice squeaking like that?

"No."

"What is it, then?"

He tapped her on the nose. "In a moment, sweetheart."

Damnation, now was William going to pick up on that annoying habit? That took away some of her anxiety and replaced it with irritation. "Do not tap me on the nose. I am not a child."

William grinned and turned his palms up. "My apologies."

Amy sniffed and walked past him to the window, then turned. "What do you want?"

"Come here, Amy." He held out his hand.

"William . . ."

"Come here."

She sighed and walked over to him. He led her to the settee and urged her to sit. Then he did precisely what she was afraid he was going to do. He got down on one knee in front of her and took both of her hands in his.

"William, I'm not sure . . ."

"I am." He took a deep breath. "Lady Amy Lovell, will you do me the great honor of becoming my wife?"

Good grief, her eyes filled with tears. Whatever was the matter with her? "Um, I wasn't expecting this." Lie number one. "I thought we were going to talk about the murder." Lie number two. "I'm not sure my papa would approve." Lie number three.

She considered him for a moment, an idea popping into her head. "Since you brought it up, however . . ."

"Yes?"

"On one condition."

He raised his brows. "Only one? I am getting off easy."

★ ★ ★

William and Amy returned to the drawing room to the expectant looks on most of the guests' faces. He held up her left hand to show off the beautiful diamond-and-ruby ring he'd slipped on her finger. "She said yes."

They were immediately surrounded by family and friends, all offering congratulations and well wishes.

"We must plan the wedding," Aunt Margaret said. "How soon do you want it?" She turned to William. Apparently it was assumed that he didn't want to wait too long to experience all that marriage had to offer.

"I leave that up to my betrothed." There. That should give him a few points with his bride-to-be.

Lord Winchester wandered in William's direction and slapped him on the back. "Welcome to the family, son. You are marrying the finest woman in Bath."

William smiled at Amy. "I know."

"I might dispute that, but I remember what a powerful punch my sister can throw." Michael kissed Amy on the cheek and shook William's hand. "Best wishes to both of you."

After a few minutes, dinner was announced, and they all proceeded into the dining room. William strolled along with Amy on his arm, feeling quite proud of himself. He had felt no panic at all when he arrived at the jewelry store to purchase Amy's ring two days earlier. Mother had reminded him that he'd inherited jewelry from both his grandmothers, but he'd wanted something new for Amy.

She could wear the other jewelry if she wished, but he wanted his ring to be for her and only her.

Mother had done an excellent job in planning the dinner. Although he had promised he would look over her menu choices, with all that had happened since, he'd never had a chance—or truth be known, the desire—to peruse the paper she kept handing him.

They dined on a clear-gravy soup, stewed eels, fricandeau of veal with spinach, roast capon, mashed potatoes with broccoli, Nesselrode pudding, fruit, nuts, and cheese.

The conversation was lively, and he was glad to see how happy Amy appeared to be, speaking of the upcoming wedding. Once in a while she would glance down at her hand, then look over at him and smile.

Yes. This felt right.

As soon as the dishes had been removed and only the tray of fruit, cheese, and nuts remained along with brandy for the men and tea for the ladies, Mr. Colbert stood and cleared his throat, reminiscent of the book club meetings. "May I have your attention, please?" He smiled down at Mother and took her hand.

What the devil?

"I would like to make another happy announcement. Lady Wethington has granted me the pleasure and honor of accepting my offer of marriage."

William almost swallowed his tongue. Marriage? He swung his attention to his mother, who was blushing. *Blushing!* Sitting next to him, Amy grabbed his hand. "Please don't spoil this moment for them."

William took a deep breath. She was right. Mother was not only blushing but looking at Mr. Colbert as if he had hung the moon, and the man was looking at her the same way.

William wiped his mouth with his napkin, stood, and held up his wineglass. "Although I wish I had known about this before an announcement was made—"

"William," Amy whispered.

"—I would like to offer my congratulations and best wishes to my mother and Mr. Colbert." He managed to eke out a smile. "Welcome to the family."

Mr. Colbert beamed, and William looked over at his mother, who mouthed *thank you* before showing everyone the beautiful diamond ring on her finger.

"It appears we have two weddings to plan," Aunt Margaret said as she joined in the toast.

Amy looked at her aunt and then her brother. "With two more to go." She dipped her head and lifted her glass, then linked her fingers with William's under the table.

EPILOGUE

The crowds had already gathered at the Atkinson & Tucker bookstore for the much-awaited book fair. Two local authors had taken their seats at tables awaiting customers who had purchased their books for signing.

A third table piled high with stacks of books sat in the very center of the store with the sign E. D. BURTON.

No one sat there.

Amy and William strolled up to the store, hand in hand, and stopped to chat with the two local authors. They also greeted the O'Neill sisters, Lady Wethington and Mr. Colbert, and Mr. Davidson with his ever-present friend, Mr. Rawlings, along with others from the book club.

Mr. Rawlings winked at her.

William nodded to Miss Sterling and Lord Temple and his daughter, Lady Abigail. The store manager, Mr. Dobish, stood in the middle of the chaos and frantically looked around.

The crowd behind them was growing restless, several of them asking about E. D. Burton.

Mr. Dobish cleared his throat and raised his hands to gain the crowd's attention. "Have no fear, ladies and gentlemen; I was assured by a representative of the publisher that Mr. E. D.

Burton will definitely appear this evening." He checked his timepiece. "We just need to give him a bit more time."

Amy and William grinned at each other. He bowed to her, took her arm, and walked her to the table with the E. D. Burton sign on it. "My lady." He pulled out the chair and she sat, placing her folded hands on the table.

William cleared his throat. "Ladies and gentlemen, may I present to you my lovely fiancée, Lady Amy Lovell, also known as Mr. E. D. Burton, murder mystery author extraordinaire."

The crowd erupted, everyone speaking at once.

Mr. Rawlings sauntered up to them and extended his hand. "Lady Amy, I am the representative of Chatto and Windus for all of Somerset County. It is a pleasure to meet you on a professional basis."

Amy grinned. "It is nice to meet you in a professional capacity also, Mr. Rawlings." She took his hand and gave it a sharp squeeze. No one would accuse her of being a mousy woman.

William bent to speak in Amy's ear. "I have met your one condition, my lady. Plan the wedding." He winked. "I will plan the honeymoon."

ACKNOWLEDGMENTS

Thanks so much to my husband and beta reader, Doug. It was the only way to get him to read my books.

A huge thank you to my agent, Nicole Resciniti from the Seymour Agency. Your diligence on my behalf is appreciated.

To my hard-working editor, Faith Black Ross for her excellent suggestions that makes my books so much better. Thank you.

Maria Connor, my personal assistant takes so much off my shoulders that I am able to write my books. Thanks a million, girlfriend.

And thank you to all my romance readers who took a chance on my cozy mysteries.